the beyond

books by
jeffrey ford

MEMORANDA
THE PHYSIOGNOMY

the beyond

jeffrey ford

An Imprint of HarperCollins Publishers

EOS

EOS
An Imprint of HarperCollins*Publishers*
10 East 53rd Street
New York, New York 10022-5299

Copyright © 2001 by Jeffrey Ford
Interior design by Kellan Peck
ISBN: 0-380-97897-0

Library of Congress Cataloging in Publication Data:

Ford, Jeffrey, 1955–
The beyond / Jeffrey Ford.
p. cm.
ISBN 0-380-97897-0 (hardcover)
I. Title.

PS3556.06997 B49 2001
813'.54—dc21
00–046645

First Eos hardcover printing: January 2001

FIRST EDITION

10 9 8 7 6 5 4 3 2 1

www.eosbooks.com

This book is for those stout-hearted readers who have accompanied me on the entirety of this three-part journey and also for those who gave me good directions along the way, especially Jennifer Brehl, who carried the compass, showed great courage, and, on this leg of the expedition, cleared miles of rancorous underbrush.

Special thanks to:
Pat Dean, tattoo guru, for lending me some interesting
books.

Bill Watkins, Kevin Quigley, and Mike Gallagher
for reading and commenting on
various parts of this novel while it was growing.

Meems, Nauk, and Air for precious Time.

the beyond

the world's imagination

I have read that some believe the world is a sentient being, a massive head spinning in space. The oceans are its blood, the wind, its breath, the earth, its flesh, the forests, its hair, and all the creatures that crawl upon it, swim through it, soar above it, are its eyes and the agents of its will. If this is so, then the Beyond, that immense wilderness, stretching from the northern edge of the Realm thousands of miles to the frozen pole and east and west as far as belief will follow, is certainly, in its danger, its wonder, its secrets and absence of reason, nothing less than the world's imagination.

I know this to be true, because, I, Misrix, now one-quarter proud monster and three-quarters sniveling man, was born there. If I had not been kidnapped into the world of men, trapped by their language, and logic, I might still be the demon I once was, swooping down from a tree perch with perfect, unquestioning grace to disembowel a white deer. A man of great genius, Drachton Below, changed all that, and now, though I still have wings, claws, fur, horns, and the eyes of a serpent, I sip tea from a china cup, eat nothing but plant meat, and am moved to tears by sheets of paper covered with wiggles of ink that tell a story about the death of love or a hero fallen in his quest.

Below awakened me to this deception long ago in an attempt to create an heir for himself. I was a dutiful child and even wore a pair of spectacles to try to appear the intellectual progeny he so desperately wanted (now I wear them simply to see, for my eyes have grown weak from too much reading). His love did not abide because it was born of selfishness, and my transformation was incomplete, cursed by his failure to go beyond himself. I am here now, stuck like too large a grain of sand in the neck of an hourglass, between Heaven and Hell, the only resident of a fallen city that had once been my father's kingdom.

Some years ago, after Below's death, I resolved to return to the Beyond and shed my humanity. I dreamt every night of the freedoms of a boundless country without conscience, where the necessary pleasure of the hunt and kill did not require an apology or carry with it the millstone of guilt. In these nightly visions, I acted with no prerequisite of thought. I wore no spectacles, and yet my vision was crystal clear, always in the moment, unhampered by shadows of the past or future. And so, I set out one morning for the Beyond with two companions—one, a black dog, the other, a man named Cley, who hoped to find salvation for himself.

It took the better part of a month to reach the boundary of the forbidding forests that marked the end of man's influence. There at the edge were the charred remains of a town. Cley told me it had been called Anamasobia, and he confessed that he had been largely responsible for its destruction. We rummaged through its ruins and managed to find supplies we would need. Cley gathered weapons that he could use to protect himself against the unknown and, more important, to hunt his food.

The day finally came when we plunged into the Beyond. Beneath immense, barren trees, more ancient than the earliest history of the Realm, we shuffled through the yellow and orange leaves of autumn. Like brothers, Cley and I bolstered each other's courage against the overwhelming spirit of fear that pervaded the place. We both had to learn how to hunt. My tools were my strength, my claws, and the power of flight. He practiced with the rifle he had found in the ashes of Anamasobia. Our apprenticeship in the Beyond was brief and brutal.

On the third day, we stopped to rest by a stream and were attacked by four of my brother demons. Believe me, these fellows weren't wearing spectacles; they had not come to discuss philosophy. The battle was fierce and if not for the tenacity of the black dog, Wood, we probably could not have got the better of them. When it was over, I was pleased to be alive, but it struck me as I surveyed the corpses of the fallen creatures that they had never recognized me as one of their own. To them, I was a man. Something in their odor disturbed me. Even when we had left the scene and were traveling deeper into the forest, that aroma stayed with me, drawing an occasional, involuntary animal squeal from deep within my chest. I thought I felt myself begin to change then.

As the days passed, I became swifter, more powerful, more acrobatic in my movement from tree branch to tree branch. There were moments when I caught myself thinking absolutely nothing. Cley was also changing. He lost his original nervous verbosity and as he did his shot became truer. His often droll sense of humor receded and was slowly replaced with a kind of grim determination to survive. We moved through the forest in near-perfect silence, and he and I and the dog learned to communicate by no more than a look or a nod.

One night I woke from a dream of the kill with the overwhelming urge to take my companion's blood. I could smell its sweetness pulsing through him just below his flesh. The trees and the wind and the moon shining down through the bare branches coaxed me to it. He was asleep on the ground, and I approached with all of the stealth I had recently learned. As I leaned down over him, the black dog stirred and barked. In one fluid motion, Cley drew the stone knife he kept in his boot, grabbed me by my pigtail beard, and stuck the point of his weapon against my throat. His action brought me back to my senses, and realizing what I had nearly done, I began to weep.

"I suppose it is time we split up," he said with a hollow laugh, releasing me.

I nodded. "I must, again, become one with the Beyond," I whispered.

He tugged on my left horn. "Tomorrow," he said. "In the meantime, don't eat me."

The following day, we parted. We stood in a clearing amidst a stand of immense oaks, and I put my arms around him and hugged him to me.

"Good luck," was all he said to me.

I told him, "If we should meet again, you will have to kill me."

He nodded once, as if I were reporting on the weather.

The dog would not come to me when I called to him, but stood at a distance and growled. I took this to be a good sign that I was very close to being a full-fledged demon again. Then, flapping my wings, I leaped into the air and left them.

In the weeks that followed, there were moments when my knowledge of language completely disappeared. I saw, for the first time since my stay among men, things as they were without the label of a word pasted over them. Entire hours went by when I did not perceive the tiresome chatter that usually raged at the edges of my consciousness. When I hunted, I was swift and brutal, reveling in the taste of warm blood and sensing the energy my prey's flesh gave to me. It was only when I met a band of demons that I came to realize my folly.

There were six of them gathered round the base of a spreading shemel tree, bothering the thoroughly depleted carcass of a wild boar. I felt full of demon strength and courage, and I longed to join them. As I approached, I barked out a greeting that sounded completely authentic. Some of them barked back, undisturbed by my presence, and returned their gazes to the exposed rib cage of the boar. This encouraged me, and I drew closer. When I was no more than a few feet away from them, my heart bursting with excitement, I saw their noses begin to twitch. They made faces as if they were smelling something unpleasant. I stopped advancing, and they broke from their group and began slowly to surround me.

You'll have to forgive me, but what happened after that, I cannot and do not wish to recall. Suffice it to say that I barely escaped with my life. My brethren looked upon me as if I were an odious pile of dung, and that hurt more than the wounds from their claws. I carried and will always carry the stink of humanity. Here is one thing I learned: demons love the flesh and blood of humans, but at the same time are repulsed by their scent of culture and reason. Human is a bittersweet repast. For me, more bitter than sweet. I fled from the Beyond, fled as if there were some shame in what had happened. There was a measure of guilt attended to my failure that, once experienced, I could not let go of, and it served to push me further into humanity.

Where else was I to go but back to the ruins of the Well-Built City? Here I have been ever since. My days are quiet and slow, my only companions the volumes from the extensive library that survived the city's destruction. At one time there were werewolf creatures prowling the ruins, products of my father's twisted Science, but I managed to exterminate them all one at a time by laying traps and utilizing some of his old explosives.

Occasionally, men will come and crawl around in the ruins for a day or two, making believe they aren't afraid of me, but the minute I get up the energy to leave my study and fly above them, they flee back to their villages at Latrobia or Wenau. They know I am here, for I fly over their homes from time to time to see how they are getting on. I've gotten quite lazy in recent years, perhaps half-hoping that one of them will get off a lucky shot and end my miserable existence.

I am especially interested in the village at Wenau, for that was Cley's home before he left for the Beyond. I have found small ways to assist them when I can in honor of my friend. They have done a great deal of building in recent years, so I fly there sometimes and tote heavy objects that it might take three or four of them to carry *to the tops of their scaffolding. This is always at night when no one is watching. One evening, I rescued a little girl from drowning in the river. I laugh every time I imagine her telling her story to her parents about how the demon swooped down out of nowhere and carried her to safety. I told her to tell them that it was Cley who saved her.*

Now, I come to the point of all this. Some months ago, I was in the study, about to turn the page of a work concerning the grammar of constellations, when I felt, like a bubble bursting inside my skull, the sudden, unquenchable desire to discover Cley's fate. I realized that through the years, I had always hoped for his return. He was the only one who had ever accepted my halfling nature as its own individual phenomenon instead of considering me either a monstrous human or an impotent demon.

I became obsessed with thoughts of him, and I began to wonder what had happened to him in the wilderness. We had been apart many many years. Although he often said he was headed for Paradise, his true mission was one of conscience—to locate and ask forgiveness of a woman he had once wickedly betrayed. He had not been a strong man in his earlier life, given to pride and cruelty and addiction, and these sins haunted him long after he had determined to make amends.

When he had been Physiognomist, First Class, of this very city whose remains are my home, he was sent to that town at the edge of the Beyond, Anamasobia. There, he met a woman, Arla Beaton, with whom he fell in love. She, on the other hand, could not love him, because of the ugliness he harbored inside. He had a revelation that perhaps his science could improve her character. It was his belief that if the physical structure of the face was a map of the soul, he might change, with his scalpel, the girl's attitude and personality by changing her face. The result was that he butchered her horribly, and she was forced to go about wearing a green veil to protect others from the sight of her.

Cley grew to understand the hideous nature of his crime, and his entire life became a quest for that woman's forgiveness. After the destruction of the Well-Built City, they both settled in the village of Wenau, not far from here. Her scars eventually healed through some miracle associated with the birth of her daughter. Cley became friendly with her husband, a strange native of the wilderness, and her children, but she always stayed aloof from him. When that family left Wenau to travel into the Beyond, back to the husband's village, the woman left her green veil with Cley. This scrap of material had haunted him ever since, and he wondered if it was to be for him a reminder of his guilt or a sign of absolution. His salvation depended upon the answer to this riddle.

Where I gave up, Cley continued undaunted. I had to know what had become of him. With that in mind, I made a journey to the Beyond, a five day's flight from the ruins. There, at the boundary of the forest, I made my inquiry. If I had been required to delve more deeply into that nightmare land again, I would not have continued. I could not have endured another confrontation with the demons. This was unnecessary, though, for all I needed to do was gather some of the elements of the Beyond and return to my home.

I brought back with me a portion of earth, a bouquet of ferns, a jar of water, and one of air. Beginning with the ferns, I bit off the tips of a spray and chewed slowly, ferreting out the atoms of Cley's story. Nothing happens in the Beyond that is not secretly known by the Beyond. It's all there, always. What is required are the finely tuned senses of a demon, and through some sampling, one can piece together a tattered history of any creature.

With that first taste of vegetation, I found a few morsels of the story. From there I continued, rubbing my hands in the earth, releasing the air under my nose, and sipping the water that had once flowed through the rivers and streams of the Beyond. I slowly digested the crumbs of the story, one by one, and when I had gathered a good portion of them, I sat for a few days, smoking stale cigarettes I discovered in the ruins or fresh ones I stole from the villages, and stitched the whole ragged thing together in my head. It was a slow, painstaking method of discovery, but I never flagged in my diligence, as if it were a second chance for me to find my own salvation.

The story is in me now, and I am poised to record it for you, whoever you might be. Perhaps you are a soldier come to kill me and you find this manuscript in the course of your duties. Perhaps you are a traveler who happens upon these ruins in your own search for Paradise and will find, in my words, sustenance to continue your pilgrimage or proof that it is all folly. Perhaps these pages will never be found but will molder to dust in the ruins, and then Time itself will digest what I have written.

I warn you that the writing will not be the smooth delineation of events as you see here, for the knowledge I have gathered lies behind my eyes like the remains of a ravaged animal. The skull still holds some hide and has all its teeth intact, but one eye is missing, and the other has become a jellied nest for flies. Scraps of hide, half a heart, the liver missing, ribs cracked and strewn, brain exposed and baked by the sun. I will coax this incomplete parcel of a tale to rise and run with the magic of sheer beauty, in the voice of the Beyond. Do not be concerned by gaping wounds in the narrative, for these are merely portals through which the years spiral and great distances breathe.

It is true that in the time since I performed my research Cley might have died, but that is of little consequence to the story. Both men and demons are born and die. It is the journey between these two mundane certainties that is everything. Will we ever discover ourselves amidst the dangers, the wonders, the impossible depths of the wilderness, or will we wander lost and alone, without meaning, till death? I am uncertain as to which of these might describe Cley's journey. What I offer is merely a fragmented record of the events as I find them. I am a halfling beast, neither here nor there, and cannot judge the outcome. Only you, who are human, can do that.

Sheer beauty, violet elixir, medium of dreams . . .

To think that I once dragged Cley from this drug's clutches, haughtily crushing vials, and admonishing, with comic asides, against his desire to sleep his life away co-cooned by its illusions. What I knew then was poison for him, I know now, in my desire to conjure him from the elements of the Beyond, is the sap that will drive his story from the root that lies buried in my mind, down my arm, across my wrist, through my fingers, out of the pen and into the sunlight of clean, white paper.

It bubbles my veins, ripples the convolutions of my brain and sets fire to the five chambers of my demon heart. Here, the first tendril of ink begins to sprout, curling inward and out, wrapping around nothing to define a spiraling plant that grows with the speed of light. It is everywhere at once, bearing heavy white fruit that splits open amidst the rushing wind of passing seasons, releasing a flock of screaming, blind birds. They fly upward with full determination to smash against the ceiling of the sky and vaporize into a thousand clouds that form one cloud. It rains, and the green land stretches, in mere moments, into a wilderness so immense that it is impossible even to conceive of crossing it.

There, like a tiny insect on the head of a giant whose brow is the mightiest of mountain ranges, is Cley, where I left him, in a clearing of tall oaks. Beside him, that insignificant black dot, is Wood, the dog with one ear.

Closer now and closer still until I can make out his broad-brimmed black hat, sporting three wild-turkey feathers, reminders of his first kill in the Beyond. Beneath it, his chestnut hair is long and twisted together in the back to form a crude braid tied at the end with a lanyard that was once a demon's tendon. A full beard descends across his chest. Amidst this profluent tangle jut a nose and cheeks, the left scarred by the nick of a barbed tail. He stares northward with unnerving determination, as if he can already see, thousands of miles ahead of him, his destination.

I have seen scarecrows in the fields surrounding Latrobia who are better dressed than this hunter. Old brown coat, removed from a skeleton back in the ruins of Anamasobia, like the hide of some weary, wrinkled beast. The flannel shirt, dark blue with a field of golden stars, he found in the intact dresser drawer of one Frod Geeble's rooms, which lay behind the destruction of a tavern. A pair of overalls. The boots have been Cley's all along, and in the left one is the stone knife he assured me cut with more grace and precision than a Physiognomist's scalpel. The rifle, luckiest find of all, is for him like a marriage partner. He sleeps with it, whispers to it, cares for it with a genuine devotion. When it comes time to kill, he kills with it, his shot growing truer and truer until he can drill a demon in mid-flight, dead center between the eyes, at a hundred yards. His backpack holds boxes of shells, but the Beyond is limitless.

That dog, potential insanity on four legs, can be as calm as a dreamless sleeper until danger drops from the trees and then his placid, near-human smile wrinkles back into a snapping wound machine. The crafty beast learns to lunge for my brethren's unprotected areas—wing membrane, soft belly, groin, or tail. I, myself, witnessed that hound tear off an attacking demon's member, slip through its legs, and then shred a wing to tatters in his escape. He has an uncanny sense of certainty about him in all situations, as if in each he is like a dancer who has practiced that one dance all his days. Wood reads Cley like a book, understands his hand signals and the subtle shifting of his eyes. There is no question he will die for the hunter, and I am convinced he will go beyond death for him—a guardian angel the color of night, muscled and scarred and harder to subdue than a guilty conscience.

■ The hunter whistled once, moving off into the autumn forest, and the dog followed three feet behind and to the left. In the barren branches above, a coven of crows sat in silent judgment while a small furry creature with the beak of a bird scurried away into the wind-shifted sea of orange leaves. From off to the south came the sound of something dying as they proceeded into the insatiable distance of the Beyond, their only compass a frayed and faded green veil.

The contents of Cley's pack as they were dictated to me by the Beyond: 1 ball of twine; 4 candles; 2 boxes of matches; 8 boxes of shells (1 dozen bullets per box); 1 metal pot; 1 small fry pan; 1 knife and 1 fork; thread and needle; a sac of medicinal herbs; a book, found among the charred remains of Anamasobia (the cover and first few pages of which have been singed black, obliterating its title and author); 3 pair of socks; 4 pair of underwear; 1 blanket.

■ The days were a waking nightmare of demon slaughter, for they came for him from everywhere, at any moment, swooping out of trees, charging along the ground on all fours with wings flapping. He felled them with the gun, and, when not quick enough with this, he reached for the stone knife, smashing it through fur, muscle, and breastbone to burst their hearts. Wild blood soaked into his clothes, and he learned to detect their scent on the breeze. Claws ripped his jacket, scarred the flesh of his chest and neck and face, and when he met them in hand-to-hand combat, he screamed in a fearsome voice as if he too had become some creature of the wilderness.

The spirit that fired his intuition so that his shots were clean and allowed him to move with thoughtless elegance when wielding the knife was a strong desire he did not fully understand and could not name. It forced him to overcome great odds and demanded with an unswerving righteousness that he survive.

■ Cley hid beneath a willow and aimed at a white deer drinking from a stream. Cracking branches, the prey bolted, a moment of confusion, and a demon dropped from above onto the hunter's back. The rifle flew from his hands as he smelled the rancid breath and deep body stink now riding him, searching for a place to sink its fangs. He supported the weight of his attacker long enough to flip the beast over his head. It landed on its wings as he reached for his knife. The demon whipped at his forearm with barbed tail, and the sting weakened his grip. The knife fell and stabbed the earth. The dog was there, seizing in his jaws the demon's tail. The creature bellowed, arched backward in agony, and this moment was all the hunter needed. He retrieved the fallen blade and, with a brutal slice, half severed the creature's head from its body.

From that point on, no matter how many he killed in an ambush, no matter how long the process took, he decapitated each and every one. The thought of it makes me nauseous, but I see him cracking their horns from their foreheads and piercing their eyes with the points of their own weaponry. "Even these foul creatures can know fear," he told the dog, who sat at a distance, baffled by the curious ritual.

■ He had learned that demons do not hunt at night. At twilight he built a fire next to a stream. Placing six or seven large stones in the flames, he would leave them until they glowed like coals. Before turning in, he would fish them from the fire with a stick and bury them in a shallow pit the length of his body. Their heat would radiate upward and keep him warm for much of the night.

Dinner was venison along with the greens he had gathered in his daily journey. Vegetation grew more scarce by the day as autumn dozed toward winter. He shared the meat in equal parts with the dog.

When the stars were shining in the great blackness above, he took the book without a name from his pack. Then he lay down by the fire, the dog next to him, and strained his sight, reading aloud in a whisper. The curious subject matter of the large volume made little sense. It dealt with the nature of the soul, but the writing was highly symbolic and the sentences spiraled in their meaning until their meaning left them like the life of a demon with a knife in its heart.

The flames subsided and he made his bed with the stones. Lying always faceup—it was his belief that one should never turn one's back on the Beyond—he searched the universe for shooting stars. Falling branches, bat squeals, ghostly birdcalls like a woman with her hair on fire, snarls and bellows of pain were the lullaby of the wilderness. The wind wafted across his face. A star fell somewhere hundreds of miles to the north, perhaps crashing down into Paradise, and then he was there in his dreams, watching it burn.

■ There were trees so wide around the trunk and so insanely tall that they were more massive than towers that had once stood in the Well-Built City. The roots of these giants jutted out of the ground high enough to allow Cley passage beneath them without his bending over. Bark of a smaller species was a light fur that felt to the touch like human flesh. Another tree used its branches like hands with which to grab small birds and stuff them down into its wooden gullet. A thin blue variety rippled in the breeze; a thicket of streamers with no seeming solid structure to keep them vertical. Most disturbing to Cley was when the wind passed through these undulating stalks—a haunting sound of laughter that expressed joy more perfectly than any word or music ever had.

■ The forest was teeming with herds of white deer, and even an errant shot had a chance of felling one. Flesh from this animal was sweet and very filling. Cley discovered that its liver, when stuffed with wild onions and slowly roasted, was the finest thing he had ever tasted.

■ Adders with rodent faces. Wildcats, the color of roses, emitted the scent of cinnamon. Small tusked wolves covered with scales instead of fur. The wilderness was a beautiful repository of bad dreams that often rendered monsters.

■ Cley had lost track of how many demons he had slain, how many wounds he had dressed, how many deer livers he had devoured. He was startled from his gruesome work on the corpse of an enemy by a tiny fleck of white that moved before his eyes. Looking up, past the barren branches overhead, he watched the snow falling. "Winter," he said to Wood, and with that one word, he felt the cold on his hands, the chill of the wind at his back. His breath came as steam, and he wondered how long he had ignored the signs of autumn's death, so caught up, himself, in killing.

The icy presence of the new season now made itself doubly known in payment for the hunter's previous disregard. The frigid wind stole the feeling from his hands, and he prayed he would not have to fire the rifle in defense against an attack. It seemed as if ice had seeped inside him and was forming crystals in his bones. His mind yawned with daydreams of the fireplace back at his home in Wenau.

The only shred of hope the winter brought was the disappearance of the demons. For two days following the first light snow, they were strangely absent. He wondered if they were hibernating.

■ He and the dog gathered dry branches with which to build a fire. They heaped them up in front of the mouth of a cave, and then he rummaged through his pack for a box of matches. Cupping his hands and using his body as a shield, he managed to ignite the barest tip of a stick. Once the tongue of flame took hold, the fire's hunger overcame the winter's best attempts to extinguish it. Smoke swirled upward as he carefully placed the box of matches back in his pack.

He fashioned a torch from a large branch and stuck its end in the fire till it burned brightly. Taking the stone knife from his boot, he edged forward into the opening in the hill. The thought of discovering hibernating demons in the closed, dark place made him shudder and begin to sweat.

It was warm inside. He called out, "Hello," in order to judge the size of the vault by the echo it produced. The sound blossomed out and returned with news of considerable space. As if his voice had lit the chamber, upon the word's return, his vision cut through the dark. A perfectly empty rock room with a ceiling tall enough for standing. Continuing forward, he found, after twenty feet, that the opening narrowed in height and width as he proceeded into the hill. Following the shaft to where it turned sharply downward into blackness, he was satisfied that the cave was free of beasts. He turned and looked out through the mouth. There, in the gray light of day, sat Wood, head cocked to one side, staring at the hole that had devoured his companion.

Cley carried his pack inside and moved the location of the fire to just inside the cave's entrance. He wrapped himself in his blanket and lay down on the hard floor. The dog followed him but whined and sniffed every inch of rock. To ease Wood's uncertainty about being within the earth, Cley took the book from his pack and read a few pages out loud. As the words streamed forth, the dog stopped pacing and curled up beside his master.

Snow fell, and the wind whistled through the forest, whipping the face of the hill. The demons were asleep, and the cold could not sting him in the shelter of the rock womb. His bones began to thaw. Now that he did not have to kill, all he could think about was the killing he had done. In the wind he heard the savage war cry he had used when rushing toward demons with only his knife.

"What have I become?" he asked the dog, who was already asleep. He put the book away and searched through his belongings to find the green veil. The feel of it clutched in his fist told him he would never return from the Beyond.

■ Four or five armfuls of branches and kindling had to be gathered every day to feed the flame's appetite. At times, the wind forced the smoke back into the vault instead of carrying it away, and it grew so thick that Cley and the dog would have to leave in order to draw a decent breath. Still, they tended to it scrupulously like a beloved infant. It was a marked tragedy when it died, for with each instance of its failure the store of matches was reduced.

■ The blankets and belongings were moved to the very back of the chamber, where it narrowed, and the shaft led down into the unknown. A warm current of air traveled up from deep in the earth. At times, Cley removed his shirt and lay about in just his overalls. Outside, the world was brutally cold. The sun barely generated enough heat even at midday to cut through the frost and bitter winds. The days were brief, and the nights seemed to last for weeks.

■ The store of bullets was quickly diminishing, so Cley cut a long, thick branch from which to carve a bow. When it was finished, he strung it with deer sinew. Through endless and

uneventful nights, by the precious light of a candle, he perfected the craft of shaping arrows. To the backs of them, he
tied feathers to balance against the barbed tips he carved from
animal bone. The bow was tall and powerful, and over a
week's time, he became accurate with it. Still, it could not kill
as decisively as the rifle.

This change in weaponry heralded a change in diet from
venison to rabbit, squirrel, and the meat of a slow-moving amorphous blob of a furry mammal with a tapered snout and pitiful,
human eyes. Cley named this slothful beast a geeble after the
tavern owner from Anamasobia. Its meat was bland and fatty,
but its coat made a fine pair of mittens and warm leggings.

■ They were returning to the cave from the eastern pond
through a stand of blue, wavering trees. Cley was preoccupied with thoughts of the nameless book. The *soul* it had told
him was that irreducible, ineradicable essence of one's being
that was both the element that defined individuality and also
the very mind of God. He thought of delicate dandelion seed
on the wind, of laughter, of omniscience atomized like a spray
of perfume, a floating ghost egg, a fart. The concept slipped
through his ear and away on the wind.

Wood barked, the clipped near-whisper sound the dog
used to indicate danger. Looking up, Cley reached toward the
geeble-hide quiver he wore across his back. An animal stood
twenty yards in front of him next to the undulating trunk of a
blue tree. The sight of it brought him up short and set his
heart racing.

It was a cinnamon cat, one of those illusive red-coated
lynx that Cley had only seen out of the corners of his eyes on
a few occasions. He knew it better by scent than sight, because in its wake it left a sweet aroma like those he remem-

bered emanating from the bakeries of the Well-Built City. Even in dead of winter, he smelled its disarming perfume, and it spoke more of home and safety than the presence of a predator. The cat crouching before him now was larger than any of the others he had glimpsed briefly. He raised his right hand to indicate to Wood to remain still.

Nocking an arrow in place, he pulled back on the bow-string. He was unsure how dangerous these cats could be, but he had on occasion come across the results of their hunting—corpses of deer that held the sweet scent with bellies split open and all the internal organs devoured. The arrow flew. Cley smiled until the shaft bounced off harmlessly onto the snow. The cat never moved. Another arrow traveled as true a path as the first and also dropped to the ground.

"I think it's dead," Cley said.

The dog barked, and together they slowly approached. He slung the bow over his shoulder and leaned down for his knife. Wood was the first to reach the lynx, and he licked the creature's face.

"Frozen solid," the hunter said as he stepped up and tapped the cat on the head with his blade. It was like hitting the head of a marble statue. "Winter's trophy," he said. The corpse was too heavy to carry back to the cave, so he marked the spot and the trail he followed home.

The following day, he returned, started a fire next to it, thawed it, and carefully removed the skin. This process took him the better part of a day, but he did not rush, hoping the pelt would make a good-sized cloak when he was finished. Back at the cave, he cured the inside of the hide with hot ash. When he was finished, he had a beautifully scented garment with a tooth-fringed hood, bearing pointed ears and empty sockets. The dog sometimes wrestled it around, unsure if it was dead since neither of them had killed it.

■ The deer had disappeared. All he carried was the carcass of a starved squirrel. Cley stood in a thicket of trees at sunset, listening to the wind. He marked the ever-decreasing length of the days, the relentless drop in temperature, and wondered if the wilderness was inching toward total, static darkness, like death. Then the dog barked, and he continued toward the cave, realizing that for a moment he had forgotten who he was.

■ On a frigid afternoon, when the sun had made a rare appearance, a black reptilian wolf dashed across the clearing where Cley had felled a rabbit and snatched it away. The hunter yelled at the injustice, and Wood gave chase. The lizard skin of the creature's body offered a good defense against the dog's teeth and claws. The rivals rolled in the snow, one snapping and growling, the other hissing and spitting—a confusion of black in a cloud of white powder.

Striking with the speed and cold cunning of a snake, the wolf gored Wood in the chest with one of its short, pointed tusks. The dog dropped to the snow as Cley shot an arrow into the sleek marauder's side, sending it yelping into the underbrush. The hunter lifted his companion from the ever-growing pool of blood. Through deep snow, he trudged over a mile back to the cave, with the dog draped across his arms. By the time they reached their sanctuary, Wood was unconscious, and Cley feared that the wolf's tusk might have held some poison.

He treated the wound with an herbal remedy he had carried from Wenau. Then he fed the fire and laid the dog down on his blanket next to it. Stroking Wood's head, the hunter begged him not to die.

Late in the night, the dog began to shiver violently, and

Cley suspected that death was very near. He removed his cat cloak and draped it over the blanket. Then, from out in the dark, as if at a great distance, came the wind-muffled sound of a dog barking.

"Come, boy," Cley called, and whistled as he always did in the forest to call his companion to his side. He yelled frantically for hours. As the day came on, the barking subsided, and then suddenly was gone.

■ Wood survived the attack, but could do nothing but lie on the blanket near the fire and stare straight ahead. Cley felt guilty leaving him alone, but they needed food. He discovered that an integral part of the process was missing when he hunted alone. The frustration marred his aim, and he cursed out loud, scattering whatever game might be nearby. He was embarrassed to return to the cave in the evenings with only a geeble or a few crows.

Although he was weary, he fed the fire and cooked whatever pittance he had brought. Dicing the meat as small as he could, he fed the dog one piece at a time, then poured a little water into his companion's mouth with each serving. By the time Cley had a chance to eat, it was late and he had little appetite.

Wood was most at ease when the hunter read. On the night he recited the section of the book that made the argument that thoughts were as real as rocks, the dog stirred and sat up for a few moments.

■ An enormous thicket of giant gnarled trees grew so closely together that in order to pass between their trunks, the hunter had to turn sideways and wriggle through. Inside the natural structure that arched overhead like the domed ceiling he remembered from the Ministry of Justice building in the Well-Built City, there was a huge clearing where the wind was all but forgotten. The branches tangled together forty feet overhead, and the trunks were like walls. Here, there was only a dusting of snow on the ground, whereas outside it was piled three feet deep. As little of the morning sun penetrated as did the snow, but in the dim light he saw, hanging above him from the roof of arching limbs, odd brown sacs, hundreds of them, each a man-size fruit. He felt a tingling at the back of his neck, beads of sweat broke on his forehead, as his eyes adjusted to the shadows. They were demons, sleeping, suspended upside down and draped in their wings.

Slowly, without breathing, he stepped backward and, as quietly as possible, slipped out between the trunks where he had entered. Once clear of the nest, he smiled and began to search for kindling. As he gathered fallen limbs and twigs, he wished the dog was with him.

An hour later, fifty yards from the enclosure, he had a small fire burning on a plot of ground he had cleared of snow. He thrust the end of the torch he had made into the flames until it caught. His eyes were wide, and his chest heaved with excitement. Turning, he headed back toward the natural dome. As he approached the wall of trees, he stopped and reached the torch toward them. Before the fire could lick the trunks, he hesitated. Minutes passed and he stared at the flame as if hypnotized. Then, sighing, he opened his hand and let the glowing brand fall into the snow. A thin trail of smoke curled upward, and he walked away.

■ The eastern pond was frozen solid, and his luckless excursions in search of game took him to its side most distant from the cave. One day, he tracked through the snow the prints of what appeared to be a type of deer he had not yet encountered—something much larger than the white variety. The promise of its size drew him farther into undiscovered territory. A few hours after noon, a storm suddenly swept down from the north. At first, he hoped the weather might pass, and he kept going since he had not killed anything. The sun receded, the storm grew in intensity, and he finally realized he would have to turn back empty-handed.

Hours flew by before he reached the edge of the pond. In order to save time, he decided to cross it. Somewhere in the middle of that frozen tract, the snow began to drive down so fiercely that he couldn't see more than a few feet in front of him. He pushed on, never knowing if he had left the pond or where he was in relation to the cave. Like a sleepwalker, he lurched along without direction, and as the snow drifted upon the drifts that had already begun to harden, walking became difficult. Fear mounted in his mind, and all he could picture was the frozen corpse of the cinnamon cat, whose pelt he wore on his back. The sky grew dark with night as he inched along, unknowingly turning in wide circles.

Thoughts became clouds as dreams and memories flew together and then melted into snow. The wind insisted that he lie down and rest. "You are tired," it said, "and the white bed is soft and warm." Above the howl of the gale, he heard the distant sound of a dog barking, and it frightened him, because he knew the phantom noise meant the approach of death. "You must continue," he told himself, but the wind was right. He was tired, and the snow at his feet appeared a pure white comforter in which he might wrap himself. The bow fell from his hand, and he dropped to his knees in a deep drift that held him upright in that position.

Death came for him, blowing down from the north—a swirling swarm of darkness mixing in with the falling snow.

He saw it in his mind's eye, he heard its soothing voice above the roar of the storm. It gathered itself up before him where he knelt, becoming a statue for the Beyond. The ice on his eyelashes cracked as he opened them to see the hunter whose prey he had become.

Wood bounded forward and rammed Cley in the chest, knocking him onto his back. The dog licked his face, thawing the ice jam of his confusion. The hunter grabbed his bow and found the strength to stand. Whistling weakly, he called, "Come, boy," but the dog was already in the lead, showing him the way to safety. The faster they traveled, the more body heat he generated, reviving the circulation to those extremities that had begun to go numb. The relentless sting in his hands and feet was a welcome sign.

No sooner, it seemed, had they begun their journey home than the wind eased and the snow diminished to the lightest flurry. Before long, the moon glared down, offering light by which to mark their way. Wood stopped for a moment in a clearing in order for Cley to rest. The Beyond was hushed with that certain calm that follows the rage of blizzards. The trees were fringed with white, and the drifts were wind-curled at their tops like ocean waves.

As they were about to push on, Cley saw something moving among the trees to his right. The figure was large and shadowy, and the only thing that gave an indication as to what it might be was the reflection of moonlight off the bone white of its antlers. "Could this be the beast I was tracking all day?" he wondered as he let his mittens drop and reached for an arrow.

His hands still had little feeling, but the bow was so familiar that he was able to place the arrow. Wood noticed what he was doing and immediately crouched in the snow. Pulling the bowstring back was difficult, and his arm shook with the exertion. The thing in the woods blew a gust of air from its nostrils, and judging from where that cloud of steam gathered in the glow from above, he figured the distance to the chest, aimed, and released. A deep, rasping squeal cut the stillness of the night.

Wood was off like a shot, circling in among the trees to drive the creature out so that Cley could get off another shot. An enormous buck broke into the clearing just as the hunter was drawing back on the bowstring. As the stag got its footing and crouched to dash off to the left, he saw his other arrow jutting from the animal's thick neck and aimed lower. The new arrow hit the mark, directly between shoulder blade and ribs. The animal went down hard, sending up a shower of new snow. Kicking its back legs, it squealed miserably in a strange, near-human voice, and thrashed back and forth.

In an instant, Cley had the stone knife in his hand. As soon as the stag rested from its death throes, he approached it from behind. The legs of the creature gave a few more quivering kicks, and then the hunter lunged in and sliced it across the throat. The life had barely left it before Wood lapped at the blood-dyed snow.

The carcass was too heavy to carry back, and it was a certainty the wolves would devour it by morning. It was as big as a small horse, with a rack that numbered ten points on either side. Cley had no choice but to take whatever he could carry. There was no telling if the Beyond might serve them venison again until spring. He cut two enormous steaks from its flanks, enough for a week's worth of meals, and they trudged back toward the cave.

It took all of his remaining energy to build another fire, and he heaped on their entire store of kindling and branches so that he would not have to tend it through the night. With his hunting cloak and mittens still on, he wrapped himself in the blanket and passed out by the shaft at the back of the cave.

He slept hard, without dreaming, for what seemed an entire day, before waking to the sound of his own voice, shouting. Immediately, he fell back to sleep again.

He came to, late in the morning, but of which day he wasn't sure. His leg and arm muscles ached fiercely, but he was pleased to find that all of his toes and fingers had survived exposure to the storm. Wood approached and he put his arms around the dog.

"Venison, for you," he said, and laughed at the thought of having beaten the Beyond one more time.

Passing the cooling embers of the fire, he walked through the entrance of the cave and into the day. The sky told him that snow would fall again before night. He dropped to his knees and began digging through the ice-crusted white in order to uncover the meat he had hastily buried. The lack of tracks indicated his kill had been safe from scavengers. After digging to the frozen earth in one spot, he found it wasn't there, and realized he had misjudged the hiding place. He set to digging in another spot a few feet away. Again, nothing was revealed. Frantically, he worked in spot after spot with twice the vigor. An hour later, the entire area of a six-yard arc in front of the cave mouth had been exhumed. Throughout the entire excavation, he found not a single drop of blood, not a single hair from the hide that would have covered one side of each steak.

Cley cursed angrily. The dog came out of the cave and stood in front of him, but turned to the side, looking out of the corner of his eye.

"Did we not kill a huge buck last night?" he asked Wood. The dog didn't move.

He thought back to the scene in the moonlit clearing—the shadow of the creature, its breath turned to steam, the perfect accuracy of his shots, the sound of its last breath when he cut its throat. Reaching down into his boot, he retrieved the stone blade and inspected it for any evidence of a recent kill. It was spotless.

From all through the forest came the sound of branches cracking beneath the newly fallen snow—the sound of the Beyond, laughing.

■ Wood recovered fully from his wound, though it left a jagged scar across his chest. The days came and went with a lethargic monotony—tending the fire, hunting, sitting through long hours in the cave, staring out at a perfectly white world. Wild imagination was more abundant than food, and the companions' diet consisted of hunger occasionally punctuated by a thin, rabbit haunch and snow soup or a geeble stew that when thoroughly cooked was no more than fat pudding. Now and then they dined on roots or, if luck was with them, a large crow. In addition to daydreaming and not eating, they spent their time reading the nameless book of the soul. The tome had lost all meaning for Cley, but he continued with it, as it was the closest thing he had to a human conversation. Each night, the dog took its weight in his jaws and carried it over to the hunter. Wood had grown dependent on the whispered droning of the words in order to fall asleep.

After the dog dozed off, Cley sometimes took the green veil from his pack, rolled it into a ball, and held it out in front of him in the palm of his hand. Occasionally, he was so enchanted by the tattered scrap of material that he forgot to tend the fire. These eruptions of emotion, of memory, were like tiny islands in the overwhelming sea of sun-starved boredom that was the winter. It was repetition and mundane ritual that kept them alive. They partook of these with a stoic determination that eschewed even the vaguest desire for spring.

◼ Cley opened his eyes and looked to the cave's mouth to catch a glimpse of the weather, but all he could make out was a dim, blue glow. The rest of the den was cast in deep shadow. A wall of ice had formed, separating them from the world. It seemed impossible that so much snow could have fallen in a six-hour period. The fire had gone out, and ice was beginning to form along the walls where the opening had been. He took his knife in hand and attacked the frozen boundary, chipping away in hopes that it was merely a thin crust, on the other side of which he would find soft snow.

After an hour of hard work, it became clear that the knife was useless. All he had to show for his effort was an indentation the size of a fist. It was obvious that the temperature outside had plummeted below anything they had yet experienced. He turned his head and put his ear to the frozen barrier. Somewhere, far away, as if in another world, he heard the fierce cry of the storm blowing through the forest.

"Buried alive," he said to Wood as he slid the knife back into his boot. The dog walked over and stood next to him.

He considered lighting a fire in an attempt to melt the smooth blue wall but realized that if it did not melt fast enough, he and the dog would be suffocated by the smoke. He entertained the possibility of waiting until the storm ended, hoping the sun would thaw the obstruction. That could take days, though, and they had nothing to eat but a few scraps of cooked rabbit and a handful of wild sweet potatoes, already beginning to rot.

Going to his pack, he retrieved a candle and lit it. The glow of the flame pushed the dark into the corners and alleviated the grave nature of the situation for a few moments. He let a pool of wax drip onto the floor and fixed the candle in it. With legs crossed, he sat back against the rock wall and tried to concentrate while Wood paced at the entrance, growling at the ice.

He knew he did not want to wait the storm out. There were no guarantees that the sun would free them before they starved to death. Besides, he imagined that the wait would be so boring, he might be forced to shoot himself. Thoughts of the rifle brought to mind a bizarre scheme that entailed his emptying the remaining bullets of their powder and creating a bomb with which to explode a passage to freedom. There were only a dozen bullets, though, and an image of his blowing his own hand off quickly followed. Desperation began to set in. The safe haven of the cave had become a prison that would soon become a tomb. He yelled angrily at Wood to stop pacing, and the dog lifted his leg and urinated on the ice.

"Nice work," said Cley, and Wood began pacing again.

Although the candle generated light, it offered no warmth. Dressed only in his overalls and flannel shirt, Cley moved back toward the shaft to catch more of its subtle warmth. Now that the normal egress was cut off, he began to think more keenly of that dark aperture that led down into the hill. The hole, though narrow, was still large enough to accommodate the width of his body with a few good inches on either side. He leaned toward the tunnel, trying to peer into the darkness, which revealed nothing, and wondered if it connected to another opening in the hill or a sheer drop to the center of the earth.

His decision was made when Wood carried the book over and dropped it at his feet. The dog lay down and prepared for the long wait he now somehow understood was before them.

"No thanks," said Cley. "I'll take the shaft."

He got a box of matches and another candle from the pack and put them in his pocket. Then he tore the lit candle off the floor. Before crawling forward into the darkness, he looked back and emphatically told the dog to stay put. He took a few deep breaths as if about to dive under water, then inched slowly forward, the flame flickering in the warm breeze that moved up around him.

Five yards farther in and the tunnel narrowed even more. He was forced to lie on his stomach in order to proceed. The shaft pitched downward at a forty-five-degree angle, and from what little he was able to see ahead, it seemed to continue that way for quite a distance. If it didn't open up and present a place where he could turn around, it would be difficult wriggling up that slope backwards. He decided to go on a few more yards. Moving like a snake, he continued as the walls of the tunnel closed in around him.

He stopped to rest and noticed how warm it was in the shaft—a pleasant place simply to lay his head down and sleep. Then he remembered this was exactly what the winter wind had told him the night he had been lost in the storm. Before he began to move again, he heard something up ahead—water dripping or loose pebbles tumbling. Suddenly, Wood was behind him, barking. The candle guttered in a strong gust from below, and everything went black. The dog panicked and tried to scrabble past Cley, unknowingly clawing the hunter's legs.

"Easy, easy," he called out to Wood, and lunged forward, trying to escape the frantic dog. In doing so, he moved himself out over an unseen ledge and the two of them fell. Cley screamed, thinking he was headed for a mile-long descent, but his cry was abruptly cut off when he hit solid rock five feet below. He landed on his side, smashing his elbow, and the wind was knocked out of him. Wood came down on top of him, and then sprung off unharmed. The hunter rolled on the hard rock, working to catch his breath.

It was pitch-black, but, even in his distress, Cley noticed that the sound Wood's nails made against the rock echoed out, indicating they had stumbled onto another large chamber. He rolled himself to a sitting position and dug the matches out of his pocket. Sparking a match to life, he lit the candle he had been able to hold on to through the misadventure. The flame revealed what he had suspected, another cave, larger than the one above, and at the far end of it a tunnel of such size that he might enter it standing upright. Cley noticed that the warm breeze, which heated his own rock apartment above, was emanating from down the corridor that led farther into the hill. He started slowly forward, holding the candle out in front at arm's length, while Wood followed close behind.

The tunnel took a wide turn, and as they followed its curve, a blast of warm air extinguished the candle again. Cley cursed out loud, then noticed that there was another light source somewhere in front of him. Stumbling forward, using the rock wall for support, he finally stepped out of the passage and into a small chamber bathed in a yellow-green light.

At first, he thought it must be the sunlight streaming through a hole in the ceiling. The glow came not from above, though, but below—an underground pool that generated its own fluorescence. The cave rippled with brightness from the water. The swirling glow was fantastic enough, but on closer inspection he saw that the walls had been decorated with drawings done in charcoal and a thick red paint possibly made of clay. Stylized images of men and women, animals, and strange humanoid creatures with fishlike heads filled the chamber. Here and there someone had left red handprints.

"What do you say to this?" Cley asked Wood, then looked around to see where the dog had gone. He whistled in order to locate him, and a bark answered from off to the right. Moving around a low wall of rock, he stepped into yet another small chamber. The glow from the strange waters did not extend to this new area, so he used another match and relit the candle.

The gleam of the flame was reflected in Wood's eyes. The dog was sitting upright amidst the remains of what appeared to be six or seven human bodies. There were dried flower petals and fragments of pottery scattered among these bones. It was obvious from the small, delicate nature of one skull and rib cage that an infant lay among the dead. Another of the skeletons showed evidence of a type of deformity—a vestigial fishtail protruding off the end of a perfectly preserved spinal column.

Set off a foot or two from the others were the remains of what obviously had been a woman whose long black hair had survived the ravages of time. The luxuriant tresses stretched out more than four feet from the skull, which still retained a large portion of withered flesh. She wore a necklace of white beads made from shells, and at the end there was a small leather pouch. The walls in this chamber were decorated with spiraled images of plants and vines and blossoms.

Standing in silence, Cley wondered how long they had lain, undisturbed in this secret place. "What lives did they live?" he asked himself, and felt the breeze of centuries passing, years turning to dust. Then, in an eyeblink his reverie became fear, and he was frantic to escape the underground for daylight.

"Let's go," he said to Wood, noticing another smaller tunnel at the end of the burial chamber. The current of warm air flowed from it, passing around him. Before leaving, he knelt and worked to remove the woman's beads over her skull. As he tried to free them, her hair fell across the back of his hand, and the touch sent a wave of revulsion coursing through him. He pulled away with the necklace in his hand, and the sudden motion severed the fragile neck. The jaw came unhinged and dropped open. Her brittle ribs cracked, sounding to him like whispered gasps of pain. With the prize tightly clutched in his left hand and the candle in his right, he fled forward into the next natural corridor.

Wood grabbed Cley by his right pant leg just in time to

prevent him from falling headlong into an almost perfectly round hole in the middle of the dark path. The toes of the hunter's boots were already out over the abyss. A blast of warm air rose from far below and lifted Cley's hair. He took a step back. Miraculously, the candle remained lit. This was the source of the tropical current that had kept their own cave temperate through the worst of the winter.

Both Wood and Cley vaulted the opening in the rock floor with ease. The passage continued on, twisting and turning and widening until it eventually broke clear into a cave with a tall, broad entrance that looked out on the day. From where they stood at the back of the chamber, it was as if they were in the rear of a theater, watching a play about a blizzard.

They slept that night back in the tunnel near the conduit of warm air. When he awoke the following day, Cley was mightily hungry and knew the dog must be too. They left the tunnel, and upon entering the cave that opened on the opposite side of the hill from their home, they saw a glorious sun shining out over a vast plain. The sight of that flatland stretching out toward the north showed Cley the way to travel once the winter was over.

Out on the plain there were no trees, and it seemed a certainty that the demons would not hunt there. Escaping this threat would allow him and the dog to make headway north without constantly having to fight for their lives. He decided then that as soon as the days began to lengthen, they would resume their journey before the demons woke from hibernation. There weren't enough bullets left to survive another season against them, and he sensed that somewhere in the cold, dark time of winter he had lost his will for slaughter.

Two hours later, after traversing the circumference of the hill in hip-deep snow, at times clinging to tree trunks against the wicked pitch of the incline, they stood outside the entrance of their own cave. Luckily the sun was bright and offered enough warmth for Cley to have survived the arduous journey without his cloak or mittens. Then began the grim task of digging out the opening while hunger twisted their guts. Every few minutes, the hunter had to stop to blow on his frozen fists, but eventually they managed to clear enough snow so that the sun could shine directly onto the ice that had formed over the entrance.

Next, they set about gathering branches that had cracked under the weight of the ice and fallen to the ground. With these, he built a small fire as close to the obstruction as possible. As they waited for the fire to do its work, Cley warmed his hands over it and set one of his boots smoldering, trying to do the same with his feet.

Sometime later, a well-placed kick shattered the remaining inches of glazed snow. Reentering their cave filled Cley with a sense of peace and comfort. He and Wood greedily devoured the few cooked rabbit parts they had stored, and then Cley went to work on one of the raw, rotting sweet potatoes. The fire was moved inside the entrance and they settled down to rest for a spell before preparing to hunt. The dog insisted on a few words from the book, and Cley acquiesced in a weary voice.

■ The white deer returned to the forest. In many places the fallen snow melted and revealed the welcome face of the earth. Flocks of crows again perched in the treetops, and an owl took up residence somewhere close by the cave, haunting the nights with its call.

■ On a hunting expedition to the eastern pond, Cley heard the ice cracking in long, wavering echoes. The sound was a signal to him that he and the dog should soon begin their journey across the plain. Although he rejoiced at the fact that the sun now shone brightly in the afternoons, pushing back the night a few minutes each day, he wondered how long it would be before the demons came forth to hunt, driven by a season-long hunger. As he traipsed across the thawing ground, tracking a deer, he began to make plans.

There were a few things that distressed him about their coming trek across the open country. One was that the store of matches had been seriously depleted. He had one-quarter of one box left, which, optimistically, he surmised might last little more than two weeks. The other concern was shelter. Out on the grasslands there would be no caves nor trees to offer a temporary haven against the elements.

He remembered that in the adventure novels of his boyhood, he had read of ways to start a fire without matches—rubbing sticks together or drawing a spark by knocking a flint against a rock. The thought of actually accomplishing either of these seemed to him more impossible than the daring exploits of those books' heroes. Still, he knew there was nothing else but to begin work on learning one of these skills. As far as the lack of shelter was concerned, he decided to take many deerskins and from them create a small tent that would at least keep the wind and rain at bay. It had to be something he could roll up and carry, but that would add extra pounds to his already heavy pack. Then the thought came to him that perhaps Wood might pull it behind him.

■ Cley's accuracy with the bow had become so good through the winter that he could fell a deer with just one arrow. He worked quickly, skinning his prey on the spot, and in this manner was able to take two or three skins a day. At night, he and Wood ate venison steaks and livers and began to regain much of the strength they had lost through the harsh heart of the winter. After dinner now they passed on the book, for the nights were filled with industry—treating the insides of the pelts and readying them to be sewn together. He calculated that he would need at least fifteen skins to make a tent large enough to cover both of them.

Killing a deer and carving it up was second nature for the hunter, and he enjoyed the work—at last a definite project other than merely surviving. It took his mind away, and he no longer sat morosely holding the green veil and staring into the past. When the tent was three-quarters sewn together, he realized he had not yet tackled the job of making fire without matches. The idea of rubbing sticks together to draw a flame seemed preposterous, so he instead opted for the technique that called for the banging of rocks.

Following the stream at the bottom of the hill, he and the dog set off one morning, searching along its bank for promising specimens. Every now and then he would stop, lift two rocks, smash them together as hard as he could, and study the results. By midday, he had broken nearly thirty rocks and smashed each of his fingers at least once without having produced a single spark. Wood grew tired of this fruitless pursuit and went off into a stand of shemel trees after a geeble.

"What idiot invented this technique?" Cley wondered, but drawing on the persistence that had kept him alive through worse trials, he continued. He knelt again by the stream's edge and brought up a large, black, heart-shaped stone. He was searching for another against which to smash this one when he heard a strange noise. It was something familiar but nothing he had heard in a long time. He stopped and listened more intently. All he heard was the sound of the tree branches scraping together in the breeze and the rushing of the water.

Minutes later, he reached out to take up another stone and heard again, from off in the forest, the distinct sound of someone weeping. He was used to the weird noises of the Beyond, but this particular one made the hair on the back of his neck stand up. Listening closely, he was sure he heard a woman sobbing. Getting up, he called for Wood. The sound of his own voice dispelled the crying, and he stood perfectly still for a long time, listening.

"Hello?" he finally called but there was only the breeze.

"Who is there?" he yelled, and with this, Wood came charging out of a thicket of trees. He realized, upon seeing the familiar figure of the dog, how momentarily frightened he had been. Listening intently a while longer, he finally decided it was nothing more than the call of a bird or the rushing of the stream over an obstruction.

In order to put the incident decisively out of his mind, he banged together the two rocks he held. A spark leaped out of the collision and landed in his beard. Moments later, a thin wisp of smoke curled away from his face, and a moment after that, he was on his knees again dipping forward into the ice-cold stream. Wood nipped him on the rear end as he knelt with water dripping off his face.

On his way back to the cave, Cley looked up from his thoughts to see where the dog had gone. In the distance, a figure stood amidst the trees where the stream turned left toward the hill. He blinked and looked again. Whatever had been there was now gone. Pocketing the two rocks, he took out his knife and began running as quietly as possible. He was positive that what he had seen was not a demon because there was no sign of wings or tail. It appeared to be a person, standing still, gazing down into the moving water. When he reached the spot, he spun slowly in a circle, staring sharply into the trees.

"Show yourself," he called out. He listened for the sound of breaking twigs or rustling in the underbrush. "A bear?" he wondered. Something inside told him to run, and he did, all the way back to the cave, Wood following at his heels.

◼ He insisted upon using the rocks to start a fire. Because of this, they did not eat until the moon had risen in the star-filled sky. As he prepared his blanket to lie down, he heard the owl suddenly call from outside the cave. Although the bird came now almost every night, on this particular visit its cry set Cley's heart to pounding. The dog looked over at him and then toward the mouth of the cave, sensing his master's anxiety. For the first time since early winter, the hunter loaded a shell into the rifle's chamber. He kept the weapon across his knees as he read to Wood, and slept that night in a sitting position, his finger wrapped lightly around its trigger.

◼ On the day that Cley took the last deer needed to complete the tent, he wandered back toward the cave past a stand of gray, barren trees he had passed at least a hundred times throughout the winter. On this trip, though, he noticed something he had never seen before. In among the trunks he spied an unusual object sticking up out of the ground. He moved cautiously over to it, and there he found, of all things, a pickax, its handle half-buried in the ground. Dangling from a strap off one of the points was an old helmet, tiny holes eaten through the rust.

He lifted the headpiece to see if affixed to the front there was a device to hold a candle. When he found what he was looking for, he knew he had discovered one of the graves of the explorers who had struck out years earlier from Anamasobia. It had been told to him by Arla Beaton that they had been dressed in their mining gear, on a quest to discover the Earthly Paradise. He remembered the story—sixteen of them, and the only one to return was Arla's grandfather. Cley could not help but smile at the ridiculous equipment they had brought, as if they had intended to excavate miracles from the Beyond. The wilderness had wasted no time in turning their tools into grave markers. Still, the hunter felt a sense of camaraderie with the fallen miner and knelt before the crude memorial. He tried to think of something to say, but remained silent. A minute later, he took up his pelt and whistled for Wood.

On a clear patch of frozen ground, he scratched out with his knife a crude design for the tent carrier he imagined. It had to be light with thin runners since it wouldn't be pulled over snow but instead the grass of the plain. He determined that the perfect branches for the device would be those of the carnivorous tree that devoured sparrows and starlings, since they were long, straight, and pliant enough to shape.

It was one thing to draw on the ground with a knife and quite another to hack the limbs off a tree with a volition to eat flesh. The one he chose to attack was not strong enough to lift him and stuff him down into the opening at the top of its trunk, but it tried to. He could hear the tree's digestive juices bubbling within as he hacked at its limbs. The grasping twigs at the ends of the constantly moving branches kept pulling at him, and it hurt madly when they wrapped around his hair and beard. All the time Cley worked, Wood paced nervously a few feet away, barking at the giant with which his friend appeared locked in combat. Occasionally the dog charged in and tried to bite the many-armed enemy but was unsure as to where to sink his teeth.

After much struggle, the required branches wriggled on the ground like a brood of snakes. From their cut ends oozed a dark green sap.

"That's the damnedest thing," said Cley, waiting for their life to drain away.

He began construction and decided that the limbs of the hungry tree were the right choice for the job. They were sturdy, but could be bent to make the frame and runners. Using dried strips of deer hide, he tied the joints fast, then bowed one long stalk into a perfect loop to fashion the harness that would fit around Wood's chest. The work took him the better part of the day, and he enjoyed the complexity of the task.

It was early evening when he finished, and pleased with his creation, he took the time to double-tie all the joints. During this process, he looked up to find where the sun was in its descent and saw a woman, dressed in skins, standing in front of him. The fact that there was someone there, watching him, was startling enough, but it was her otherworldly presence that made him reel backward onto the ground. Her form was slightly transparent, wavering like a heat mirage, though the air was still cold. Her eye sockets were perfectly empty and dark as any tunnel through the underground. She appeared a magic-lantern projection from another time—her hair blowing behind her in a phantom wind, her flesh shrunken against her cheekbones and pulled tight in a thin scrim across her forehead.

"What?" he yelled, his entire body trembling.

When she put her arms out toward him, as if pleading, he knew instantly who she was. Reaching into the cloak by his neck, he pulled out the beaded necklace he had worn since the day he discovered her grave. Slowly, as in a dream, she dropped to her knees and began digging at the thawing earth. From everywhere, came the sound of her sobbing. Cley got to his feet and backed away. She reached toward him again, then motioned back to the ground.

He had never thought to see what was in the pouch because it had always felt empty, but now he understood that it contained something that was important to her. Nervously, he lifted the beads to get at it. Pulling apart the gut drawstring, he turned it over onto his palm. Out rolled a small, green seed half the width of a thumbnail and tapered at either end. Fine roots like hairs grew from each of the tips. He looked back to her, holding it forward, but she had vanished, leaving behind only the diminishing sound of her sorrow.

Cley shuddered as he lifted his knife off the ground where it lay next to the sled. He knelt and dug a shallow hole in the earth. Very carefully, he dropped the seed in and gently covered it over, tamping the cold dirt with his palms. As soon as he was finished, he leaped to his feet and gathered his mittens and rifle. Grabbing the sled by its harness, he whistled for Wood and set out quickly for home.

When they arrived at the cave, he did not bother to remove his cloak but went directly to the back, to the shaft that led down into the burial chamber, and threw the necklace in as far as he could. Even after an hour had passed, he still sat against the rock wall, staring out at the sky.

■ Before the sun rose, he made an inventory of his belongings and placed them neatly in his pack. Since the temperature had risen in recent days, he rolled up the cat cloak, the mittens and leggings, and stuffed them also into the pack. He was pleased to be able once again to wear only his overalls, shirt, jacket, and the black hat adorned with wild-turkey feathers. Once he was fitted out for the journey, he slung the bow over his shoulder and took up the rifle. Before leaving the cave, he looked back into it once with a perverse sense of nostalgia.

He had rigged the tent to the sled the night before, and now all that was needed was to get Wood into the harness. It took some doing to convince the dog that dragging the weight was a good idea. For this purpose, he had saved a few strips of venison from the previous night's dinner, and with these he was able to coax his companion into the job of mule. Cley felt a measure of pride when the rig slid over the ground with ease.

They started around to the other side of the hill, and had not gone fifty yards, when they found a demon blocking their path. It lay facedown on the ground, unmoving, its wings folded in as if it was either asleep or dead. Cley stopped and brought the rifle up in front of him. He was wary of the beast, knowing the demons were not beneath a form of simple trickery. Wood was beside himself in the harness. Unable to attack, he growled in warning and frustration.

Cley advanced slowly, keeping a strict aim on the head of the creature. A wing lifted slightly, and without a second passing, the hunter fired, missing the base of the skull and instead chipping off the tip of the right horn. Then he realized that the movement of the wing had been caused by the wind. He walked over and, using his foot, flipped the body onto its back. The face the demon wore was so horrific, Cley almost fired again out of fright. Its eyes protruded as if momentarily frozen in the act of exploding, and its bulging tongue draped down across its chest. He knelt and touched the carcass. It was still quite warm, and he figured it had probably been killed within the past half hour. Now he noticed the necklace of shell beads wrapped tightly around its throat, cutting deeply into the windpipe.

They navigated the hillside with minor difficulty and reached the plain by late morning. Out on the huge expanse, they moved quickly, half-fleeing the forest of demons, half-rushing toward the promise of the future. A sweet breeze blew in from the east, and beneath their feet were the first signs of green, sprouting out of the mud.

"i know you."

Although I dare not neglect Cley's impossible journey, something miraculous has happened in my own insular world that has transformed the tenor of my existence. While I wait for the sheer beauty to begin to percolate and guide me back to the Beyond, I will record these recent events that have had the same effect on me that a new pair of stronger, cleaner, spectacles might.

Two days past, after having stayed up all night in the thrall of the drug's dictation of Cley's months in the demon forest, I was completely exhausted. Although demons' lives are long in comparison with the normal span of a human's, I admit I am now getting on in years. The aftermath of the beauty has more of a deleterious effect on me than it once did. When younger, I could take the needle, experience its influence, and after a few hours be done with it until next I needed a touch of existential levity. Now, it dries me out, droops my lids, sags my wings, and leaves me feeling as if I could learn my wild brethren's practice of hibernation. The one thing it has never been able to do is trap me in addiction—I think.

I came away from this writing desk late into the following morning. Thoughts of Cley's cave, the black dog's wound, and those off-putting empty eye sockets of the ghost woman still swirled through my mind. The packs of cigarettes (stale ones this time from among the ruins), I'm sure only added to my pitiful condition. Instead of going off to my room to sleep, I decided to step outside and take some fresh air to disperse those nightmarish images.

It was a clear summer day, and I welcomed the sun as an antidote to the frigid landscape of the Beyond. The ruins appeared as they now so infrequently do to me, namely, as truly wondrous as they are—more exotic than when the city was whole and vibrant. I flew up to perch on one of the more prominent piles of rubble. From my research I knew that it had once housed the Ministry of Justice. I often sit in this spot, where two slabs of coral have settled at right angles, creating a comfortable throne that allows my wings to hang over the back. Resting my arms on my knees and my head upon my arms, I stared sleepily out across the static mayhem that is my kingdom.

As I was making a mental note to fly to Latrobia that evening to filch some fresh cigarettes from the back room of the blind mask maker who lives on the outskirts of town, I heard the sound of a human voice. There were no particular words I could discern, but I distinctly heard it, someone trying too hard to whisper. My initial reaction was anger. The last thing I needed in my present exhaustion was to be playing hide-and-seek with a troop of idiot treasure hunters. I saw it all in an instant—greedy, gun-toting fools eager to make off with Below's broken-down wonders. It would be easier to kill them than to scare them, but my all-too-human nature would not allow me that option.

Instead of leaping to action and crawling on all fours through the rubble in order to sneak up on them, the aftereffects of the beauty insisted that I sit still and wait for them to pass below my perch. While I waited, I could hear their voices grow more distinct. I sniffed at the air, and it brought me news of one female and either two or three males. I was pleased it wasn't the invading army I keep expecting. In my dotage I have become, in some ways, as paranoid as my father was. Minutes crawled by, and with each my anger grew *until my tail was dancing and I half considered the consequences of merely damaging one of them.*

Then they appeared from around the corner of the blasted Ministry of War and began crossing the intact plaza, which lay fifty yards beneath me. My mind seized, my anger instantly deflated. There were three of them—children. My first thought was to sit stone still as not to frighten them. My second thought was, "What irresponsible parent allows his children to go exploring among dangerous ruins where it is a known fact that a demon resides?"

They were neither very young nor very old, if that tells you anything of their age. The tallest was a boy with long brown hair, wearing a red shirt. He carried a sharpened stick in his hands with the same tenacity with which I had pictured Cley holding his rifle. I could tell by the way his gaze constantly roamed and he moved along in a partial crouch that he was scared. In fact I could smell his fear and that of the other, smaller boy with the peaked cap. The girl appeared second oldest to the boy with the stick, and she moved without care, leading the others onward. Her hair was long and blond, and she was thin, her arms gracefully swinging at her sides. The instant I saw her, I knew it was not the first time.

I could feel my anxiety rising. It was one thing to play rough with treasure hunters, but what does one do with children? I didn't realize until that moment how much more I would have preferred the invading army. Just then the girl looked up, and I could see her catch sight of me.

"There he is," *she shouted, pointing up the mound of debris at me.*

Her companions ran, screaming, and it was the last I would see of them. She not only stood her ground, but she smiled and waved to me. I tried to pretend I was a gargoyle made of stone, but she moved closer to the bottom of my hill.

"I know you," *she yelled.* "Do you remember how you saved me from the river?"

And so it was, that girl from Wenau I had pulled out of the river some years ago. "No good deed goes unpunished," I thought. My gargoyle disguise was too flimsy even for my addled sensibilities. I lifted a hand and waved to her.

"I know you," I said.

She began straightaway to climb the blocks of coral to where I sat, and, afraid she would fall and hurt herself, I called down to her to stay put, that I would come to her. Since she was the first person to have come to the ruins actually to visit me, I decided to do my best.

Shaking off my fatigue, I slowly stood, sucking in my paunch and thrusting out my chest. Regal was the look I wanted, so I let my wings spread completely on either side before I flapped them and leaped into the sky. Not until I was on the descent did I see what effect my show was having, but when I saw her face she appeared mightily pleased with me.

I landed with a spectacular but unnecessary fluttering that lifted the coral dust off the plaza and sent her hair up over her head. The last thing that I expected was that she would point at me and laugh. At first I was wounded by her reaction, but the sound of her joy was infectious, and I could barely restrain myself from joining her.

"Do I amuse you?" I asked.

"The spectacles," she said, covering her mouth with her hand. "When they draw you in the newspaper at Wenau, they make you a fierce monster."

I had to smile.

"You're not, though, are you?" she said quietly.

"If only you knew, my dear," I said.

"Do you remember the river?" she asked.

I nodded. "Was it four years ago?"

"Six," she said. "I was seven then."

"Very good," I told her, and then didn't know what else to say.

"Those boys were frightened of you. The one with the hat was

my brother, Caine. The other one is our friend, Remmel. My name is Emilia." She held her hand out to me.

Those long fingers, that thin arm, looked too delicate for me to touch. I bowed slightly instead, and said, "Misrix."

"I've come to tell you that not everyone in Wenau is afraid of you. Many have read the books of Cley and know that you helped him and us. Many don't believe the Physiognomist and think you are a wild animal. Those in the church say you are the spirit of evil," she said as if performing a speech she had memorized.

"It is likely that they are all in some part correct," I said.

"Because you pulled me from the river, I knew you were gentle. You will not hurt me, will you?" Her eyes went wide, and she lightly touched a locket that hung from a chain around her neck.

"That would never do," I said. "You are my first guest. Would you like me to show you the ruins?"

"Yes," she said.

I started walking, and she followed me. This was an opportunity I had long waited for—someone to whom I could explain the ruins. Throughout the long, lonely years, I had become a kind of archeologist, digging artifacts out of the chaos, researching the lives and lifestyles of its citizens, reading the histories in the library, poring over surviving documents from each of the ministries. Now that I had the chance to expound, I was tongue-tied by the youth and honesty of the only one ever interested in listening.

We had walked a hundred yards in silence, and I was beginning to sweat, when she said, "Can I touch your wings?"

"Of course," I told her.

She came close to me and reached out her left index finger, running it along one bone and then down across the membrane.

"Not as smooth as I thought," she said.

"Smooth is not my specialty," I told her.

"Tell me about this place, Misrix," she said.

So I began, and although she was only a child, I decided to be as honest with her as possible. "All of this you see around you," I said, "all of this destruction, this coral mess, and the metal and human remains that lie amidst it, when added together, combine to tell a story. A great, grand story. A tragedy for sure, a cautionary tale, but a love story nonetheless . . ."

I showed her the laboratory with its miniature lighthouse that still projected the forms and sounds of songbirds, the only remaining complete statue of a miner, in blue spire, brought here from Anamasobia, those sections of remaining architecture that might give an idea of the original grandeur of the place, the electric elevator that once led to the Top of the City but now only traveled four floors, the underground passages, and the blasted shell of the false Paradise. There was, of course, much more. She was a great listener, only speaking when she had a question that could not wait. I appreciated her silence, her focused attention, her mere presence.

I ended the tour after two hours in my room, where I house the Museum of the Ruins, my own natural history installation of those objects I believe to hold an integral part of the essence of the Well-Built City. We strolled up and down the rows, and I showed her the head of the mechanical gladiator, the old shudder cups, etc. When we came to the back row, I took down the core of the fruit of Paradise that Cley, himself, had eaten, and let her smell it.

"I see a beautiful garden surrounded by ice," she said, as I held the core up to her nose. For some reason, the look on her face almost made me weep.

From the museum, we went down the hall to the library, and I showed her the volumes and my writing desk with the pen in its holder and the pages from my previous night's work neatly piled.

"What are you writing?" she asked.

"About Cley," I said. "I'm trying to find him with words."

"People who believed Cley's writings in Wenau gathered money and sent an expedition a few months ago to the Beyond to also find him," she said.

"A mistake," I told her. "I wish them well, but I'm afraid what they will find there is death."

"They took a lot of guns," she said.

I could not help but laugh.

She was unfazed by my reaction. "Cley has become a hero for them," she said.

"I wish them well," I repeated.

Then she pointed to my desk, at the jeweled box I keep in the corner of it. It is fixed with red stones and fake gold—just a trinket, but something that I have always liked since finding it underground by the site of the false Paradise.

"What is that for?" she asked.

"Nothing," was the real answer, and I was going to give it to her, but at the last moment, I had an idea. After our tour through the ruins, she knew most everything about them, but I thought as long as there was some element of mystery here, she might return again.

"That box holds a powerful secret," I told her, knowing by her obvious intelligence that she would be susceptible to wonder. "I'm not ready to show it to anyone," I said. "I would have to know that person very well indeed."

I thought she would ask me to open it for her, but she didn't. All she said was, "I understand; I have a box like that at home, myself."

"And at home, they do not mind that you and your brother have run off to the ruins?" I asked.

She looked away from me, down one of the long aisles of the library, as she spoke. "We were supposed to be going to Latrobia to visit relatives. I made the boys follow me to the ruins by telling them they were cowards if they didn't come."

"How were you traveling?" I asked.

"On horseback. We had two horses—Caine and I on one and Remmel on the other. I know they have probably taken them and gone back to Wenau to tell my mother that I have become lunch for the demon," she said.

"Come quickly," I said. "We will easily beat them to the village."

As it turned out, I flew her home. I cannot recount the details of that journey because as I now fly in my memory, I do not pass over the fields of Harakun, but instead, move at the speed of thought over the flat land of the Beyond. The beauty has me in its arms, and I am empty-handed, searching for Cley. Below, the wilderness is shaking off the spell of winter.

the hunter is hunted

Wildflowers sprouted, and the grass came up so quickly that the hunter could swear he heard it growing in the stillness of the night. Every day was deep blue, warm sun, and a soft breeze blowing from the north. In the late afternoons, the light shone down in golden shafts through billowing white clouds. The plain appeared endless in all directions, perfectly flat and treeless. An ancient glacier had, in its retreat, deposited smooth oblong boulders here and there, and Cley thought of them as giant loaves of bread. He and Wood were like ants traversing the dinner table of the Beyond. Through the winter, the nights had seemed to last for weeks, but now, it was the days that were near-infinite.

■ Fresh water was plentiful, for there were streams that crisscrossed the land. They hunted, always with the bow, small game—rabbits, diminutive hogs with bushy tails, a tasty red lizard that ran on two legs, and a tall, flightless bird of beautiful green plumage. This same awkward creature's eggs made good breakfast food. Its nests were so easily discovered, small mounds of mud and twigs, that Cley wondered how the species has been able to survive. It was a disappointment not to find the herds of deer he had hoped for, but he was more than willing to trade them for the absence of demons.

■ Wood pulled the tree-branch sled, which glided over the new grass as effortlessly as a boat on water. It carried the tent, the rifle, and Cley's winter clothes. The hunter hefted his own pack and carried the bow slung over his left shoulder, the quiver, over his right. The dog's chest and shoulders had thickened with the daily exercise, and Cley's calf muscles had swelled to make his pant legs tight at the bottoms. Although he wore the wide-brimmed hat every day, he removed it at the noontime break to let the sun penetrate his head and melt away the memories of slaughter. With this practice, his face tanned to the same deep brown as his arms.

■ Nights were still cool, but the hunter had perfected his use of the stones in building a fire. For fuel, he used a type of gnarled bush that, when given one tug, pulled right up out of the earth. These grew everywhere, and to Cley's surprise never put out leaves or flowers. They burned very slowly, their branches filled with a thick, aromatic resin that when lit gave off a scent not unlike jasmine.

No longer in the forest, beneath the demon-haunted canopy or in the darkness of the cave, Cley viewed the night sky in its entirety. There were so many stars—bright dust scattered as if by a maniac's hand. He often thought, while lying on his back and staring straight up, that he was gazing into a kind of ocean. His mind wandered out past the moon, diving like a swimmer into the spiraled depths of the universe. Its immensity no longer frightened him as it had during his first night on the plain. One moment he was flying toward the constellation of Sirimon, the serpent from whose womb, mythology told, the world was born, the next, he felt the sun on his face and Wood tugging at his boot to continue the journey.

■ On the second day of the fifth week of their trek across the flatland, Cley decided that they had put enough distance between themselves and the demons. It took Wood well into the morning to comprehend that it was a day of rest and that they would not be starting out, as usual, toward the north. The dog pulled at the hunter's boot and barked. He trotted a few yards off and then looked back and growled. Cley brought out the book to divert the dog's attention from the demands of routine.

Breakfast was eggs and hog steaks. Cley checked all of the joints of the sled to see if they were secure. He inventoried his pack to remind himself of what he had and what he had used. When he came across the last box of shells for the rifle, he took one out and held it in his hand. He had not fired the weapon in more than a month.

By the side of a stream, he trimmed his hair and beard with the stone knife while whistling the tune of "That Soft Eclipse," a love song he remembered from his days in the Well-Built City. Then he washed himself, his underwear, his socks, and set the laundry out to dry in the sun. It was in the midst of this task that he got a strong urge to fire the rifle. "It would be a wonderful thing," he thought, "to hear the report of the gun split the silence of the plain."

After lunch, he took the weapon off the sled. He knew it was wasteful to fire it for the sake of hearing the noise, so he decided to at least go in search of a rabbit. When the dog saw the rifle, he started bounding around the hunter. They left the camp, heading in a westward direction toward a pile of boulders that looked, from a distance, like the form of a sleeping giant.

Not so much as a lizard showed itself. Cley scanned the sky for crows or buzzards. It was perfectly blue and empty all the way to the horizon. Since natural cover was so scarce on the plain, he held out hope that something would be hiding in the shadow of the boulders.

As they neared the huge rocks, Wood ran ahead, barking, and disappeared behind them. Cley stood a few yards back with the rifle aimed and ready for whatever was flushed out. He waited, but nothing bolted into the sunlight. The dog's bark changed to a growl, and, bringing the gun down, the hunter ran around to the opposite side of the formation. He worried that Wood had cornered a snake. In their travels they had seen some large ones, all a startling bright yellow, slithering through the new grass.

What he found was not a snake, or not the snake he had envisioned. Wood crouched in his attack stance, the hair along the ridge of his back raised, his teeth bared, facing off against the skeletal remains of what had once been an enormous creature.

The skull itself was nearly as large as the dog, resembling a cow's but with a much longer snout. Its mouth was open and filled with rows of perfectly preserved needlelike teeth. The eye sockets were big enough for Cley to easily pass his fist through. Stretching out for fifteen feet behind the head was a body composed of a spine with pointed, half-circle ribs curving down and resting their tips on the ground. Both the length of the ribs and the width of the spine diminished toward the tail, which ended in a three-foot-long, tapered bone needle.

Cley circled the remains, rubbing his hand on the smooth, sun bleached bones. He noticed the lack of legs or arms. "Sirimon," he whispered, and the thought that one or more of these things might still be roaming the plain made him nervous.

"Just old bones," he said to Wood. The dog relaxed somewhat, but was still visibly agitated by the skeleton. The hunter put the rifle butt to his shoulder, took aim, and, without hesitation, pulled the trigger. The gun's report was like a violent explosion that, for a heartbeat, devoured the serenity of the plain. Smashing through the skull, chips of bone flying in its wake, the bullet lodged in a rib halfway to the pointed tail. Cley instantly regretted the reckless act.

He moved away quickly and whistled for Wood to follow. A few yards later, they both stopped in their tracks. The dog was silent. The hunter scanned the empty sky. "Where are the birds?" he asked. They hadn't seen a rabbit or any other creature all morning. He squinted as if trying to see more keenly—no lizards, no ants, not even the gnats that had been their constant companions from the first day on the plain. Now, even the breeze had vanished.

"Where are the damn bugs?" he said.

■ At midafternoon, Cley sat up from where he had been trying to relax since their return from the boulders.

"Let's get out of here," he said.

He began quickly to gather the clothes and supplies laid out around the camp. Refilling the pack, he readied himself to resume the journey. His hands shook as he fixed the harness over Wood's head and chest. Before they set out, he packed the bow and arrows on the sled and again lifted the rifle. Removing his pack, he rummaged through it for the box of shells and loaded the gun.

They moved away from the campsite at double their usual pace, and it didn't take long for motion to alleviate the vague anxiety that had beset them more than the gnats ever had. He wondered if the problem was simply that they had broken their routine, but continued to hold the rifle close with both hands. After the first mile, they slowed to their normal pace.

■ From a great distance, he saw them shining in the late-afternoon light, and knew from their reflection that they were not boulders. Although he meant to avoid them, for some reason he continued on a path leading directly into their midst. Three more skeletons of the Sirimon creature lay clustered together in the ankle-deep grass. Two of the specimens were perfectly preserved—tail, ribs, and skull intact. The third had broken apart, its skull lying on the ground with a purple wildflower growing up through the left eye socket. He did not stop to touch them. In fact, he increased his pace. When he looked back and saw Wood sniffing the remains, he yelled angrily for him to hurry. For the miles that followed into evening, the ground they crossed was littered with fragments of skull, short lengths of spinal column still supporting a rib or two, and even one sharp, tail end, sticking straight up out of the dirt.

■ Night was upon them when they made camp in a spot that might have been any other at which they had stopped since entering the plain. He removed the harness from the dog and wondered, for the first time, if they would ever escape the flatland.

During the day's march, they had seen and killed only one rabbit, and that they found sitting out in the open, shivering and confused. When Wood barked the sorry creature did not even run but waited for Cley to remove the bow from the sled and nock an arrow into place. The ease with which he killed it made him suspicious, but there was no other meat.

"Like a painting," he said, considering the stillness of the landscape.

The fire was built, and they ate the confused rabbit along with some roots of the kierce blossom he had collected on previous days. For all of his uneasiness about it, the food tasted fine. Wood moved up close to Cley after the meal, and they read a few pages about the energy in nature that linked all individual souls together. "What a poozle," he said, and laughed in the midst of his reading. The dog growled quietly, as if to say, "Read on, you fool."

When he bedded down beneath the open sky, his errant thoughts brought him images of the Sirimon, slithering through the grass. The night, though, was as static as the day. When he finally held in check his imagination and really listened, he heard nothing. Still, he drew the loaded rifle closer to his side.

■ While they slept, the half-moon that had cast a silver glow on the plain disappeared behind a bank of dark clouds that moved without a breeze, flying, as if of their own volition, in from the west. Eventually, the stars were also obliterated from view. Early in the morning, just before sunrise, a fine misty drizzle began to fall. Cley tossed and turned in the dampness, deep in a dream of Doralice, the prison island upon which he had once been incarcerated. He stood on the shore, close to the breakers, staring out to sea, and beside him was the monkey, Silencio. When the waves crashed, the spray washed over the pair, and this spray stood in for the soaking Cley took in reality from the weather of the Beyond. The monkey pointed out to sea at a ship in the distance, opened his mouth wide as if to scream, but instead there came an explosion that blasted the hunter into consciousness.

He cleared the water from his eyes in time to see a bolt of lightning tear the western sky. Thunder quickly followed, and, with it, the rain began to fall in torrents. He looked around for Wood and saw him already cowering in submission to the storm. Cley's first thought was to pitch the tent he had made. They had used it only twice when first entering the plain and then not against rain but cold night winds. He felt well rested and wanted desperately to find a way out of the flatland. "We are going to get wet anyway," he thought. "We might as well move on."

They broke camp and started out just as a weak, diffused light began to spread across the sky. No sooner had they begun to walk than the wind that had been absent for nearly an entire day swept down from the northwest, driving the rain at an angle. Cley now carried the bow, having wrapped the rifle in a skin and stored it on the sled.

■ The ground had begun to turn to mud, and the rain gathered in puddles. Wood was having a hard time pulling the sled, its runners occasionally getting stuck in the soft earth. Cley got behind and pushed the contraption in order to get it going again. The downpour never tapered off, but constantly increased in strength until it was difficult for him to see more than a few feet ahead. Once, when trying to free the sled, Cley slipped and fell in the mud. He landed only a few inches from one of the nest mounds of the flightless bird. Discovering a clutch of half a dozen good-sized eggs, he carefully gathered them and put them in his pockets.

■ By the time they stopped to eat, it seemed that most of the plain was covered by an inch or two of water. In certain spots the puddles were deeper. He pitched the tent to allow them a few minutes of refuge from the storm and as a canopy beneath which he hoped to light a fire. It was difficult trying to get the demon-horn pegs to hold in the wet earth, and he had to search for a time before finding a piece of ground that was a foot or so higher and still relatively dry. Once the pegs were fixed, he slid the willow sapling rods, which gave the thing its boxlike structure, into the sinew notches sewn to the deerskin cover. The shelter was tethered in place by ropes woven from vine. He and Wood sat beneath it and rested, safe from the persistent battering of the storm.

"If you shake the water off you in here, I'll cut your other ear off," Cley said with a grim laugh.

The dog moved over next to him and looked into his eyes.

Cley petted him on the head. "A little water," he said. "How about some eggs?"

The hunter went outside and yanked up one of the bushes they burned nightly. Returning with it to the tent, he placed it inside to dry for a few minutes. Then he went through his pack and pulled out a small copper pot. Taking the pot, he walked a few yards away from the cover to where a deep puddle bubbled wildly beneath the driving rain. He was about to dip the pot into the water when he noticed something dark moving through the shallow pool. Leaning over, he looked more closely, past the agitation on the surface. There, swimming through the grass, was a school of tiny, black fish.

"Fish born of nothing," he said. Knowing there wasn't anything he could do about this miracle, he siphoned some water off the top of the puddle and returned to the tent.

"Fish in the puddles," he told Wood.

The dog barely lifted his head at the news.

Cley took the stone knife out of his boot and used it to gouge a deep hole in the ground that was the floor of their shelter. He then hacked some choice branches off the bush and threw the remainder outside. Next, he dug through his pack and brought out the book.

"Sorry, Wood," he said as he ripped the first few pages out.

The dog lifted his lip and gave an unconvincing snarl.

"We've read them already," said the hunter. He replaced the book, then wadded up the loose paper into balls. Placing these at the bottom of the hole, he took the cut branches of the bush and built a pyramid structure around them. As good as he had become with the stones, it was obvious that this operation called for matches. He retrieved them from the pack, and in minutes the smoke was rising, streaming out of the sides of the tent. He hoped that the branches, though still damp, would dry enough as the paper burned to then ignite. The words concerning the nature of the soul wrinkled brown and vanished in the flames. A short time later, the eggs of the flightless bird rolled in the boiling water of the copper pot.

■ The respite from the storm was so welcome that Cley did not want to leave the shelter. He sat, listening to the rain battering the skin, its rhythm now almost comforting. Wood rested his head on his paws, his exhalations forming puffs of steam in the cold air. Eventually the water infiltrated their haven, lifted the scattered eggshells, and washed them away.

◼ A fierce gale whipped around outside, tugging at the vines, and one by one the demon-horn pegs shot up out of the ground with the sound of buttons popping. The willow-sapling frame snapped and buckled in a dozen places. The deerskin cover flapped against the travelers like a giant wing closing over them, and then it was gone. Cley looked up and, in the sudden brightness of a flash of lightning, saw the tent being carried away like a sheet of brown paper on the wind. He acted quickly to save his hat from the same fate.

He stood, dripping wet, and surveyed the situation. The plain was clearly sinking beneath a lake of rainwater. On closer inspection, he saw it was not a lake but an immense shallow river. Now that the water was ankle-deep every-where, he noticed that there was a slight current to it. He watched as the bush whose branches he hacked off to make the fire gained buoyancy and began moving, along with sticks and loose blades of grass, off toward the north.

It was with great distress that he left the sled behind. He knew it would put a strain on Wood, constantly bogging down and getting stuck in the deepening water. There was also the absurd consideration that eventually they might have to swim, and then it would put the dog in serious jeopardy. All he salvaged from it was the rifle. With the pack and bow slung on his back, he carried the gun, and they started slog-ging through the sinking landscape.

◼ The drag of the water made every step like the weighted plodding of a nightmare. Cley thought the idea of drowning out on the flatland totally insane, but as the hours and the miles passed by it seemed to become more and more a real possibility. In those instances when the lightning flashed, he searched desperately ahead of them for some kind of shelter, some sign that the plain had a boundary. They continued, mindlessly, the persistence of the rain drilling their reason until they proceeded in a state bordering on the unconscious.

■ Cley looked up and realized that they had walked all night and into the next day. He was shivering so badly, he had to stop for a moment, maneuver the gun into the crook of his arm, and put his hands under his armpits for warmth. The hat brim had wilted and hung low, almost covering his eyes. He turned and looked for Wood, but the rain was falling so heavily he couldn't see two arm lengths in front of him. Then he heard the dog bark and staggered forward a few feet to find him sunk three-quarters of the way to his neck.

■ Somewhere in the day, they stopped to rest. There was nothing else to do but sit down in the flow. Cley found a small rock under the water and perched on it, with the ever-growing, lethargic river reaching to just beneath his chest. He positioned the gun across the back of his neck and slung his arms up over each end. Wood sat next to him, the water passing around his shoulders. Cley tried to think of a good excuse to continue, and did not move for a very long time.

■ The second night came on early since the day had been little more than a bright smudge on the horizon. The rain had slightly abated to what might be considered, in the Realm south of the Beyond, merely an incredible downpour. It seemed as if they had been traveling through the sunken world for years. Cley wondered if he and the dog had wandered blindly into some quadrant of Purgatory. The only things that convinced him otherwise were the hunger and the fierce burning of every muscle in his body.

■ It didn't seem possible that the sky could hold so much water and not, itself, fall from the sheer weight. Wood was swimming, and the waterline was nearing Cley's waist. The hunter had a mad vision of them two days hence still traipsing slowly along the bottom of an ocean, a school of sea horses passing above in the lime green water.

■ He stopped and peered into the dark. The lightning came again, but this time, a few hundred yards ahead, he saw, in the split second of diminishing brightness, a formation of boulders. The current had grown stronger, and it helped them along in their frantic charge for the safety of the granite island.

When they reached the rocks, Cley wasted no time, but threw the rifle, bow, quiver, and pack up onto the lowest one. Then he bent over and helped Wood scrabble up out of the water. The dog reached the top of the low, flat boulder. He did not stop there but jumped to the next highest one and then on to the most immense one in the clutch of six.

Cley reached his hands up and tried to hoist himself out of the water, but found that with the added drag of his wet clothes his arms didn't have the strength. Wood barked again and again, and with the dog's encouragement, the hunter took one last leap and barely managed to get his upper body high enough above the surface of the rock to lock his elbows beneath its weight. He grunted and struggled and kicked his feet, and, after a long battle against gravity, rolled forward onto the flat surface of stone.

Now, out of the water, he was energized enough to move the equipment to the next highest rock. From there, he reached each item up to where Wood was waiting for him. When he began to climb onto it himself, he slipped on the slick surface and hit his head. The concussion left him dizzy and nauseous, but he finally succeeded in scaling the boulder. Once there, he fell to his knees, then forward to lie flat against the cold surface. The sound of water falling, running, rushing was everywhere, and the world was spinning.

"All is lost," he whispered to the dog.

Wood moved closer and watched as Cley's eyelids fluttered and closed.

■ It was still raining, though less fiercely when the hunter woke, shivering. He reached over to where Wood lay and put his hand on the dog's back. The wind had shifted and now came from the south, blowing steadily but warmer than before. His dreams had him trudging through deep water, but his head was clearer now. The blood had dried from the gash. He sat up and tried to look through the dark.

He and Wood were stranded more thoroughly than if they had been shipwrecked on a desert island. He had never conceived of the journey ending in this manner. Maybe one day, in a hundred years, a traveler might discover their skeletons perched atop the boulder and wonder as Cley had when finding the remains of Sirimon. Even in the demon forest, when things were most grim, he had managed to reserve a place in his thoughts for his success. Now, in searching his memory, he could no longer find the image of his being reunited with Arla and Ea in the true village of Wenau. His hope of handing the green veil to Arla Beaton had been dissolved by the rain.

He reached into his shirt pocket and took the veil in his hand. Laying it on the rock in front of him, he smoothed it out flat. Since there was little chance now of his ever delivering it, he decided to send it on alone. He stood and held the piece of green material by one threadbare corner above his head. The wind lifted it, and it fluttered as if eager to be released. He cursed once, then opened his fingers, and it was gone, soaring upward on the warm southern current.

For the remainder of the night, he sat recalling the long chain of events, like an enormous coiled serpent, that had brought him to this rock. He no longer noticed the wind or rain, and near dawn, as the clouds broke and the moon became partially visible, he paid no attention. "The shortcut to Paradise," he murmured. By the time the eastern sky began to lighten, he had come to the end of his own story and fallen asleep sitting up, his arms locked around his bent knees.

■ With great care for the slipperiness of the boulder and his still-aching joints, he stood in order to view their situation. The sun felt wonderfully warm upon his skin, and before looking out over the water, he turned his face to stare straight into the burning disk. When the orange spots cleared from his eyes, he noticed that it was perhaps the clearest day he had yet spent in the Beyond. The sky was cloudless, and all around them flowed the transparent, jade green river, carrying in its slow current, bushes and sticks, wildflowers and grass.

Measuring the height of the water against the base of their boulder island (the one he had hoisted himself onto was now completely submerged), he estimated that the depth must be a uniform seven feet. He wondered if it was possible that so much rain could have fallen in two days. It was a certainty that to the south, at higher elevations, rivers had breached their banks and emptied into the flatland. It was all heading somewhere, and he tried to picture its destination—an immense whirlpool, a limitless ocean, or perhaps Paradise, which would accept all the Beyond had to offer.

■ He removed his shirt and pants and set them out on the rock to dry in the sun. Wearing only his underwear, he lifted the rifle and began to explore the confines of his tiny kingdom. Each step had to be planned and executed with care, for to slip and fall could easily have been fatal.

"We are in the Country of Six Boulders," he told Wood, whose toenails tapped against the rock with every step.

Down the other side of the tallest boulder, there were three more of decreasing size. The entire half dozen set was not arranged in a straight line but in a clutch and closely enough together that moving from one to another did not require leaping. The reconnoitering of the new country took all of five minutes. There was nothing remarkable to report from any of the provinces—all hard rock and water.

When they reached the last one (the second lowest of the six that had not been submerged), Cley stopped and peered out toward the horizon. He thought he had caught something on the very boundary of his sight out to the northeast. Using his hand as a shade, he looked more intently. At first, he was unsure if what he was seeing was a mirage, the reflection of the light on the water mixed with his own desire, but he swore there was the very faint trace of a tree line.

"Land ho," he said.

■ Cley sat on the highest of the boulders, trying to think of ways to gain sustenance enough to survive until the flood receded to a depth that would allow them to escape. Nothing came to him, and eventually, all of the thoughts of filling his stomach made him ravenously hungry. He left his perch and retrieved the copper pot from his pack. With Wood at his side, he descended to the lowest boulder that had not been submerged. Kneeling, he reached out over the rushing water and scooped up a good measure. Although the sudden river was a deep green, he was pleased to see that the portion of it he had taken appeared to be clear. He sniffed at it and found it had no foul odor. Then he put the pot to his mouth and drank deeply. The water was cool and refreshing, and it served to fill his stomach for the time being. After he had his fill, he again leaned out and brought in a potful for Wood.

■ Cley's clothes dried quickly in the heat of the bright sun. He dressed, put on his hat, and sat down on a lower boulder with his back against the tallest one, waiting for whatever might happen next. The Beyond was in complete control, and he knew it would do no good to struggle against it. Either it would destroy him or send him an opportunity for survival. It took Wood longer to come to the same conclusion, for he moved restlessly from one province of the Country of Six Boulders to another and back again.

■ The sun grew more intense as it reached its apex, and Cley could feel himself baking on the hot surface of the rocks. He considered a swim but feared the current might snatch him away from his island nation and drown him. Wood nosed through the pack in search of the book, but the hunter told him, "No." He motioned for the dog to come and sit beside him. His companion uttered something like a sigh before giving in. The two of them did all that was left to them. In sleep, Cley dreamt of the green veil, flying high over the wilderness of the Beyond.

■ He was awake and staring up into the bottomless blue sky of late afternoon before he even realized it. The heat had diminished somewhat, and there was a slight breeze. He could hear the water moving and the black dog breathing. Something sailed through the sky, crossing his line of sight. At first, he thought it was the veil, having flown out of his dream. When he squinted, he saw it was instead a bird—a large one at that. "A crow?" he wondered. The bird circled back into his field of vision, and he squinted again. He determined it was not a crow by the fact that, even at the great height at which it flew, he could see it was not black but a deep scarlet color. "The wings are too large," he said to the dog, who was still asleep.

It was a beautiful sight the way it spiraled down and then upward with an absolute minimum of wing thrust. The knot in his stomach then tightened a notch, and he came completely awake to the possibility. Nudging the dog in the ribs with his boot, he whispered, "Wood, time to hunt." In an instant, he scrabbled up to the highest rock and grabbed the rifle. Making sure the chamber was loaded with two shells, he pushed off his hat and brought the gun to his shoulder. Before he could sight the bird, the black dog was next to him. He prayed the rain had not ruined the weapon or bullets.

He followed the progress of the elegant creature as it slowly spiraled above them. The task was to shoot when the bird was at its lowest point and also off to the south of the island so that if he managed to fell it the current might sweep it past them. He waited for it to break from its course and fly off, out of range of the rifle, but it never did. As he continued to aim, he gave a grim laugh, realizing that the target might be a species of carrion bird, like a vulture. It could very well have had him and the dog in its own sight as two likely prospects for a future meal.

"The hunter is hunted," he said to Wood as he watched the large, red figure swing southward in its orbit of the island. He pulled the trigger and the report of the gun was startling. The bird neither dropped nor fled. It didn't change its course in the least.

"I didn't lead it enough along the arc," said Cley, and Wood growled either in agreement or admonishment.

The bird circled southward again, and when it dipped low in its spiral, Cley aimed and shot. It continued to glide for a few moments as if nothing had happened, and then, suddenly, it plummeted straight into the water, three large feathers drifting after it.

The hunter yelled, the dog barked, as they looked to find the carcass riding atop the green water. They immediately spotted it bobbing toward them on the flow, its bright scarlet like a moving wound. Cley hastily set the gun down and, forgetting the danger of the slick rocks, leaped to the lowest dry boulder. Wood followed his lead and beat him to a safe landing. The bird was floating toward them, only thirty yards away. It appeared that all he would have to do was lean over, stick out his arm, and it would be his.

At twenty yards away, their dinner began to drift out toward the eastern side of the island. Cley moved left on the rock and, leaning out as far as he could, waited for the bird to pass. It seemed to take forever to come even with the boulder, but when it finally did, it moved rapidly past, just out of reach of his fingers.

"Shit," Cley bellowed, but it changed nothing. Wood bounded twice, leaped over his companion's body and into the swiftly moving jade river. The dog surfaced immediately and began paddling toward the kill. Cley called to him to return, afraid he would be swept too far off to fight the current back to the rocks.

"Come on, boy," Cley yelled, as Wood took the huge bird between his jaws and turned against the current. The dog paddled with all his strength and began to make slow but steady progress. When Wood finally reached the side of the boulder that Cley lay on, the hunter reached down with both hands. He placed one on the scruff of the dog's neck, one at the base of his tail, and with a mighty heave, pulled him up out of the water and to safety. Wood dropped the red bird at Cley's feet, and although exhausted, moved in close to be praised and petted.

■ The sun descended toward a pale orange horizon. Cley sat atop the country of boulders, the bird laid out before him, and took his stone knife from his boot. Wood watched quizzically, his head cocked to the side. The hunter studied the carcass—the iridescent wing feathers shifting from red to purple to pink in the dying light. The eyes were an unsettling pure red with no obvious pupil, and the beak was as black and shiny as onyx.

"Not my first choice," he said, "but it's the specialty of the house." Bringing the stone blade to the bird's neck, he sliced the head off with one deft cut. Then, lifting the body as though it was a flagon of mead, he let the blood run into his mouth. At first, there was no taste, just a warm sensation passing down his throat. When the blood did reveal its flavor, it was not bitter or salty but almost unbearably sweet, like a wine made of sugar. He could feel the life liquid charging his body with energy as he drank it.

When he had taken as much as he could stand of the cloying sweetness, he held the carcass up to the dog's mouth. He tilted the bird, but Wood growled, closed his mouth, and backed away.

"It's all we've got," Cley said, but when he again approached with the bird, Wood leaped down to another boulder and sat, watching.

Cley knew there was not much chance of it, but he wondered if the bird might be a female carrying eggs. Wood's favorite meal was bird eggs. Lifting the knife again, he sliced open the body from the neck to where the tail feathers began. A dark smell rose from the innards of the prey. He gagged momentarily and then went to work, digging into where he believed the bird's womb might be. At first, he felt nothing but a sickening, wet mess. Still, he continued probing, and his fingers actually closed around something substantial. He pulled whatever it was out into the dim twilight.

In his hand was not an egg at all but a human ear, severed neatly where it would attach to the side of a head. Cley felt the sweet blood begin to rise in his stomach. He retched twice without vomiting. As soon as he had control of himself, he lifted the remains of the creature and tossed them out into the flood.

■ As the dark came on, he fetched water in the cooking pot for himself and the dog and then enough to obliterate every trace of the bird's remains. Only when the surface of the rock had been cleaned did the dog again approach the perch at the top of the island. Cley noted the uneasy look in Wood's eyes as the moonless, starless dark clamped down over the Beyond. He fell off to sleep in spite of the dog's soft whining.

■ He woke into darkness, half-delirious, with chills and sweat. His teeth chattered, and he could not control the spasms in his legs and arms. It was all he could do to remain awake while vomiting, afraid that if he lost consciousness he would choke on his own spew. The dog sat next to him, staring down at the shivering invalid he had become. The blood of the red bird had poisoned him, infected him, was turning him inside out. What he had thought was an opportunity offered by the Beyond for him to save himself he now knew was to be the agent of his demise. The wilderness had grown weary of entertaining his quest. Amidst the involuntary groans that welled up from his tortured gut, he cursed the land.

■ Hours passed, and his condition worsened. There was nothing for Wood to do but sit by and watch. Near morning, bright colors flashed in front of Cley's eyes and the sounds of the water rushing by, his own frenetic heartbeat, seemed heightened to a deafening decibel. His head felt as if it would split down the middle in the manner in which he had cleaved open the bird. Blood ran from his nose and across his lips. Its taste was anything but sweet.

■ He drifted in and out of consciousness. Once, upon waking, he saw before him the apparition whose necklace he had taken back in the demon forest. She knelt above him, rocking forward and back, her long hair reaching down at times to cover his face. Her eye sockets were, as before, empty, and when he cried out in fear of her, she opened her own dark hole of a mouth, emitting a piercing note that drilled the night. The touch of her bony hand upon his chest quelled his shivering. He believed he was dying and that the worlds of death and life were mingling. The terror of her presence overwhelmed him. When something red and feathered shot from her mouth and into his left ear, he lost consciousness.

■ Cley heard Wood barking as if at a great distance. He was still burning inside, and the pain in his head made his vision blurry. The sun had risen either in reality or in one of the thousand dreams through which he flew. In the midst of his wavering awareness, he sensed that there were people nearby. He looked up through watery eyes and saw a man standing over him. The fellow was tall, with long, tangled hair and perfectly naked. His skin was the oddest shade of gray, the color of cold cigarette ash, and marked everywhere with blue designs that looped, swirled and turned into pictures of birds and bees and plants. Across his chest was etched the skeletal head of Sirimon.

Cley felt many hands upon him. He was being lifted and carried. In his helplessness, he cried out for Wood and heard the dog answer his call. Following this, he blacked out for a short time. When he revived, he found himself surrounded by others like the man—naked with decorated flesh. They all seemed to be moving together through the flood on a boat or barge. These images and sensations ran together like watercolors in the rain, eventually mixing into black.

■ Motes of dust whirlpooled through thin beams of sunlight that pierced a thatched roof. All else was bathed in soothing shadow. There was a woven mat of reeds beneath him and some kind of animal skin covering his naked body. It was warm inside the narrow structure composed of young tree trunks and branches. He caught a glimpse of a young woman with long black hair, her ashen skin a backdrop to a wild garden of blue vines. He did not notice her eyes, but he would never forget the intricately petaled florets whose centers were her nipples. Her face held no scribbling but for the finely rendered blue flies inscribed on either of her cheekbones. She poured water on his forehead and made him drink a bitter, herbal potion. Even in his debilitated state, he knew that one of the ingredients was flowering akri, a natural antibiotic.

"Thank you," he tried to tell her, but when he spoke, she covered her ears as if the sound of his voice was painful.

She gently put the fingers of her left hand to his mouth to quiet him.

■ He wanted desperately to stand as proof, if only to himself, that he would not die, but the mere movement of pressing his arms against the ground exhausted him and sent him again into a dreamless sleep that seemed to last for days.

■ When he woke again, he found that a good portion of his strength had returned. His mouth was no longer bone dry and his head had lost the whirling sensation that made him feel he was spinning in circles when his back was flat against the ground. He sat up slowly and stretched his arms.

The first clear thought that entered his mind concerned

the fate of the black dog. Before he attempted standing, he put his lips together and whistled. There was no response. In fact, there was no sound coming from anywhere. He wondered where his rescuers had gone off to. He whistled again, this time louder, and a moment later, he heard Wood bark. The sound of the dog's reply filled him with energy. He scrabbled to his feet and found his way, haltingly, to the animal-skin flap that was the doorway of his infirmary.

The sunlight was bright, and he was forced to close his eyes at its insistence. A refreshing breeze swept around him as he stepped away from the entrance. The movement of it across his body suddenly reminded him that he was naked. He stood there, a little weak now, wavering slightly from side to side. Then he heard Wood bark again, directly in front of him. He tilted his head back and rubbed his eyes to clear the glare from them. The twin dots of bright orange finally dissipated from his field of view, and he beheld a sight that startled him.

Sitting before him at ten paces was Wood, a garland of purple flowers draped around his neck. Gathered closely together in a semicircle behind the dog, as if posing for a group portrait, were twenty or thirty of the gray, tattooed people. Although men, women, and children were all naked save for the blue drawing on their skin, they all covered their eyes with their left hands, embarrassed at Cley's immodesty. The young woman who had ministered to him in his illness came running forth, one hand still over her eyes. She slipped past him and into the hut. In seconds, she reappeared with his clothes. After dropping them at his feet, she fled back to the safety of the group.

Cley laughed out loud. He gathered up the pile of his belongings, finding both his knife and hat among them, and retired back inside to dress. When he stepped forth into the day again, he found that the people had dispersed to different areas of the small village. Wood had waited and leaped up to greet him. Cley hugged the dog to him and rubbed the top of his head. Just then, an old man approached. He was bent over, and his decorated skin hung loose. His face was a web of design and wrinkles, his head, bald but for one long, white tress descending from the back. He lightly touched Cley on the shoulder, then pantomimed eating. When the hunter nodded that he understood, the man pointed to a hut at the far end of the village.

"Thank you," said Cley.

The old man turned to lead him, and the hunter noticed, with a stab of revulsion he dared not give voice to, that his guide was missing an ear. In its place was a ridge of ugly scar tissue surrounding a dark hole.

As they passed through the middle of the village, Cley noted its circular design—huts of various sizes, like the one he had recovered in, made of thin logs and branches and reeds, were positioned to form a perimeter. Within that ring there were places where men and women were at work, weaving reeds, cooking on small fires, using stone knives, not unlike Cley's, to fashion either weapons or tools out of wood. Amidst this scene of industry, the children, also tattooed but not as thoroughly as most of the adults, ran and played. With the exceptions of the crackling of the fires and the knives hacking away at branches, the place was perfectly calm and quiet. Cley realized, as they reached the destination the old man had pointed to, that not one of the people had uttered so much as a single word.

He followed the old man into the hut, which was much larger and longer than the others. It was dimly lit by a small fire in the center of the dirt floor. Above the flames there was an opening in the roof of braided branches through which the smoke rose. It was warm inside, and a fragrant aroma of wildflowers mixed in with that of the burning wood.

Two virile-looking young men and a young woman sat around the fire. The old man took his place in the circle and motioned for Cley to sit next to him. The hunter smiled as he got down on his knees and copied their posture with legs crossed in front. They smiled back, and he noticed it was not genuine but more an attempt to imitate him. He nodded in a feeble show of thanks for their courtesy, and they nodded back. Wood then stepped up to the old man and sat close beside him. The old man put his head forward for the dog to lick his nose. For this, Wood was given a piece of meat from a gourd bowl resting on the fire stones.

Cley was impressed that the dog had already ingratiated himself to the tattooed people, for the animal repeated this act with each of those present and at each stop was fed a piece of meat. Then Wood approached Cley and waited as if expecting his companion to follow the ritual. The hunter tried to ignore him, but Wood sat and waited. Cley noticed that the others were watching, so he gave in and leaned forward. There was also a bowl of meat set by his place at the fire, and he fed the dog a piece.

"You sly bastard," Cley thought.

Wood glanced at him from the corner of his eye and then walked over near the entrance and lay down.

The others began eating from the bowls, and Cley did not hesitate to join them. The meal, whatever it was, was delicious. The meat was cooked to tenderness and seasoned with a variety of spices, both sweet and hot.

"Very good," said Cley, but the sound of his voice seemed to annoy them, for they winced when he spoke. For the rest of the meal, he remained silent, satisfied enough to be filling his stomach with real food.

Cley decided that the fellow sitting across from him must be the chief or the mayor of the village. He alone wore an elaborate necklace made of formidable-looking animal teeth and was decorated more profusely than the others. There was also the fact that his muscled, lean physique exuded an aura of strength and confidence.

When they were finished eating, this young man reached behind himself and brought forth an object of considerable size. Cley was surprised to see that it was the book he had carried with him on the journey. The chief passed it to his right to the young woman, who took it and handed it to the hunter. He looked up and around at the circle of faces. The other man to the immediate left of the chief squinted and fixed Cley with a piercing stare. The old man with the one ear opened his eyes wide. The young woman winked her left eye and the chief winked with his right.

Cley understood the seriousness of the situation but could hardly prevent himself from laughing. He wondered what he was to make of all this mugging and eye language. The old man leaned over and opened the singed cover of the book. Turning to the first full page of remaining text, he gently brushed his gnarled fingers across the words.

"Book," said Cley.

They stared at him.

"Words," he said.

They sat as if waiting for something to happen.

In the tense silence, he finally realized what they wanted. He lifted the tome and began quietly to read. As he read about the nature of the soul, they sat perfectly still, and when he looked up at the break between the third and fourth paragraph, he saw that they were not even breathing. He refocused his attention and hurried to the end of the page so as not to suffocate them. When he was finished, he saw their bodies relax and heard, only faintly, the air passing through their nostrils.

He looked around to see if they wanted him to continue. The old man leaned over again and took the page that Cley had just read between his fingers. The hunter waited for him to turn it and indicate that they wanted him to continue; instead he suddenly ripped it out of the book. Cley was startled, but he did nothing, knowing he owed them much more than the entire book for having saved his life. The page was passed around to the chief, who balled it up, put it in his mouth, and started chewing.

The old man now indicated that the hunter should read the next page, and he did. Again they held their breath, and when he came to the end, he, himself, ripped the page out and passed it over to the young woman, who he guessed to be the chief's wife. She crumpled it and put it in her mouth. This process was repeated so that the old man and the other fellow next to the chief each also were given something to chew on.

To Cley's bafflement, they chewed the wadded paper for the longest time. He smiled at them every now and then, and they mechanically returned his smile. Finally, the chief swallowed and the others followed his lead. Cley nodded to them all as if to say he hoped they enjoyed it, but then he saw that they were not finished. The chief, his wife, the old man and the one to the left of the chief moved from their sitting positions in order to get on all fours. They did this slowly, and each movement of their limbs was like some part of a ritual.

When all of their heads were facing in toward the fire, they suddenly spit in unison. Cley jerked back, partially at the abruptness of the coordinated act, but more because their expectorations had a luminosity about them, like copious gobs of quicksilver. The instant the spittle hit the fire, there was a sizzling noise, and smoke began to rise. It did not trail upward as before like a twisting, turning, blue-gray vine. Now it rose in a wide, undulating sheet. Within this living veil of smoke, an image began to appear.

Cley leaned back in awe at what he witnessed, but his

wonder turned quickly to fear when he recognized that the figure in the smoke was that of the eyeless ghost woman who had visited him on the island in the midst of his fever. He saw her open her mouth to cry out as he had in his delusion. There was no sound, but the clarity of her image made him believe there would be. He sat stunned, with his own mouth open. Then, as before, without warning, a perfect miniature of the red bird darted from her mouth toward his ear. Cley screamed, but fast as a snake striking, the old man reached out and caught the terrible creature in his hand. As his fingers closed around it, the bird, the sheet of smoke, the apparition, all disintegrated into nothing.

The chief stood up, and the others of the tribe followed. The young woman had to help Cley to his feet, for he was still sitting motionless with an expression of terror on his face. He rose slowly and was led out into the sunlight. The chief, the woman, and the other man each touched the hunter lightly on the forehead before they walked away. The old man remained and led him back, with Wood following, to the hut in which he had recovered. Before departing, his guide also touched his forehead. Although he was shaken, Cley nodded in thanks. The old man turned away, and the hunter noticed that the venerable fellow now had both ears intact.

■ He came to think of them as the Silent Ones, for they neither spoke nor sighed, laughed nor sang. When the children cried, the tears rolled down their faces, but they voiced not the slightest peep of anguish. At times, he was convinced that they were physically unable to utter a sound, and at others, he wondered if he was witnessing the greatest collective act of stoicism ever encountered. His own voice often seemed to disturb them, but there were times, especially when he read from the book, that he could tell they were listening carefully, almost entranced by the cadence of his words.

■ Every day that passed in the village, Cley pledged would be his last. He did not forget his destination, which lay somewhere far ahead, an eternity or so away, but the silence of his rescuers was an enigma that sparked his curiosity. They proved themselves to be such a gentle people, such a calm and content society, that he saw something in them that he knew he would need if he was to be successful in his quest. What that quality was, he felt ever on the verge of discovering when waking each morning in his hut. He followed them in their daily routines, watched them work and hunt and play, but at night, when he rolled back onto the reed mat, he fell off to sleep with the frustrating realization that he was no closer to the answer than when he had first arrived in the village.

■ He stayed on for two weeks, casually studying their body art, their subtle communication of furtive glances, their desire to ingest the pages of the book. He hoped that in a wink, a spiral of blue line, he might find the answer to how they knew he was stranded on the rock island in the middle of the flood, or, more importantly, why they had made the effort to save him.

The gravity of the second question became clear to him on the day he accompanied two young men of the tribe back to the edge of the drowned flatland and saw out, across the now decreasing waters, the Country of Six Boulders, an insignificant dot on the horizon.

He couldn't tell if they were pleased to have him as a guest or if he was a burden. As with most things, they seemed neutral on the subject and continued to conduct their lives in the same unassuming manner from day to day.

■ The body images had been rendered with such incredible precision that Cley was constantly tricked by the design of a large spider on one young man's shoulder and tried, on more than one occasion, to brush it off. The fellow appeared unfazed by the hunter's foolishness.

■ In order to avoid unknown social blunders, Cley attempted to decipher the power structure of the Silent Ones. It was plain to see that he was correct in assuming that the young man with the necklace and the Sirimon skull tattooed on his chest was the chief. The others seemed to pay him deference by looking at his feet when first in his presence. There were only two individuals among the tribe who appeared to contradict his command at certain times. One was his wife, or the woman Cley at first guessed to be the queen. On a certain morning when the chief was casting symbolic glances all over the place and motioning with his hands, she asserted herself by thrusting out her own left hand, making a fist, flipping out the thumb, and jabbing it at the ground. Upon seeing this sign, the head of the village immediately ceased dispensing his silent commands, rushed to their hut, and returned with a bright yellow plum for her, which she devoured on the spot.

When none of the adults were nearby, Cley tried this same hand motion out on one of the many children who followed him through the course of his daily activities. He wondered if the boy would bring him fruit. Instead the child crossed his eyes and made a hand gesture involving the middle finger.

The only other person who seemed to hold a position of power was the bent old man. Cley learned that he was the body scribe, supplying all the members of the tribe with tattoos. He worked outside his modest hut. The subject either lay down or sat on an animal skin. The hunter watched as the old man mixed together different ingredients—plant sap, berries, and the secretions of a fat toad—to create a blue ink, the color reminiscent of the spire rock once mined in Anamasobia. The artisan's tools were a series of long thin needles with stone-ground points that had been crafted from the tail spikes of Sirimon skeletons. Cley sat beside him as he rendered a depiction of the flood on the stomach of a middle-aged woman.

■ Cley woke one morning to find the chief sitting in his hut, patting Wood's head, and holding across his lap the long spear that was the Silent One's weapon of choice. The native pointed to the hunter's clothes and closed his eyes, indicating that Cley should get dressed. As soon as he dressed and put on his hat, the young man somehow knew to open his eyes. Then he pointed to the rifle. Cley picked up the gun, and the chief rose and left the hut.

With Wood following close behind, they traveled out past the perimeter of the village. The surrounding landscape was not so densely wooded as the demon forest. There was not as great a variety of trees and none so giant as where Cley and Wood had wintered. This was a territory of shorter, gnarled, fruit-bearing trees that grew in clusters of thirty or forty amidst green, rolling hills. It was a serene place with pockets of wildflowers and occasional streams running through the minor valleys. The branches were alive with all variety of birds that joined, each with its specific call, to create a kind of symphony.

Cley loaded the gun as they walked along, and as he did he noticed the chief watching him. Wood was ecstatic to be out on the hunt again. He had sloughed off the daily garland of flowers the children bedecked him with and was bounding ahead, searching for the scent of prey. As soon as the chief looked away, Cley took the opportunity to become the spy, himself, and studied the young man.

Although the grayness of his flesh was a hue that might, in any other instance, appear mordant, in the case of the Silent Ones, all of whom were in incredible physical condition, it was an indication of vigor and health. The young man's black hair, which shone like the wing of a crow, was looped into a single, large knot. He was lean-muscled and carried himself perfectly straight. Now Cley could see that the Sirimon skull depicted on the chief's chest was not all there was to the design, but the blue line image that was the entire skeleton of the dragon wrapped around his body. The trail of rib bones tapered down one leg, around the back and then up the front of the other leg to end at the groin, as if his member was meant to stand in for the tail spike. In keeping with the nature of the design, this part of the chief's anatomy remained perpetually in a state of semierection.

It was true summer now, and the day was hot with little breeze. They trekked across the gently rolling hills for most of the morning. The chief moved effortlessly through the heat, and Cley had a sense that if he hadn't been along for the hunt, the younger man would most likely be running. Although slightly weakened by his recent illness, Cley had no problem keeping the pace and actually welcomed the exercise.

Sometime past noon, Wood flushed a large creature with a hairless, wrinkled brown hide and enormous eyes set into a misshapen cow head out of a grove of trees. It made a horrid gasping noise as it lumbered into the open on toed feet instead of hooves. Cley, almost on reflex, lifted the rifle and fired one bullet. The beast staggered a few more steps before falling to the ground. The hunter reached down to retrieve the stone knife from his boot as he approached his kill. Wood raced up behind the thing where it lay twitching on the grass. As was his practice, Cley moved in to finish the job with his blade, but before he could make the cut across the throat, he felt a hand on his arm.

With a powerful shove, the chief spun Cley around and onto the ground. The hunter rolled over twice, dropped the knife, but managed to keep his hold on the rifle. The young man then leaped backward himself, away from the dying creature, bringing his spear up in front of him for protection. Seeing this, Wood also backed off. The chief leaned over and lifted Cley's knife off the ground. Once it was in his hand, he shoved the tip of his spear into the prey's forehead. The beast grunted, its bottom jaw opened as if on hinges, and a snake as long as the rifle shot out from deep inside the animal's bowels. In the same instant, the chief threw the knife. To Cley's amazement, the blade twirled end over end and pierced the head of the serpent, affixing it to the ground. The snake wriggled wildly until its host died a few minutes later. Then it expired at the same moment, as if the two had shared a common life force.

Cley, having learned the signal for "many thanks," shifted his eyes back and forth repeatedly. The chief pulled the blade out of the head of the yellow snake and handed it back to the hunter. Both men stared at each other. Cley smiled, and the chief made his imitation of a smile. The hunter, not to be outdone, tipped his hat and bowed. The young man then rolled his eyes, stuck out an exceedingly long, gray tongue, and touched his nose with the end of it. Cley understood that there was no topping this last amenity and turned to continue the hunt.

They traveled on for another hour until coming to a vast

grove of fruit trees. No more than a hundred yards inside of it, Cley heard a thunderous racket in the distance that sounded like the stampede of a herd of large creatures. The chief stopped walking and began moving from tree to tree, gathering leaves. He walked slowly beneath the branches as if inspecting closely the leaves he would pick. Cley and Wood looked at each other with a shared confusion. When the chief had collected a handful of leaves, they continued walking.

The noise that filled the day grew more deafening as they proceeded through the grove. Cley moved cautiously, expecting to come upon its source at any moment, but they walked for another full hour, the sound steadily increasing in volume. When they finally broke clear of the trees, they were standing on a cliff overlooking a waterfall, the enormity of which made Cley clear his eyes. He now knew the destination of the river-flood of the flatland. More water than he ever thought existed fell, every minute, over the brink and down into the huge canyon below. Spray billowed up and obscured the view of the river at its base. The vapor washed over them, and multiple rainbows arced through the sky above the natural wonder.

"Beautiful," Cley said aloud, knowing the chief could not hear him.

Wood hung back by the tree line, obviously afraid of the bellowing waters of the flood.

The chief turned to Cley and put his hand out, indicating that he wanted the rifle. The gun was given over. With the leaves in one hand and the weapon in the other, the native proceeded to the edge of the cliff. Cley steadied himself and then also moved up next to the rim. He watched in disbelief as the young man, with no show of emotion, tossed the rifle out over the edge and down into the cataract of water and mist. The chief then turned to the hunter and stared at him.

Cley was reeling from the sudden loss of the weapon that

had been his security for the extent of the journey. "Why?" he asked, unable to conceal his anger at the reckless act.

The chief headed back toward the grove, tossing the handful of leaves over his shoulder. The flat green ovals flew out above the canyon and were buffeted into the sky by the updraft from below. Cley stared, still in a state of shock over his loss. The leaves ascended, and at one point, came together with the appearance of joining in midair. Their texture changed from the slick, stiff petals into a billowing, twisting, scrap of material of the same color. The veil flew northward for a few hundred yards before breaking apart into the leaves again, which fell slowly out of sight.

■ It had been three days since his journey to the waterfall. In that time there had been no change in his relationship with his newfound community. Even though the chief had undone him by throwing his rifle into the falls, and Cley had shown his anger to the young man, on the walk back to the village, it had been as if nothing had ever happened. Then there had been the vision of the veil drifting high over the thundering water. The hunter couldn't decipher what this piece of magic had been meant to show him. It was obvious that when the chief had insisted he bring the rifle on their journey that day, it had been his intention all along to dispose of it. "Is this treachery?" he wondered. "Or is it a sign meant to assist me?" The only thing that was certain was that he still felt at ease among the Silent Ones and was loath to set out again into the lonely Beyond.

■ Wood had begun to grow restless. He would no longer allow the children to place the strands of flowers around his neck, and when the members of the tribe offered their noses for the dog to lick, he growled menacingly. Cley promised him one night in the hut that they would soon be on their way. The dog quieted down and brought him the book, which was a much slimmer volume than before. Someone had apparently been sneaking in when Cley was out and stealing pages from it. As far as the hunter cared, they could chew the leather cover if they so desired, but he understood that these thefts were upsetting his companion.

■ It was a hot night full of stars and mosquitoes. Cley sat cross-legged on the ground along with the rest of the tribe. Within the center of the perimeter of huts a huge fire blazed. Silhouetted by the flames, the queen danced with impossibly acrobatic flips and sensuous gyrations. Some type of drink was being passed around in gourds—a liquor that tasted of the yellow plums and orange berries that grew in groves nearby the village. Its inebriative quality was slight but enough to alter Cley's usual blindness to the nakedness of the Silent Ones and recast her highness's movements in the realm of the erotic. He swallowed hard and looked around to see the rest of the men doing the same.

Again he concentrated on the queen, who was by then directly in front with her back to him, bent over and wagging her rear end to some inaudible music everyone else seemed to hear. Cley felt a certain stiffening in the loins and noticed that tattooed onto the left hemisphere of her shapely hind section was a portrait of a man he recognized. The face was heavy, the eyes small and set close together, the hair sparse. It was so clear to him that he knew this fellow, but the otherwise sexual nature of the dance threw his mind into such a state of confusion that he couldn't recall from where.

The queen leaped away, tumbled on the ground toward the fire, and then came up with her arms waving above her head. Her speed of movement decreased, and she turned lethargically in tight circles. Each time her backside was to him, Cley tried to get a better look at the figure of the portrait. Suddenly, he looked up and saw that the queen, peering over her shoulder, noticed him focusing on her rear end. It was fleeting, but she shot him a look so obviously full of desire he instantly averted his glance. This was when he noticed that the chief had been watching the entire exchange between himself and the queen. Cley smiled, hoping the chief would return the imitation smile. He didn't.

Luckily, the queen soon finished her dance. As she walked back to join the others gathered on the ground, she again glanced at Cley. He nodded to her to be polite, and she returned the sign by rolling her eyes so far back that the pupils disappeared beneath the upper lids and showed only white. She took her place next to the chief, who rubbed his left hand on the top of his head and blinked three times. At this signal, the aged body scribe slowly stood and hobbled out before the crowd.

He took a position in front of the fire and then he too began to dance. His movements, unlike the queen's, were halting and awkward, so comically ungraceful that Cley wondered if he was simply a bad dancer or if he was drunk. His controlled stumbling lasted only a few minutes, and when he stopped, he lifted his hands to show that he now held a small songbird in each. The tiny creatures glowed unnaturally, like embers in the night. All around Cley, the people tapped their closed lips with their right index fingers. The hunter joined in. The old man threw the birds into the air, but before they flew five yards they burst into showers of sparks that rained down harmlessly upon the crowd. Next, he approached the onlookers and held up to them what appeared to Cley to be a small crystal. It glinted in the firelight for a moment before he placed it in his mouth. Then he turned and walked directly into the fire.

Cley almost shouted. He was about to lunge to the old man's rescue but quickly changed his mind and held himself back. He had been duped too many times by the parlor tricks of the Silent Ones. Through the wavering flames, Cley watched as the tattoo artist disintegrated into a pink pillar of smoke. What began as a ball of smog the color of sunsets and certain flowers soon became a profuse trail that rose from the center of the fire. It started to take on a definite shape. At first it wriggled upward in a long, wide column, and then it turned downward and headed for the crowd. As it approached, a head grew out of the smoke—a monstrous snout, large, lidless eyes, pointed ears, and from between them, tapering down the vibrantly pink snake body, a row of spikes. It was an image of Sirimon as that creature might look in life, complete with skin and scales. The serpent, whose tail spike remained in the fire, slithered through the air, twisting in and out among the seated people, who inhaled deeply. Its jaws opened and closed, and there came from everywhere at once a terrible roar that startled Cley. The last thing he expected was a sound.

Eventually, the Sirimon drifted apart into misty tatters that melted into a pink haze and hung in the air around the village. Standing before the fire was the old man, his head bowed, his eyes closed as if he was asleep on his feet. Cley assumed the celebration was over when the members of the tribe began to rise and head toward their huts. He followed their lead and made his way in the direction of his own place, where Wood sat waiting for him. On the way, he passed the body scribe, who was now miraculously before him instead of behind. The old man took no notice of Cley but stared straight ahead. As the hunter passed him, the artist reached quickly over and slipped something into his hand. Noting the secretive nature of the act, Cley did not make a show of looking at what it was but stashed it quickly into his pocket.

■ In the hut, by candlelight, Cley inspected the secret gift. It was a crystal, much like the one the body scribe had put in his mouth before stepping into the fire. The stone was a perfectly clear, smooth oval—most pleasing to hold. The hunter took off his clothes and lay on the reed mat, staring into the stone. He wondered what prompted the gift and why the clandestine nature in which it had been given. These thoughts would have to wait, though, because Wood was beside him with the book.

They could not read fast enough to keep up with the theft of pages. Each night they landed in the middle of a completely new subject. The dog was genuinely put out by the lack of linearity in the reading, but Cley found a certain amusement in trying to guess what hobbyhorse the metaphysical author would be riding. One night it was "the power of faith," another, "the connection of the mind and the universe through a certain pealike structure in the brain," and on this particular occasion, "the souls of inanimate objects." He thought the subject mildly interesting, but could go no further than two pages owing to the effects of the drink served at the celebration.

Wood, for all of his insistence on hearing the words, was asleep before Cley closed the singed cover. The village outside was still, and the cry of a lone night bird sounded from a distant grove. Before extinguishing the candle, he rested back on the mat and held the crystal up to look at again. In his memory, he saw the old man step into the fire and become a cloud of smoke. "How?" he whispered. What was yet more difficult for him to figure out was how the pink illusion of Sirimon was made to roar.

If he had learned anything valuable from the Silent Ones it was that he needed to change the way he thought about the Beyond. This, he saw, was a key to his survival. Somehow he had to find harmony with the wild territory. All of his long-held beliefs, garnered from a lifetime in the Realm, were causing him to struggle against the wilderness. He was an infection, an invading parasite the land had identified as alien. The secret was to become like the snake that lived in the belly of the creature he had shot on the trip to the waterfall. In order to accomplish that, he decided he would have to prolong his stay in the village.

As he rolled over to blow out the candle, he was interrupted by the sound of movement just outside his hut. He turned back and saw the animal-skin flap being lifted. Slipping through the entrance was the queen. She came toward him, holding a drinking gourd, with a most seductive look on her face. Cley reached over quickly and covered himself with the animal skin that was his blanket. Although he knew speech was useless, he asked, "Can I help you?"

She crouched next to him and handed him the gourd. He looked at her and she at him, and he knew he would have to drink. Thinking it was the same mixture that had been served at the celebration, Cley leaned back and dashed off three-quarters of the brew. Only when he had finished the rest of it did he realize that this drink was something completely different. It was much stronger, more bitter, and he choked on the aftertaste. He handed the gourd back toward her, and she nonchalantly knocked it out of his hand. She grabbed the edge of the animal-skin blanket and pulled it away from him.

"Excuse me," said Cley.

He looked at her and she was beautiful, but the look on her face was one of such fierce determination that she also frightened him. For the first time, he noticed that her eyes were a dazzling shade of green, and that etched everywhere upon her shoulders, along her neck, across her forehead were tiny blue crickets. She leaned forward and licked his throat. He reached forward to touch her breasts.

"Trouble," he thought, but the intimacy was something he had longed for.

She moved one leg over him, straddling his middle and then reached down and maneuvered his member inside herself. Cley felt the drug she had given him begin to work. It moved as swiftly as fire from his toes to his chest, a wave of paralysis sweeping up the length of his body. He could no longer move his feet, his legs, his arms, his hands.

The condition galloped on to his neck, and, as he tried to cry out, his tongue went paralyzed and all that came forth was a grunt. Although he was completely numb, he could see perfectly in the flickering candlelight. The queen sat up straight above him and looked down past her breasts. Now he heard others entering his hut. The chief was there, looking over his wife's left shoulder, smiling mechanically, while the old man peered from over the right shoulder. Behind them there were other members of the tribe. As Cley began to lose consciousness, the queen swept down and licked his right ear.

"Pa-ni-ta," she whispered.

The last thing the hunter was aware of was the raucous laughter of the Silent Ones.

others

Believe me, I have kept my vigil every evening here at the desk, juiced to the tips of my horns with beauty, waiting for the wilderness to seep out onto the paper. I could feel the Beyond behind my eyes, like a ball of ice with the potential to melt into a river of words, but the blackness in which I had last left Cley kept it frozen, and I could not generate the creative warmth necessary to get things running, no matter how many cigarettes I smoked or how I grimaced and muttered.

I poked around in the old, dust-covered files of the Ministry of Justice, reading some of the prosecutions Cley had been involved in when he had been Physiognomist, First Class. A good many of these had fanciful titles—"The Latrobian Werewolf," "The Grulig Case," "The Unseeing Eye," "The Guilt of Flock"—and read much like fictional stories. I had hoped that reading about my subject in a different context might help me find him again in my own thoughts, but the Cley of those older times was a different man entirely.

My frustration even led me down beneath the remains of the Academy of Physiognomy, through a tight aperture in a passage choked with wreckage. There, in a well-preserved marble room, one massive wall of which was lined with three-foot-by-three foot metal *vault doors, I paid a visit to number 243. Behind each of those doors was the body of a mechanized human being. These individuals were victims of Below's experiments. He had created a small population of organic automatons that could be brought to life by pressing the backs of their necks. From what Cley had told me, they were wired from within and their neurons had been replaced with those of dogs. Though they looked in every way like normal people, the Master's abilities were not capable of capturing the inner humanity. On our journey to the Beyond, Cley had confessed to me one night that when he was a student he had fallen in love with the physical beauty of one of these monstrosities.*

Years ago, when I had first returned to the ruins, I remembered his story and came in search of them. I found the very one he had mentioned and brought her to life for an hour. The sight of her elicited in me an overwhelming reaction of pity, for her as well as myself. I can't say why I recently thought another meeting with number 243 would somehow focus my vision of Cley in the Beyond, but I went and brought her to life. Perhaps it was just the peripheral connection to my subject, perhaps something else entirely. The movements of her beautiful body made me think, for a short time, that I was onto something, but her first horrible grunt in response to a voiced thought of mine was enough for me to lead her back to the rolling slab behind the door and return her to merciful sleep. I fled the basement of the Academy more confused and depressed than when I had entered. I swore to myself never to return to that hell.

Following the ill-fated meeting with 243, I injected myself with so much beauty one night that I thought I was going to drift out of my own body. No writing came of it, but I was visited by many apparitions of those whom I had known and those I never knew. My father, Drachton Below, made an appearance and admonished me for my desolate existence. He told me he wished I had never discovered the secret trove of the drug he had stashed away in the underground tunnels. "Face it," he told me, "you are a man. Now start acting like one. Guilt is the food of the weak and the useless." At the end of his speech, he forgave me for my sins and moved close to put his arms around me. Yes, I wanted to feel that embrace, the comfort of it, even though he had been a murderer and a tyrant, but, alas, he fizzled into nothing and was gone.

In that same monumental stupor, I saw the girl, Emilia, who had come to visit me, and it struck me that my problem was not that I could not find Cley in the Beyond, but that I longed to speak with her again. I could not go on with the writing until I settled this dilemma in my own life. Although the beauty had never been able to catch me up in addiction, I was now addicted to the notion of having a friend. Her visit made my loneliness so much more apparent to me, and it became clear that this was the very winter that kept the particulars of Cley's journey frozen like a ball of ice behind my eyes.

The discovery stayed with me when I again became sober, but I was, of course, too much a coward to act upon it. What was I to do, fly to Wenau and sneak up to her window at night to speak with her? When I flew her home, I did not enter the village, but left her on its outskirts. I had no idea which of the many houses was hers. Now, with all of the new growth of that village, there are so many buildings. Instead, I spent my nights stealing and smoking fresh cigarettes and staring at the moon.

Then, two days ago, she returned, this time in the flesh, with others. I was in the ruins of the laboratory, marveling at a green, female human head with long black tresses that I remembered had once floated in a giant jar of clear liquid until the werewolves had ransacked the place and broken all of the glass. The many years the thing had been exposed to the air had mummified it. Though it was shriveled, it still retained all of its features. I had never put it together before that this was either the prototype or the corporeal conclusion of the Fetch, that disembodied head that flew through the Master's memory palace. How he expected to achieve the same ends with it in reality, I had no idea. For Below, imagination, memory, reality, were all one and the same. I wondered, "How might that belief govern one's life in the world?" and at that moment, I smelled them approaching.

Perhaps I should have been more cautious, but I knew from my senses that Emilia was among them. If it was to be a trap, I didn't care. I instantly lit into the air through a hole in the roof and was above the city before they had left the fields of Harakun. From my vantage point among the clouds, I watched them approach in wagons and on horseback. The girl was there, and there were no fewer than twenty others, men and women and children. Some of the men carried rifles, but they walked away from their mounts without fear, and Emilia was leading them. I swept down to my coral seat atop the pile of rubble and anxiously waited.

They came in a close group, creeping across the plaza below as had Emilia and the boys. I had to admire the girl as she led them, out in front of burly fellows carrying weapons. She spotted me again and pointed for the others to see. They did not run, but many of them looked as though they would have liked to. For a moment, it entered my mind that this was a dangerous situation. I was sure that Emilia could be trusted, but I wasn't sure that one of the others might not, at the last second, balk at the undeniable "otherness" of my form and drill me through the heart. The girl told me, herself, how much negative propaganda had been leveled against me, how my species was for them a religious symbol of evil portent, a living nightmare.

I dispersed these cautions with the flapping of my wings and went down to meet them. Of course, when I landed, they backed up a few steps, and one or two of the men brought up their guns as a precaution. I held out one of my hands and said, "Peace be with you," a line I had stolen from one of the thousands of volumes I had devoured in my seclusion.

"Misrix," said Emilia, pointing to me and looking back at the others.

They nodded and smiled.

I nodded but did not smile, knowing how ghastly it might look to them to see my fangs. "I am so pleased that you all have come," I said. When I uttered these words, I intended them as a pleasantry, but in the midst of speaking, I suddenly understood the depth to which I meant them. There were tears in my eyes. I removed my spectacles and brushed them away. It was this unguarded show of emotion that I believe convinced them more than any stolen lines of literature that I was to be trusted. Then, the rifles were lowered and one by one, they stepped forward and offered me their hands. This time, I shook each one.

One middle-aged woman wearing a flowered scarf over her hair introduced herself to me as Emilia's mother. She took my huge hand in both of hers and thanked me for saving her daughter from the river. I told her it was my pleasure to count Emilia as my friend, and she gave way to tears that, I could tell, had to do with many other things besides my rescue of her daughter.

The official leader of the group was a tall, bright-looking young man named Feskin. He wore a pair of spectacles like my own, and I liked him immediately. I learned that he was a schoolteacher back in Wenau and had carefully studied the manuscripts that Cley had left behind and gathered, over the years, a good deal of history concerning the ruins and the culture of the Well-Built City. He had been the first one to extend the theory that I might be more civilized than given credit for. Through the logic of his argument and because of Emilia swearing I had saved her from the river, the others were not unwilling to believe that the lurid stories told about me had been false.

Mr. Feskin inquired as to how I spent my days, and I told him of the books I had read. He seemed mightily impressed and, right there, we had a discussion about Brisden's Geography of the Soul, a classic from the early days of the Realm that had had a most limited print run of three copies. While the others listened, we waxed somewhat erudite, and although it was boorish, I wanted desperately for them to know that I was learned.

I gave them all a tour of the ruins, with Emilia at my side. She was very proud of herself for being able to point out details of the remaining architecture I had discussed with her on her last visit. When I stopped among the ruins of the Ministry of Science for them to see the preserved remains of the monkey who had been taught to write the line, "I am not a monkey," a woman came up to me and asked what my diet consisted of. When I told her plant meat and fruit, she then seemed confident enough to ask if she could touch my wings. I said it would be fine. She ran her hand over the membrane. Upon seeing this, the others stepped up and touched me in different places. The children wanted to feel the sharpness of the barb at the end of my tail, and I warned them not to prick their fingers since it contained a poison. One young woman reached up on her toes and, closing her hand around my left horn, stroked it up and down repeatedly. For a moment I considered returning her touch, but then thought better of it.

In the Museum of the Ruins, they each had many questions to ask about the history of the city. They marveled at the core of the fruit of Paradise, and I allowed each to hold it and smell its aroma. I attested to its ability to produce miracles and told them that there was a specimen of that tree growing within the confines of the ruins.

"You are a miracle," said Feskin, placing one of his long, thin hands on my shoulder. "More human than many of those who would damn you back in Wenau."

He would have continued with my praises, but an older woman had just found among the shelves the head of a doll she remembered owning when she was a girl, living in the Well-Built City. I told her to take it with her, but she shook her head.

"It belongs here," she said.

In the way she said it, I wondered how many of them still thought the same of me.

We walked in a group out to the broken wall through which they could return to their wagons and horses. One by one, they thanked me for the tour and asked if there was anything they could bring me or that I might need. I told them I couldn't think of anything. As the others departed the ruins, Feskin and Emilia stayed behind.

"I want you to come and visit us at Wenau," he said to me.

"That would be wonderful, but I doubt the entire village would want that," I said.

"Give me some time to speak to them. A week is all I need. Come to the schoolhouse in a week. It is the building . . ."

"I know the building," I told him. "Where the old market used to be, by the bell."

He nodded. "Come in the evening, an hour after sunset. I'll be waiting for you."

I agreed to it.

"One other thing, Misrix," he said. "A rather delicate matter, so don't take offense. This may sound presumptuous, but you must do something to clothe yourself if you want to move freely among the people of Wenau."

He was looking down at my loins as he finished speaking, and I could not help but laugh.

"I'll see what I can do," I said.

Emilia, to her credit, looked at Feskin as if she had no idea as to what he was alluding. When the schoolteacher left, she remained with me for a few minutes.

"I brought you something," she said, and reached into her pocket. Out came a long, thin object wrapped in brown paper.

"What is this?" I asked.

Her mother called to her to come and she said good-bye to me and ran through the opening in the wall. "It's candy," she called back.

For three days, I did nothing but bask in the glow of meeting the people of Wenau. At night I would fly over the village and look down at the lights burning in the dark and wonder which of my new acquaintances was sitting by each flame, reading or sewing or rocking a child to sleep. I did not eat the stick of candy that Emilia had given me. I did not even dare to unwrap it, but I would run its length under my nose. It smelled sweetly of orange, and its aroma was more lovely to me than that of the fruit of Paradise. This afternoon I was doing just this, when I saw in my mind's eye an image of Cley, kneeling next to a pool of clear water. Then I knew it was time again to write.

The taste of that candy now mingles with the intoxicating warmth of the beauty. What was once an iceball behind my eyes is now a ripe orange, dripping its sweetness into my bloodstream. I see the Beyond, and the late-summer sun hanging in the sky. There is the hunter, alone with only the black dog for companionship. I begin to write, knowing I have fared better than he with the natives of my own respective wilderness.

empty book of the soul

It was dark, unmercifully hot, and he could feel a flat surface pressing upon his face. The first clear thought that came to him was that the Silent Ones had buried him alive. In reaction to the fear of suffocation, he tried to sit up. When he did, the hard leather cover of the book, now empty of all of its pages, slid from his face down into his lap, and the bright sun suddenly blinded him.

Although he was relieved that he had not been entombed, he was sweating profusely, and his head ached. There was an infernal itching at the center of his forehead, and he scratched it. He sat quietly with his eyes closed for a few minutes and worked to compose himself and regulate his erratic heartbeat. Slowly, he opened his lids against the harsh light and saw Wood lying in front of him, tongue drooping down, panting wildly.

Beyond Wood, there was a landscape composed of nothing but pink sand. He turned to the right and left, and saw everywhere tall dunes without so much as a single weed growing among them. To his left, there lay on the ground a bulging waterskin. To his right were heaped his bow and quiver of arrows, his striking stones to make fire, his hat and knife. His pack was missing.

"At the bottom of the waterfall with the rifle, no doubt," he thought. Staring straight ahead at the horizon where reality rippled in the intense heat, it slowly dawned on him that he had been abandoned in the middle of a desert.

"So much for my friends, the Silent Ones, and so much for their silence," he thought as he recalled the chorus of derisive laughter—the last sound to grace his hearing before the drug had done its work.

"Pa-ni-ta," he said in a whisper, repeating the queen's message. "It most likely means 'Fools will burn,' " he said.

Then, at once, the weight of what had happened descended upon him, and he felt all the bitterness of betrayal. A mournful sound came, unexpectedly, from deep within. His body heaved, and he cried without tears. He was alone, left to perish by the very people he thought would teach him to survive in the Beyond. Grabbing the corner of the empty book of the soul, he tossed it away onto the sand. The dog stood with great effort, as if the heat had in some way increased gravity, and moved slowly up next to the hunter.

"I can't go on," Cley told his companion. "We are more lost than ever and not an inch closer to our destination." He had no desire to stand and decided simply to sit where he was, letting the sun bake him into unconsciousness and then death. As he reached for the waterskin in order to allow Wood to drink, he heard the distinct sound of a birdcall from behind him. At first he believed the heat had cooked his mind, but then he heard the sound again, and, from a different location, another bird answered the first.

Curiosity finally won out over his depression, and he slowly, unsteadily, stood and turned to see what type of heat-generated illusion was croaking at his ill fate. He was dizzy from getting up, and the sight his eyes fixed upon made him dizzier still. There, lying a hundred yards away, was a huge oasis, a veritable city of lush vegetation, like a green jewel set in the burning pink sand. He cleared his eyes with his hands, unsure if what he was seeing wasn't a mirage. After blinking repeatedly, turning around and then back three times, the swaying trees, the fan-leafed ferns, the bright red and purple blossoms, static explosions of color amidst the undergrowth, were still there. A bird, a flying rainbow, with an exceedingly long tail and wings that rolled like waves, lit into the sky and disappeared among the trees.

■ This forest was like none other that he had encountered. All of the vegetation, from the boughs of almond-shaped leaves to the tangled riot of brush beneath, was a resilient green. It was as if the force of the desert's heat had compressed the very possibility of life into a circular area of two hundred acres. "Another island of sorts," thought Cley as he pushed the ferns and thick, dangling vines aside with his elbows. Above, the ceiling of lush growth was teeming with birds while all around him was the whir and buzz of insect life. He wondered what other creatures might dwell in such a magical place and kept the bow, arrow in place, at the ready in front of him.

As he brushed past a certain branch, its many leaves came to life in a storm of butterflies. The backs of their wings were dull, but now they revealed the powder blue shade of the fronts. They swarmed upward, all together, twisting and looping, sharing one mind, and when Wood barked at their sudden flight, the sound dispersed them, and they were like a shattered pane of clear summer sky. Cley watched as they joined together again on a single branch, turning back into the drab leaves they had begun as.

■ A shiny black, hard-shelled insect, as big as a rat, with twitching antennae and vicious-looking mandibles, scuttled up the partitioned trunk of a tree that bent toward the ground beneath the weight of its prickly, yellow fruit.

■ In a clearing, the floor of which was made up of pink sand that reminded Cley of coral dust swirling through the ruins of the Well-Built City, they discovered a half dozen man-size mounds of varying heights. Moving between them, around them, and into them were red ants engaged in a hundred single-file parades. At the peak of one anthill, a cluster of workers struggled to fit the eyeball of some unfortunate creature down an opening they could not seem to grasp was too small.

■ When it screamed at him, drawing his attention, Cley took aim and fired an arrow at what at first appeared to be a disembodied female head hanging by its hair from a thick vine that had grown horizontally between two trees. The shot hit its mark, and when the hunter and the dog inspected their prey, it became clear that it was a bat, whose strange markings, when upside down, wings folded, looked for all the world like a human face with wide eyes and a mouth full of sharp teeth. Although the arrows were precious, he did not retrieve this one. The false visage reminded him too much of another from a false world.

■ They passed through a thicket of plants with stems that reached four feet above the top of the hunter's hat. Drooping down were prodigious white blossoms, the width of which he measured against his outstretched arms and found his reach inadequate by a few inches on either side. The petals overlapped and spiraled toward the center of the blossom, where a black circle oozed a clear viscous fluid. Every so often a droplet of this sap fell, and, in its descent, hardened into a small pebble before hitting the sand. These floral diamonds did not last for long, though. Before a minute could pass, they evaporated into a thin trail of white smoke that carried the scent of citrus.

■ Cley washed his face in the pond. Kneeling on a bed of moss, he leaned out over the still water and cupped some into his hand to drink. He told Wood it tasted clean, and the dog joined him. When Cley was finished drinking, he removed his hat and brought up another draught of water to splash on his head. The coolness of it quelled the headache he had had since waking in the desert.

As he hunched over the pond, letting the water drip from his face, he peered down at his own reflection. He had not seen himself for a very long time, since well before his hair had grown long enough to tie back and the beard had come in. The man below, looking up, momentarily startled him. Now he knew the person that the Silent Ones knew, and he wondered if his frightful aspect had made them ill at ease. He looked every bit a man of the wilderness.

Bringing his hand up, he touched the scar on his cheek where the demon had drawn blood with its barbed tail. It was while inspecting this feature of his face that he saw another. Upon noticing it, he could not believe he had not spotted it sooner. In the center of his forehead, directly above his eyes, there was a design. He leaned closer to the water and now could make out clearly the image of a thin blue snake coiled eight times around a central point that was its head. The final loop came halfway around the spiral, and the end of the tail bent, pointing due north.

■ Just before nightfall, they reached the opposite end of the oasis and stared out on more pink dunes rolling off toward the setting sun. It was as he had expected it would be. Still feeling the wound of his betrayal by the Silent Ones, he did not have the will to continue north. He decided to stay in this new forest for a few days of rest before starting his journey across the sands.

They left the edge of the desert and returned a quarter of a mile into the green island to a clearing Cley had noticed earlier. It was difficult finding firewood, because everything was so alive and full of sap. Eventually they came upon a lone tree that had died of some disease, and the hunter hacked its branches off easily with the stone knife. By the time he managed to get a spark to leap from the stones and set the kindling going, night had come, and the area around their camp was made fantastic by the intermittent blinking of fireflies.

In addition to the flying squirrel Cley roasted for Wood, he had collected a variety of the different types of fruit that grew plentifully in every quadrant of the oasis. Some of them he had already tried, and although a few specimens were bitter to the point of being inedible, many more proved to be sweet and full of juicy pulp.

As the dog ate the charred strips of squirrel and Cley worked away at one last white plum, a refreshing breeze began to blow through the forest. Yellow moths circled the fire, a few giving their lives to be one with the flames.

"What do you say?" the hunter asked the dog. "Is this the Earthly Paradise?"

Wood looked at him. He rose and began moving around the area as if searching for something.

Cley laughed. "We left it in the desert," he said, yawning.

The dog whined and finally came to rest by his side.

"There were no more pages. They were all devoured by our hosts," he told his companion.

Wood continued to complain.

"I'll tell you a story," he said, and pretended he was opening a large book.

The dog closed his eyes and rested his head on his front paws as Cley began speaking.

"Once there was a man, who woke one day to find a blue snake tattooed on his forehead. He wondered where it had come from and why it was there. 'What can this mean?' he asked his friend, the dog, but the dog had never heard of such foolishness, and wasn't about to start. The blue snake twirled around itself in a spiral whose center was its head. At first the man wondered if it was there, between his eyes, to help him focus. Then he wondered if the snake was supposed to be the snake, Kiftash, in *The Legend of the Alluring Woman of Constance and Her Last Wish,* or just meant to represent a circle without end. Some snakes, as you know, are poisonous, and yet sometimes this poison can be made into a medicine to cure the sick. Perhaps this was a snake that rattled its tail or danced to music or, being blue, was discovered curled up in a rock in the heart of Mount Gronus. Snakes have always been treacherous fellows, but . . ."

Cley stopped speaking and listened to the crackling of the dying fire. One lone moth still circled the flame. Wood lifted his head, then returned to sleep. The night wind moved among the trees and carried the scent of blossoms. Something was creeping through the underbrush, and Cley thought to himself, "I need my knife," but in the process of acting on that thought, he forgot about it, and his eyelids closed.

■ Perhaps a butterfly, a falling leaf, a blossom on the breeze, brushed against the hunter's right cheek, and he brought his hand up to swat it away. In his slowly rousing consciousness his last thought from the night before fired like a spark in his mind. He sat up quickly, reaching for his knife, and opened his eyes on a new day.

Wood was still asleep, which was unusual. Now Cley noticed that lying on the sand in front of the dog was the empty leather binding from the book of the soul.

"So much for my stories," Cley whispered to himself. He pictured the dog, sneaking away from the camp, tearing through the forest at night and then breaking free of the trees onto the pink sand illuminated by moonlight.

"That flinking book is a curse for sure," he said, then poked Wood in the rear end with the toe of his boot.

The dog woke immediately.

"Let's hunt," Cley said.

Wood rose and stretched, his front legs forward, his back in the air, while Cley looked around for where he had laid his hat. He remembered taking it off just before they had sat down to eat dinner, but now it was nowhere in sight. He was about to question the dog, suspecting retribution for having left the book out in the desert, but then he noticed something in the sand.

The hunter dropped to his knees and spread his arms for support, bringing his head down close to the ground. The dog came up next to him and also looked at the ground. Cley traced the outline of it with his index finger as if to validate the discovery.

It was a footprint, not an imprint of one of the soles of his boots but a large vague outline of what appeared to be a human foot. He looked up at another spot in the sand. There were more, leading off into the forest.

A scream came suddenly from behind them. Cley reached

for his knife and spun around on his knees with the blade pointing out just in time to see the yellow bird in the branch overhead scream again. He looked back at Wood and motioned with his hand to his mouth—their sign to stay quiet. The hunter stood, and with the distinct sensation that he was being watched, turned slowly, peering into the tangle of growth.

■ They followed the shaggy footprints west through the oasis toward an area they had not yet explored. Cley wondered if the hat thief might be one of the Silent Ones left behind to spy and play tricks on him. "Who else would be about in such a far-flung place?" he asked himself. He ruled out the apparition of the eyeless woman, since she left no prints when he had encountered her in the demon forest. Then he had a sudden memory of the face that was inscribed in blue outline on the queen's backside. He saw it again in his mind's eye, and realized where he knew it from. "Brisden," he said, and stopped walking. Wood held up and waited for him to continue following the trail.

"I'll be damned if it wasn't Brisden, that tub of words," he said. He thought back to his journey through Drachton Below's memory and recalled the corpulent philosopher, who had saved the dream woman, Anotine, and himself from death at the hands of the Delicate. It seemed like another lifetime when last Cley had known him as the symbolic representation of a concept in the mnemonic world. As he later learned, all of those he had met in that reality had antecedents in this one, in real life. How could the queen have his portrait on her left buttock if he had never been or was not in the Beyond? Perhaps the Silent Ones had brought him to meet the man, since he was also pale-skinned and had obviously at one time been a subject of the realm like Cley. "But what are the chances?" the hunter asked himself. "And why would he steal my hat?"

■ Late in the morning, just before Cley was about to stop and pick some fruit, he and Wood passed a shallow pond covered with lily pads. From each of the round leaf bases grew a violet flower whose petals were sharp spikes. Half-submerged in the water and surrounded by the floating blossoms was the skeleton of a Sirimon—the bones gone green and the left horn cracked off. The sight of its sharp teeth startled the hunter, and he raised the bow in self-defense before he knew what he was doing. At the last moment, he held the arrow back.

■ Sitting beneath an overhanging frond, surrounded by the gnawed cores of a red fruit, Cley and Wood dozed in the afternoon heat. They had searched for hours and eventually lost the trail of prints in the sand. The western end of the oasis seemed much like the area they had traversed the previous day. The hunter had killed a small wild pig for dinner, which was lying next to the waterskin. He kept his bow close by and the knife in his hand should anyone or anything try to steal another of his meager belongings.

He began to doubt that what they saw that morning in their camp were human footprints. The possibility that some other creature could have made them seemed all the more likely. He remembered his ruminations about meeting Brisden in the heart of the Beyond and laughed quietly to himself.

"Madness," he thought, and as the notion passed from his

mind, his hat passed along over the tops of a stand of tall ferns that lay across the sandy clearing before him.

The hunter sat upright and watched as the black, broad-brimmed shape sailed by. "Wood," he called quietly to the dog. His companion looked up and saw the hat moving off into the forest. In seconds, they were on their feet. Cley grabbed the bow and arrows and was off after the thief. They broke through the ferns and saw in the distance, through the mesh of tree trunks, vines and tall ferns, a vague figure disappearing into the green. Cley began running, and the dog was soon bounding ahead of him.

■ For the remainder of the afternoon the hat led them on a chase through the exotic forest of the oasis. They stumbled past tranquil pools, gigantic flowers, birds with the most outlandish plumage, a million insect wonders, but noticed none of it, their sights fixed firmly on the quarry which seemed always to stay at the same distance—close enough for them to make out the black lid but far enough away so as to keep its wearer's identity a mystery.

Near dusk, they realized that they had not seen the hat for an hour and were running blindly with no purpose. Cley called Wood to him, and they turned back, the hunter trying to remember the direction toward the spot where he hoped the pig he had killed would not have been set upon by scavengers.

As they made their way around the undergrowth and between the trees in the failing light, Cley was no longer nervous about the stranger, who was obviously much more afraid than he and Wood were. In fact, he desired a confrontation, his curiosity now ablaze.

Just as he was considering forsaking the wild pig and

stopping to make camp in the next clearing, they came upon the site where they had left their kill. He realized that while he had been walking, his mind turning wildly with thoughts of the day's pursuit, he had been unconsciously following Wood. The dog obviously knew all along where he had been headed, driven by a desire to eat roasted pork.

Luck was with them, for no scavengers but the ants had bothered the meat. These were easily scraped off. Firewood was searched for and a fire started. In their toil to prepare for the coming night, Cley did not notice the hat sitting atop a large bush off to the right of the clearing. Just as the dark completely swamped the oasis, and he was carving up the kill into strips to affix to his makeshift spit, the hunter noticed the hat. In astonishment, he began to laugh out loud and shake his head.

"Our neighbor is a trickster," he said to Wood.

The dog looked where Cley was looking, saw the hat and walked over, lifted his leg, and urinated on the bush.

"Revenge," said the hunter, and turned his attention back to preparing dinner.

■ That night a sweet wind carrying the narcotic scent of blossoms slithered again through the forest. Cley had already read the sleeping Wood a confabulated nonsense story from the missing pages of the book cover the dog had insisted on carrying in his mouth all day. The hunter leaned back on a tree trunk well within the flickering bubble of light cast by the fire's glow. He was exhausted by the day's exercise. Through lowered lids he looked across the clearing at the hat perched atop the bush and let his thoughts unravel. In his hand was the stone knife and lying next to him in the sand was the bow and quiver of arrows.

The sizzle of a moth in the flames woke him from a doze, and he looked around the clearing to see that everything was as it should be. He glanced at the hat and jerked himself forward to sit upright. Squinting in order to focus his sight, he scrutinized the bush atop which the lid rested, and confirmed what he, at first, could not believe. Some inches beneath the broad black brim, two burning eyes, like tiny fires recessed in twin caves, had opened in the matrix of leaves and seemed to be staring straight at him. Confusion paralyzed the hunter, and though he wanted to stand, he could only sit where he was and stare back.

A moment later, a dark opening, obviously a mouth, appeared below the eyes. Then, the bush began to slowly move in unnatural ways. A leafy arm spread itself from the whole and reached out, followed by another on the right side. There were hands of tangled vine with delicate sprouts continuing like thick hairs from the tips of root digits. The body of the bush began to rise on incredible legs composed all of leaves and tangled twigs. It stood upright, like a man, but a man of vegetation, with tiny white flowers growing here and there amidst the thatch of its body. The black hat riding atop this green impossibility was the most absurd thing Cley had ever seen, and he could not help but smile through his amazement and terror.

The plant creature walked toward him, and still he could not move. Already he sensed that it did not mean to attack. Its movements were as gentle as the wind-rocked fronds of the tree above him. It stepped carefully over the sleeping dog and came to a halt before the hunter, where it slowly lowered itself to sit only inches away, facing him. Then the two arms that seemed cut from a hedge rose simultaneously and lifted the hat with leafy hands off a head of spiraling, tendriled hair. It reached over and placed the hat on Cley's head, and the dark opening that was the mouth almost formed a smile.

Cley was reeling, but in the whirlwind behind his eyes, he suddenly remembered Arla Beaton's writings about her grandfather's journey through the Beyond. In certain fragments of that story there was mentioned a man of green, what Beaton had referred to as a *foliate,* named Moissac, who guided the beleaguered party of miners toward their elusive goal of Paradise.

"Moissac?" asked Cley.

The thing shook its head, reached to its viney throat, and plucked a leaf. It motioned putting the green oval in its mouth and then handed it to Cley. The hunter accepted the gift, and without hesitation opened his lips and placed it on his tongue. The taste was rich with the essence of fruit and flower. Like a perfume he was smelling with his taste buds, this vapor rose through his palate, infiltrated his sinuses, and gathered in his mind to form sounds that slowly evolved into words.

"I am Vasthasha," said the voice in Cley's head.

"Do I hear you through this leaf?" asked the hunter.

"No, you understand me," it said. "The leaf carries me to you."

"Why are you here? Why did you steal my hat?" Cley asked.

"I had to know if you were the one. The hat carried the residue of your thoughts and dreams. I needed to be with it for a time to discern if you were my liberator," it said.

"Your liberator?" asked the hunter.

"The seed you planted back in the place you think of as the demon forest. In the new, green time, after the ice, that seed produced a plant, which grew and grew with the speed of rain falling, until, in the early days of the sun's strength, when I had become complete and the spark of life burned in my head, I pulled my legs up by their taproots, snapped off those anchors, and began my search for you."

"You have found me," said Cley.

"And now, I am to serve you," the voice said.

"I am heading to the village called Wenau," said the hunter.

"I know," said the foliate, "the green veil? I thought it in your hat."

"All of it?"

"Much."

"Am I close to Wenau?" asked Cley.

"In comparison, if you were a child beginning on the journey of your life toward your goal of death, and you were to live a hundred years, you would not yet be born for a hundred years."

"That close?" said the hunter.

"There are some places in this wilderness you call the Beyond that cannot be reached by traveling through space. The possibilities will simply not align for you to arrive," said Vasthasha.

"Then I will not reach Arla Beaton?"

"I am here to guide you. The woman whose necklace pouch you found my seed in, Pa-ni-ta, was the last of a lineage who could direct the energy of the Beyond to her will."

Cley recalled the last word of the queen of the Silent Ones.

"Yes, her spirit has been with you throughout your journey. She needs you to help her. If you come with me and perform the task she requires, you will reach your destination."

"And what is that?" asked Cley.

"I cannot reveal it to you until the time of new growth, the spring. While I lie in the frozen ground, the snow piled upon me, she will tell me in my dreams what we are to do."

"I thought she was dead," said Cley.

"You might have considered me the same until you put my seed in the ground," said the foliate.

"How does she know me?" asked the hunter.

"She knows you through your desire. She knows what you want . . ."

Here the leaf in Cley's mouth began to lose its flavor and the foliate's words quickly diminished in volume until they were replaced by a sound like barren branches scraping in a winter wind. Vasthasha reached over and touched one of the gnarled, tapered roots that were his fingers to the tattoo on Cley's forehead.

"We will talk more tomorrow," the hunter heard the foliate say. "You must sleep, for with the sun, we must leave this place if you intend to find your way."

"Through the desert?" asked Cley.

"The desert, indeed," said the green man. Following his words came the sound of rain falling on dry autumn leaves, and Cley realized that the foliate was laughing.

■ While he slept, the hunter unconsciously chewed on the leaf given to him by Vasthasha and its sap flowed through him, into his dreams. There, he saw the woman, Pa-ni-ta, as she was in life—black hair flowing in the wind, eyes bright with knowledge. She walked through a field of growing foliates still attached to the ground. Some were only half-formed, and some were near maturity, but as she passed, they turned their leafy heads and reached out, the tips of their branches brushing against her legs and arms. Even in sleep, Cley was somehow aware that they had been created to serve as an army.

■ Cley woke the next morning, half-expecting all that transpired through the night to have been no more than part of one fantastic dream, but when he opened his eyes, he saw the foliate sitting in front of Wood, lightly stroking the dog's back.

The hunter rose and walked over to them. As he approached, Vasthasha pulled a leaf from his throat and offered it to Cley, who placed it under his tongue.

"You have become friends with Wood," said Cley.

"The name is interesting considering the circumstance," said the foliate, and Cley heard the laughing sound again.

"That dog has saved me more than once," said the hunter.

"Yes, your fates are bound together," said Vasthasha. "I just told him that it was I who fetched the book for him the other night."

"I thought that was his work," said Cley. "Can I give you a message for him?"

"There is no need for that with a creature like this. He knows all you would tell him."

"Do we leave then?" asked the hunter.

"We must go now if we are to make progress."

Cley gathered up his fire stones and put them in his pocket. He took a quick bite of a piece of pork left undevoured by Wood and then slipped the stone knife into his boot. Lifting the bow and arrows, the waterskin, he whistled around the foliate's talking leaf and motioned for Wood to take up the book cover. With Vasthasha leading the way, they headed for the northern side of the oasis.

■ Before setting out across the pink sands, each of them took a long drink from the waterskin. Cley was amazed, watching the foliate tip his head back and gulp like any other thirsty man. Although he was seeing it before his eyes, it remained as strange to him as if some piece of furniture in a parlor had suddenly come to life—like a large rock writing a letter or a fence post making love.

Vasthasha handed Cley another leaf for his mouth, and as

soon as the verbal effect commenced, he told him that after a few more of the leaves, the hunter would not need them anymore for days to come.

"Aren't you especially concerned with the heat of the desert?" asked Cley.

"After we have traveled through the sands for a few days, you will have to carry me," said the foliate, and stepped out of the shade of the oasis and into the bright sun.

Cley was troubled by the thought of hoisting the foliate on his back while traipsing through the deep sand. "We'll never make it," he thought to himself.

"Why should I believe all you have told me?" said the hunter.

"At the end of the autumn, when I have to leave you, Pa-ni-ta has arranged to show you a sign so that you will believe that she understands your desire. Until then, you must trust me," said Vasthasha.

Cley realized right then as he began to walk in the hot sun that he had no other choice but to follow.

The travelers climbed a set of tall dunes like a miniature mountain range, descended into a valley of sand, then faced another three times the size of the first.

Even Wood had a hard time getting a foothold in the shifting sand. The ascent was steep, and with every two steps they took, they slid back another. Cley stopped climbing three-quarters of the way to the summit and worked to catch his breath.

"It's got to level off soon," he said to the foliate, who slid back down the incline to help him.

Wood kept charging and sliding back and charging until he reached the top. Once there, he turned back and barked down at the hunter and the man of green.

Vasthasha stayed with Cley on his climb, helping him along. The hunter looked down and saw that the foliate had grown, in mere minutes, wooden spikes out of the bottoms of his feet. By the time they reached the top, Cley had been reduced to crawling. As he came up over the top of the rise, he saw spread out below him the shoreline of a violet ocean. The water sparkled in the bright sun all the way to a distant horizon, and waves rolled in and crashed in foam explosions on the pink sand. A half mile to the north, along the beach, there was a tree line and the beginning of grass-covered hills.

"You knew all along," said the hunter. In his head, he heard the foliate laughing.

"We made it, Cley. There are no deserts so unforgiving as those that lie within."

■ Vasthasha told the hunter that they would follow the shoreline of the inland ocean northward, for he knew of a place a few hundred miles ahead where Cley and Wood could winter with members of their own tribe—an expeditionary force from the western Realm that had some years earlier come to the Beyond to set up a base camp.

"Then I am not alone," said Cley, as they walked side by side along the edge of the violet sea.

"There have been others. There will be others," said the foliate. "The wilderness is more ancient than you can imagine. I will show you something in our time together before the season of frost that will help you understand. There was a war in the Beyond, a disruption to the balance of nature that changed everything."

"I believe I saw in my dream last night that you and others like you were created to be warriors in that battle. Am I right?" asked Cley.

"You were not the first, Cley, but I am most assuredly the last. We were brought to life by Pa-ni-ta, physical manifestations of nature energy. Imagine how difficult it is to defeat an opponent that regenerates itself every spring. Still, our enemy was powerful enough to find a way. Moissac was a deserter. That is why he was still alive to help those who came in search of Paradise."

"And what about you?" asked Cley.

"It will become clear in the days to come," said Vasthasha.

The foliate turned away from the shoreline and headed inland toward a grassy plain. He motioned for Wood to come to him and relieved the dog of the book cover. Putting the empty binding under his arm, he pointed toward the trees.

"We will stay near the ocean but travel where you can hunt for food," he said.

"Tell me," said Cley, hurrying to catch up to the foliate, "why does the dog care about that damnable piece of book?"

"He thinks it is a device that helps you to tell stories," said Vasthasha, and the twin fires of his eyes blazed for a moment.

"Why would a dog care about stories?" asked Cley.

"He knows they are what the world is made of," said the foliate.

They traveled on through open country for days, the sea always to their left. Each time Cley encountered the sight of it from the top of a hill or when rounding a thicket of trees he was startled by its immensity and beauty. The landscape they passed through was teeming with game—white deer, wild pigs, long-legged turkeys, and a type of diminutive three-toed striped horse. The hunter found Vasthasha to be a first-rate teacher in how to survive in the Beyond. The foliate expounded on the properties of the exotic flora they passed, and Cley questioned how the specimens might interact with an animal system. Since the green man had a root in both worlds, so to speak, he could readily surmise their effects.

At night, around the fire, Cley related the wonders and terrors he had lived through in the Realm and the foliate questioned him about human love and treachery. While they conversed, Vasthasha grew, in the course of an hour, from the root that was his left index finger, perfectly straight shafts of branch that Cley could turn into arrows.

No night was complete until the book cover was opened and Cley extemporaneously confabulated a tale for the dog and their green friend. The foliate wanted to hear about the stars, what they were made of, and why they were there. He told Cley that Wood liked best those stories with at least one dog in them. The hunter became adept at creating such yarns, and spun them with greater and greater ease as the days passed.

One afternoon, he heard the foliate warn that a giant bird was diving for his head. Cley fell facefirst on the ground as the huge creature, a yellow sparrow the size of a fox, with a razor beak and piercing talons, swooped dangerously close to him. He came up with an arrow on his bow but missed the shot. As he watched the monstrosity fly off, he realized he did not have a leaf beneath his tongue.

■ At the top of a wooded hill overlooking the ocean, they found a pickax jutting straight up out of a mound of stones. Hanging from the head of the ax was a rusted miner's helmet. Cley thought back to Anamasobia and to Arla Beaton. He saw her in his memory, walking down the main street of that now ruined town.

"She was beautiful," he told Vasthasha. "I wonder what she looks like today," he said.

The foliate pulled a small white flower from his chest and placed it on the miner's grave. "Like the summer, now," he said, "moving toward autumn but still carrying a bright sun."

There was a moment of silence, and then they turned and

continued down toward the sea. Wood urinated on the ax handle before running to join them.

■ It was a night of falling stars, and Vasthasha feared the heavens were collapsing. Cley took an object from his pocket and held it up in the light of the flames in order to divert the foliate's attention from the meteor shower.

"We are in no danger, my friend," said the hunter. "Think of it as the sky shedding old leaves. They will burn to cinders before they reach the world. But here, look at this." In the palm of his hand rested the crystal given to him by the body scribe of the Silent Ones. "What do you make of it?"

Vasthasha nervously diverted his attention from the sky and looked at the stone. "Where did you find it?" he asked.

Cley told him the story of his rescue and stay among the tattooed people—how they ate the book, disposed of his fiercest weapon, duped him, and marked his forehead.

"Yes," said the foliate. "I know of them. They have lived in the wilderness longer than I can say. The other tribes of the Beyond call them Shantrei. It means 'the Word.' They worship language in all its forms. The fact that you thought of them as the Silent Ones is not without humor, since they know a multiplicity of languages—human, animal, and vegetal. Each of them is decorated with an array of images that combine to form an original idea, and each individual body is the expression of the word for that idea."

"I have my own word for them," said Cley, staring into the light captured by the crystal.

"They have marked you. That is unusual since you come from the other side of the demon forest. Through wearing the hat, I felt your sense of betrayal concerning them. They are trying to help you. Do not lose that stone."

"Are they in league with Pa-ni-ta?" he asked.

"They were at one time her enemy, but things change. They obviously left you where you and I could find each other," said the foliate, and then looked back overhead.

"Am I a word now to them?" asked the hunter.

"You are the word for you," said Vasthasha.

Cley shook his head. "When I came to the Beyond, I thought I would be escaping such complications and convolutions. The farther I travel, the more complex and confusing it all becomes. Back in the demon forest, I understood—kill them before they kill you, find food, make fire."

"The life of one termite here is more complex than all the history of your Realm," said Vasthasha. "Simplicity will be yours in the grave."

"Comforting," said Cley.

Then the foliate suddenly sat upright, the fires of his eyes flared, and the tendrils that were his hair straightened.

"What is it?" asked the hunter.

Wood got up instantly, reacting to Cley's distress.

"It's coming," said Vasthasha.

Cley got onto his knees and reached for the bow. "A creature?" he asked.

"No, the autumn," said the foliate. "It is close."

The green man bowed his head and fell into silence. Cley watched the sky, waiting for Vasthasha to speak again, but he did not.

■ The waves of the ocean broke a hundred yards to their left. It was an overcast day, and a light drizzle was falling.

"There are demons in this forest," said the foliate.

"Can we avoid it?" asked Cley.

"No, I want to show you something important at its heart," said Vasthasha.

In among the trees, whose trunks were straight and tall, the sand of the beach gave way to a carpet of brown needles and leaves. Cley lifted the bow, and Wood hung back beside him as if understanding that danger might be close by.

They continued through the dim morning, Cley now recalling the terror engendered by demons. He tried to remember how he had found the courage to battle the creatures with such tenacity, and all he could dredge from his mind was his fear of them.

■ It was late afternoon and though the rain had tapered off the sun had still not burned through the mist. They stopped to rest and eat some roots and mushrooms. For Wood there was a piece of deer meat left from the previous night's meal.

The large, round, orange heads of the fungus tasted like cooked apples and the roots like licorice. As the foliate split the last disk to share between them, Cley noticed that the small white flowers that had dotted the thatch of his green guide's body had all turned brown as if singed at the edges. Then he saw, across Vasthasha's chest, a pattern of red leaves mixed in with the usual emerald.

He was about to note the change to his companion when he was interrupted by the cry of a demon as it swooped from branch to branch above them. The hunter looked up and spotted three of the creatures in the tattered autumnal canopy overhead. He lunged for his bow as two of them dived, their wings outstretched.

Wood rose to the attack as if it was only yesterday that they had left their cave. Cley drew an arrow from his quiver, but fear made his hands tremble, and he fumbled in the act of nocking the shaft onto the string. In the next moment, he was flat on his back, with the weight of a demon upon him.

The creature reared back and opened its mouth to display long fangs. The hunter tried to reach for his knife, but his arms were pinned. He waited for the thing to sink its teeth into his face, but then saw a green vine twirling rapidly around his attacker's throat. In the next instant, five sharp roots poked through its chest where its heart might be. Blood splattered, covering the hunter.

The demon fell backward onto the ground, dead, to reveal Vasthasha, whose fingers and hair were now growing back into themselves. Cley wasted no time, but loaded an arrow and looked to see where Wood was. The dog was running madly in circles, chased by two demons. The hunter fired at the larger of the monsters. The arrow pierced one side of its head and the tip of the shaft poked through the other. There was a shrill scream as the wounded demon fell into the arms of his brother. The unharmed creature lifted the dying one, flapped his wings, and ascended into the treetops.

■ They survived three demon attacks in as many days. Vasthasha proved to be a more than able warrior. On one occasion Cley watched as the foliate shoved his sharp root fingers into a demon's back. A moment later, branches poked out of the creature's eyes just before its skull literally exploded outward with the force of a spiked bush growing with incredible speed from within.

"I am invisible to them," the foliate told him. "They think I am any plant or tree in the forest. Not being meat has its advantages here."

▣ They pushed on through the dangerous landscape, killing when they had to, running when they could. In the very hour of the particular day on which Cley began to question, to himself, the prudence of the course they were taking, they passed through a thicket of tall, white birch, and there, before them, across a large field, lay the ancient city of dripping spires that the hunter recognized from his dreams and mnemonic journey as the Palishize.

▣ As they trod the winding, shell-cobbled streets, passing around the broad bases of the mounds, Cley half expected to see the ghostly form of Bataldo hail him from one of the dark openings that riddled the sides of the crude structures.

"I have been here before in both my mind and that of the demon's, Misrix's," Cley explained to Vasthasha.

"And now in the body," said the foliate.

"Why does this deserted city figure so prominently in all that has to do with the Beyond?" he asked.

"This is not a city, Cley," said the foliate. "The best I can describe it, using the words and ideas I gathered from your hat, is that it is an earth machine."

"It is not a dwelling place for an ancient people from the sea? This is what I had gathered from my psychic and psychotic machinations," said Cley.

"It was created by our enemy, the O, who were a people from beneath the surface of the inland ocean. Although they walked upright with the stature of men, like ourselves, they had long fish tails, webbed fingers and toes, a shimmering red, scaled flesh, and a sharp fin that ran from the forehead to the center of the back," said the foliate.

Cley whistled to Wood, who was about to enter one of the

dark holes at the base of a mound, the spire of which reached a good two hundred feet in the air.

"I know that the Palishize is laid out in a large spiral," said the hunter.

"Yes, it draws and focuses the energy of the earth. Its presence disrupted the power of Pa-ni-ta. I and the other foliates were sent here to kill the O. They died easily when we could wrap our vines around their necks, but they were a shrewd people. They had many inventions, many strange and miraculous devices."

"How many did you kill?" asked Cley.

"More than I can count," said Vasthasha. "Then they infected my kind with a type of mite that caused us to be unable to regenerate each spring. When our raiding parties were hacked to pieces, they ceased to be. Pa-ni-ta saved me and carried my seed when she fled. One of their assassins overtook her as she was nearing the boundary of the Beyond. She had gone south in search of help."

"There was the body of a fish-tailed creature in the burial chamber where I found her remains," said the hunter.

"Yes, she and a small contingent of her people were wintering in that cave. Those who were not killed off through the autumn by the demons were slain by the O assassin. Pa-ni-ta's ghost reached across the boundary of death to kill her murderer. She took him down in the burial chamber as he was laying the last of the children's bodies next to hers," said Vasthasha.

"And then, in the form of a seed, you waited to be reawakened?" asked Cley.

"In the sleep of the seed I was told to find one from outside the boundary of the wilderness. Only an outsider can reverse the treachery of the O," said the foliate.

"And I am that outsider?" asked Cley.

"You will profit through helping by success in your journey," said Vasthasha.

"What is the nature of my task?" asked the hunter.

"We will know this only in the spring," said the foliate.

"What is at stake?"

"The very consciousness of the Beyond."

■ On their second day within the walls of the Palishize, Vasthasha led Cley and the black dog into one of the openings. The tunnel ran through the center of the mound and then angled downward. They traveled through a pitch-black corridor for over an hour before a circle of light could be seen far in the distance. As they made their way slowly toward it, the foliate told Cley that the experience was like being reborn.

"But you could have told me the history as we walked along the shore, around the Palishize," said Cley. "Why did we have to enter it?"

"The shoreline south of the structure is planted with a thousand traps and devices of death. This route is the only one through which I can ensure your safety. I remember, so long ago, the day Moissac and I discovered it. We took down five of the O in this very passage," said Vasthasha.

An hour later, with Wood leading the way, they exited the dark catacomb beneath the Palishize and found the ocean lapping the wall that was built right at the edge of the sea. Luckily it was low tide, and they were able to make their way along the beach, in water only to their knees, before the waves grew and thundered in to smash against the foundation of the incredible structure.

■ The landscape north of the Palishize was composed of wooded hills rolling down to a mile-wide field of sand dunes that bordered the sea. Vasthasha insisted that they follow the beach as much as possible for it was a faster route than through the woods.

On those days when they had to cross the dunes in order to hunt in the forest, Cley noticed very readily that the season was changing. The leaves of the trees had turned orange and gold and fell in droves. At night, as they sat around a drift-wood fire in the hollow of a large dune, the air was cold, and the hunter's speech came forth in puffs of steam. Vasthasha had begun to move more slowly as the leaves of his body dropped off, a few each day, and were carried away on the wind. More of his viney thatch had gone brown, and the fires in his eyes were dimmer.

One night the foliate woke the hunter from his shivering sleep, and said to him, "If I should leave you soon, do not be alarmed. Continue along the shoreline, and you will come to a fort inhabited by people like yourself. They will take you in for the winter. In the spring I will find you, and we will do our work."

Cley could only nod at the message, for the prospect of losing his new friend saddened him. He lay awake for a long time, staring at the full moon cast in a golden hue. It was so clear in the crisp air that he could make out its mountains and craters.

■ Wood found a leviathan stranded on the sand. He barked wildly at the amorphous black body, as the immense crea-ture's tentacles, each fifty yards long, weakly swept the air. The noise the thing made was like a soprano's aria. Cley asked Vasthasha what the monster's song meant.

"Help, I am drowning," said the foliate.

They waited for the thing finally to die, and then Vasthasha instructed Cley in how to cut open its bulbous head and find the brain. They climbed upon the body of the leviathan and hacked away until, beneath its shiny black flesh, buried in a thick layer of fat, the hunter discovered a little red parcel amidst the oozing, green blood.

That night they cooked the brain and ate it—the taste, something like oysters in chocolate sauce. Vasthasha claimed the thought organ of the Wamlash, when devoured, was supposed to increase the clarity of one's thought process. He abstained. The hunter later dreamt of the civilization of the O deep beneath the waves of the inland ocean.

■ The violet sea was wild, huge waves breaking against the shore, and the wind blowing down from the north threatened to snatch Cley's hat with every gust. The sun was high, but the day was very cold. They walked along a wide swath of beach, huge sand cliffs to their right. For the past two days, Vasthasha had been unable to keep pace with the hunter, and Cley found that he had to wait after every half mile or so for the foliate to catch up.

Above the crash of the surf, Cley heard Vasthasha's voice yell to him, "Keep going." When the hunter turned back to look, he saw the foliate pass into a small whirlwind of sand. In the blink of an eye, his vegetal friend came apart, everywhere at once, and existed for a moment as nothing but a swirl of dry brown leaves. A gust blew from the north, and the makings of the foliate flew off on the wind, carried up over the cliffs toward the forest.

Cley ran back to where Vasthasha had stood moments before. All that remained were a few dry, brown lengths of branch and vine, a few rotten leaves, and the cover of the book. Wood whined as he lifted the leather binding between his jaws. The hunter felt the wind of the coming winter pass right through him. With an overwhleming sense of resignation, as if this lack of emotion was an emotion itself, he continued on along the shoreline.

■ It was in the middle of the following afternoon that Cley spotted, at a distance, a ship run aground on a sandbar. At first, he thought it was another enormous sea creature drowning in the cold air. Then he made out a scrap of tattered sail and the cracked spire that was the mainmast.

To get to it, he had to wade through an ankle-deep tidal pool of frigid water. Wood was reluctant to follow but did so after leaving the book cover on the beach. They walked out along the wide sandbar, the surf rolling in to their left. As they drew closer to the vessel, Cley spotted a gaping hole in the front end of the hull. The ship's stern still sat in the surf, and the whole structure moved slightly from side to side as larger waves broke against it.

"A ruined ship of the explorers from the western Realm?" Cley wondered. He hoped to find useful items to scavenge within the wreck.

As they drew up next to it, he saw how large the vessel really was. The deck towered above him, but he could still gain access where the hull had been staved in. As he approached the splintered opening, Wood hung back and barked as if in warning.

Cley climbed through the hole and looked inside the long dark expanse of the innards of the ship. Enough light was let in behind him so that he could make out barrels and tools lying all around as if the ship had been lifted by the hand of a giant and shaken madly before being smashed down on the sandbar. Toward the back of the ship, the deck had rotted away and the sunlight beamed in to illuminate the chaos. Cley could still hear Wood barking outside as he stepped through two inches of bilge. There was the pervasive smell of the sea, everything encrusted with salt and barnacles.

Just after he found the remains of a dead sailor, who obviously had had his chest crushed by a flying keg, the fractured rib cage now a home for tiny crabs, the hunter noticed something standing in the sunlight at the far end of the hold. He took a few more steps toward this large block and saw that it was clear, like a man-size cube of crystal or ice, and then he realized that the ship did not hail from the western Realm.

This ship, he now knew, had sailed from a port called Merithea. Embedded in the heart of the block of unmelting ice, was the naked form of a beautiful, dark-haired woman. He placed his open palms against the boundary that was as warm as the touch of a lover's hand. The imprisoned woman stared out at him, and he sensed that she was still alive.

"Anotine," he whispered, and the merest corner of her lip turned up. The past rushed back upon him and brought him to his knees in the stinking bilge. He did not leave the hold until the sun had set.

■ That night in the dunes, next to a crackling fire, the hunter held open the covers of the missing book and recounted for Wood the story of his time with Anotine in the imagination of Drachton Below. Although the wind blew cold, he did not feel its sting, for he was heated from within by the constant feverish schemes to release his dream woman from the unmelting ice. Nothing was resolved, because he had no tools with which to work. Then he considered that the ship itself might hold an ax, a cask of gunpowder, that could be employed in her release. This blizzard of thought gave way to his trying to understand what it must be like for her, unable to move but still alive and seeing only the shadowy hold of the wrecked ship for years upon years.

He took the spirit of this frustration into his sleep, and the force of it shattered the ice. Anotine stepped forth, and he held his hand out to her.

"I dreamt of you," she said to him.

"I dreamt of you," he said, and when he put his arms around her, he woke suddenly to a cold, gray day. There was a light snow blowing down from the north.

■ Although he and the dog had eaten nothing, Cley headed immediately back to the beach. When he came over the last dune, he cried out in an anguished tone that might, itself, have drilled through ice. The sandbar had disappeared beneath the waves, and the wrecked ship, lying low in the water, was being drawn by an inexplicable current toward the horizon.

■ The snow fell in large wet flakes and began to gather on the forest floor. The sound of the ocean was ever-present, the crash of the waves like a distant summer thunder coming to them from over the field of dunes. The hunter and dog were exhausted and hungry, not having eaten for two days. Through the curtain of blowing white, Cley saw ahead the outline of a building—a large white fort with parapets and a tall wooden door. He walked up to the structure and, slinging

his bow over his shoulder, began pounding on the oaken barrier with his fist while Wood barked repeatedly.

"Who is there?" asked a voice from above. A man's face
appeared over the top of the white wall.

"I am from the Realm," shouted Cley.

"Who are you?" asked the voice.

"A hunter in the Beyond."

devil's dog

Since I have already twice interrupted this record of Cley's travels through the Beyond, I see no reason not to continue the practice, especially in light of the portentous changes that are occurring in my own life. I am more certain than ever that my investigation as to the hunter's fate is intrinsically bound to my own recent growth. In the same manner in which the sun draws upward the stem of a flower, I have been drawn from my own insular seedpod of the ruins toward the warm glow of community. I have been to Wenau to visit my friends, and, here, I will tell you about it while I wait for the needle of my compass, sheer beauty, to stop spinning and point the way back to the Beyond.

I could do no writing since my last installment, in which Cley meets the foliate Vasthasha, for I was so filled with nervous tension from the thought of taking Feskin up on his invitation to go to the schoolhouse in Wenau. During those days, I did not even bother to lift the pen, but spent the first two or three deciding if I should disregard the obvious issue of my vulnerability, both physical and emotional, and extend myself those last few increments that might result in my becoming completely human.

Of course, I was going. I knew it from the moment he had asked.

But I had to weigh it in my mind, worry about it, lose sleep over it, in order to draw the last delicious drop out of the decision. Once this foolishness had been thoroughly squeezed dry, I remembered what the young man had told me about the importance of clothing. I intermittently laughed and shook my head in confusion over the idea that the citizens would be more likely to accept what they saw as the symbolic representation of evil as long as it wore trousers.

"The demon must be clothed," I said aloud, finally breaking the spell of inaction. With that, I went in search of the perfect outfit.

In living alone for many years amidst the aftermath of a monumental disaster, I have come to know the corpses quite well—where they reside, what postures they ended their lives in, what they are wearing. Among this static community of the skeletal, I knew of one quite large fellow, well dressed, who met his fate with feet trapped by fallen debris and a bullet to the rear end. He stood upright at the ravaged entrance to the Ministry of the Territory. I had always marveled at his undiminished dignity, even in the face of a conspicuous lack of flesh. His monocle still rested between cheekbone and brow, and he was decked out in a charcoal gray with pale pink pin-striped suit and vest. The stately black top hat with pale pink band was a crowning monument to his fashion sense.

Through past research, I had come to know that this large person was none other than Pennit Dresk, the father of the young girl who, in Cley's own "Case of the Unseeing Eye," was convicted of producing subversive stick-figure drawings and sentenced to having her eyes removed. Other documents made it clear that Dresk had become part of the conspiracy to topple Drachton Below's beneficent rule. My wardrobe had a fitting lineage.

I scrubbed the outfit thoroughly, then read a book about sewing. Threading the needle with clawed hands was more difficult an exercise than having a camel pass through its eye. The opening for my tail was not so much a problem, for all I had to do was widen the bullet hole and sew around it. The jacket and vest, in order to fit comfortably around my wings, took real planning. I was more an architect than a seamstress in this matter. I forgot about the shoes. Wing tips and hooves are an impossible union. The white shirt was too much to conjure. "They will have to do with demon hair instead of linen in this case," I thought. The hat nestled smartly between my horns. I put a twig of leaves from the tree that bears the fruit of Paradise in my buttonhole, checked a mirror eight times, and was ready.

After circling at a considerable altitude for over an hour, I landed at dusk in the street outside the front entrance of the schoolhouse. The lanky schoolmaster, Feskin, was waiting to greet me. He wore only shirt and pants, and I instantly worried that I had overdressed for the occasion. I moved toward him in as dashing a manner as possible.

"You look incredible," he said, and laughed.

At first his mirth stung me, but I quickly overcame my embarrassment and laughed too. "We always dress formally in the evening at the ruins," I said.

"Very good," he said, smiling. He shook my hand and motioned for me to come inside the already lighted schoolhouse.

I went up the steps, my hooves clunking against the wood. He stepped aside, allowing me to enter first. When I did, I was met with a shout that nearly blew my top hat off. I immediately crouched in attack mode with my claws out, my horns lowered, the hair on the ridge of my back rising. It was in this posture that I met my supporters in Wenau. Slowly, I realized that the shout had been their collective voice, yelling the word "Surprise!" I rose up to my full height and then I saw them, gathered around in front of the small desks and blackboard. On the board was written, in large chalk letters, "Welcome, Misrix!"

Quite a surprise it was too. Feskin took a huge risk in startling me, for I might have just begun slashing the air in self-defense. This proved to me his faith in my humanity. Men and women and children were crowded into the building. There was a table full of food and drink. My neighbors came forth to greet me, and, closing my wings in tightly, I instantly became one with the crowd. I again met some who had come to the ruins, and it was a great pleasure to re-live old memories, even though they were not so old and there were not many of them.

Of course, Emilia was there, and she jealously stole me away from a conversation I was having with a man whose brother was part of the expedition that had gone to retrieve Cley from what they considered his self-exile in the Beyond. She took me by the hand and showed me her desk. I told her how much I enjoyed the gift of the orange candy, and said it was the sweetest thing I had ever tasted. She laughed at this, very pleased, and the sight of her innocence and joy was staggering to me. Then she told me that she had another gift for me, and she led me over to the wall, where papers were hung in a row. It soon became clear that these were samples of the students' work. We walked along the row of documents—labored testaments of cryptic penmanship illustrated with drawings. She stopped in front of one written in a beautiful looping style. On the cover was a portrait of me. The title of this piece was, "My friend, the Demon."

I read the pages as carefully as I could through tear-filled eyes. More than once I had to take off my spectacles and brush them against the exposed hair of my chest. I need not go into detail here, but it was a history of our meeting, a testimony to my good character, and an affirmation of our bond.

"Why are you crying?" she asked.

"I am a mawkish old demon, for sure," I said, and laughed for the first time in a new way.

Someone began calling for order, trying to draw everyone's attention to the front of the classroom. Before turning away, I handed Emilia the small, carved wooden dog that had sat for years on a shelf in my Museum of the Ruins.

"Here's a pet for you," I told her. "Take good care of it."

"What's its name?" she asked.

"Wood," I said.

She got half the joke and smiled.

It was Feskin who was calling for everyone to pay attention. He motioned for me to come to the front of the classroom and take a seat. I did as was requested. Then began an explanation, I suppose for my benefit, as to how and why this group of brave souls had decided to make the proverbial leap of faith and invite a demon into their midst.

I learned that night that after Cley and I had originally struck out for the Beyond, the town of Wenau almost came apart by reason of introduction of the drug, sheer beauty. The citizenry who were able to keep their wits about them had a hellish task of restoring order. Many died as a result of the effects of the drug and many more were left mentally depleted. Below's newer, stronger strain of the narcotic was taken by some without any caution or knowledge of its ultimately debilitating properties. Cley was seen as a deserter and a scourge because of the chaos he had wrought.

For a long time, his name was a curse among the survivors of Wenau. They never took into consideration how many more would have died had he not put a halt to the sleeping disease with which Below had infected them. The complexity of that thought lay beyond their grief. Then Feskin found the two manuscripts that Cley had produced, sitting in a back room of the schoolhouse under a stack of old books deigned too mature in their content for the children to read. He sat down one day in the middle of a snowstorm, having let the children go home early, and began reading. As he told it, he read through the night and finished the two manuscripts by morning. It became clear to him then that Cley was really a hero, and that I, the local scourge, was something of a hero myself.

It took the schoolteacher a number of years to convince a goodly amount of people of his discovery. Once the idea began to catch on, some of the older inhabitants, whose children had been delivered by the healer, or who had personal dealings with him, came forth to admit that what Feskin was saying was probably true.

Funds were eventually raised and an expedition mounted to bring Cley back to his rightful home. As Feskin said, "It was the least we could do, considering how we had for so long spurned his very name." A young fellow named Horace Watt, whose father had been a personal friend of Cley's, led the expedition. They had already been gone three months and were expected back in two years' time.

When I heard that part of the tale, I had to hold up my hand and stop them. I could not speak at first, understanding how my words might dash their hopes, but finally I found my voice out of a sense of honesty.

"My good people," I said, "I would love to give you encouragement for your plan, but you must understand that the Beyond is a tremendous expanse. It is a place of continents. Even if they should escape all of its myriad dangers, which I pray they do, how would they possibly hope to find him?"

"Bloodhounds," said a woman from the back row of desks. "They took with them the best bloodhounds ever born and a few of Cley's items from his home. If he is there, those dogs will find him."

At hearing her words, I wanted to laugh, but seeing the seriousness of all of my friends' faces, I nodded as if such absurdity sounded reasonable.

"Have no fear, Misrix," said Feskin. "Cley will be back among us in no time."

"Very well," I said.

Someone in the crowd said, "Let's eat," and the meeting was adjourned.

I gorged myself on pastries and produce, and drank more than I should have of the rum punch. My third stomach had begun to gurgle when one corpulent old man shoved a slice of bloody beef in my face and told me the cow had come from his farm. I almost lost my balance from dizziness. I told him that I never touched red meat.

"Well, in your case, I won't take that as an insult, if you know what I mean," he said, and patted me on the shoulder.

I spoke to him of the weather instead and found him to be a fine gentleman.

The hours I spent there were the most glorious of my life until our attention was drawn to some commotion in the street. Feskin was immediately at the window.

"It's Lengil," said the school teacher.

"Who is that?" I asked the young lady to my right.

"He is an agitator against your visit. He and a few others do not trust you and want to see you dead," she said.

"They are mostly the religious who are unable to extend their love beyond the mirror," said Feskin over his shoulder. "You are to them what they see in their books. I tried to explain it to them, but they will not listen."

I moved next to the schoolteacher and looked out the window. There was a mob of fifteen or so men carrying rifles and torches.

"Send out the devil's dog," a voice called from the street.

Those around me appeared nervous.

Feskin turned again to us, and said, "Who will keep them busy until I can get Misrix out the back entrance?"

No one made a move to help, and I did not blame them. Then Emilia pushed her way through the crowd and made for the door. Her mother grabbed after her, but she was already going through the entrance onto the porch.

"Here is the devil's dog," I heard her yell at them, and somehow I knew that she was holding up the carving I had given her.

The schoolteacher was moving me out of the room through a back hallway, but I could hear the men saying things to her in sheepish voices and Emilia yelling back her replies without fear.

As we came to the end of a dark passage, Feskin said, "You will have to give me a little more time to work on your behalf. We are making real progress, though. We thank you for coming."

He opened a door at the end of the hall. It led to a field where I had in my previous reconnaissance flights seen the children playing their games in the afternoon.

"A wonderful time," I told him.

"We will come and see you soon," he said.

Then I was off, mounting into the clear sky. I circled around to the front of the building at a great height in order to see that Emilia was unharmed. She was still standing her ground, giving the zealots a tongue-lashing. I could not help myself, but unzipped the infernal trousers and extracting my member from this useless second skin of cloth, made a mighty piss of rum punch down on the angry mob. Their torch flames sizzled and turned to smoke in the downpour. Leaving in my wake a fart like a clap of thunder, a message from their angry God, I took wing and sped off through the night sky, feeling for all the world like a mischievous child myself.

I returned to my ruins, but instead of the broken stalk that was the Top of the City, I now see before me a white fort in a clearing of a forest, lying very close to the shore of the inland ocean. The snow is falling, and there is one lone man accompanied by a black dog. He is pounding on a huge oaken door, pleading to be admitted to the company of his own kind.

the walls of this fort

The small whitewashed room had a single window that let in the dim light of the gray afternoon. On one side of a scarred table, atop which rested a long green bottle holding a lit candle, sat Cley, the black dog at his feet on the plank floor. Across from him sat Captain Curaswani, a heavyset man with a great white beard and mane of white hair. He was dressed in a rumpled yellow uniform, complete with black buttons and epaulets at the shoulders. Between each of his statements he drew on a pipe, the thin stem of which was nearly as long as his forearm. The bowl of the instrument had been fashioned to resemble the face of a woman, staring up at the ceiling, her mouth a wide, screaming aperture from which puffs of a bluish smoke occasionally issued.

"So," said the captain, "you are in search of Wenau? I have never heard of it."

"It's toward the north," said Cley.

"To be sure," said the captain. "There are worlds upon worlds toward the north. I suppose you would like to winter here with us?"

"If I may," said the hunter. "I will do my fair share of the work. You see, I've spent a winter out there in the wilderness, and, without the happenstance of some very lucky occurrences, I know I would have died. As it was, I found a cave with a draft of the earth's heat coming up from below. Still, we almost starved."

"You and the dog?" asked the captain.

"Wood is his name," said Cley.

"He seems like a fine fellow," said the captain, who smiled, smoke leaking out at the corners of his lips. "Of course, you may stay, but I have to tell you two things. At the fort, I am in charge. You must be willing to take orders from me."

Cley nodded in acceptance of this rule.

"The other is that with the state of things as they are, you may be safer out in the wilderness. I just arrived here, myself, this past autumn. I was dispatched with a group of fifteen soldiers to protect the small contingent of citizens of the western Realm, who had come a few years ago to farm and trap and make a monetary gain from the resources of the Beyond."

Before continuing, Curaswani shook his head and sighed. "It seems that in the relatively brief span they have been here, they have managed, in the time-honored tradition of western Realm arrogance and stupidity, to completely incense the local population. By the time I and my men arrived at the fort, there were only five individuals left out of sixty-five. Those who were out on the land retreated here for safety, and, one by one, over the course of the past year, they have been brutally butchered."

"Who is it you have made an enemy of?" asked Cley.

"The Beshanti, who, when our settlers initially arrived, were a peaceful group. Then our people started grabbing land they shouldn't have, killing game they shouldn't have. Look, Cley, as a military man, I don't mind fighting wars that are unavoidable, but I have an aversion to having my men killed over petty acts of greed."

"Can't you retreat back to your ship and go home?" asked Cley.

"When we were sent, we had no knowledge as to how bad the situation was. We were merely coming to try to restore order. The ship won't be back until the spring. We're trapped here, and already in the past month, two citizens and one soldier have been diced up within the very confines of the walls of this fort." The captain set his smoldering pipe down on the table and rubbed his eyes.

"Within the walls?" asked the hunter.

Curaswani laughed. "Not exactly cozy, eh?"

"How?" asked Cley.

"From what I can ascertain from the settlers, the Beshanti have a group of warriors that can somehow physically blend in with their surroundings. You know the lizard, the chameleon? Well, these fellows have the same attribute. The settlers have named them Wraiths after the old tales of angry ghosts. They are reportedly flesh and blood, but I've yet actually to see one. I have, though, seen their work. Two days ago, Private Ornist Heighth had his throat cut and his stomach split open so that his vitals lay in a steaming heap on the ground. It happened in front of two other men. They said a patch of wall came to life, wielding a nine-inch blade. Once the knife was dropped, they could no longer make out any aspect of the attacker."

"Wraiths," said the hunter.

"Welcome to Fort Vordor," said the captain, and gave a mocking salute.

Curaswani showed Cley around the inside of the compound. His quarters were in a low building that was separated from a larger structure housing the barracks and the rest of the living quarters. There were also two outhouses positioned at the southeast corner and the northwest corner of the rectangle. All of this was surrounded by a high wall that had but one egress, the tall oaken doors that were now barred by three thick wooden beams. Along the top of the perimeter wall there was a catwalk on which five or six soldiers stood guard. The two structures and the entirety of the wall had been coated in whitewash.

The captain carried a long-barreled pistol in his belt and a short sword at his side. He limped across the snow-laden enclosure at a weary pace, followed by the hunter and Wood. At the midway point between his quarters and the larger structure, he stopped and called out, "Attention." Those on the walls and the others in yellow uniforms passing to and fro turned to face him.

"This is Mr. Cley. He will be staying with us for the winter. And his dog, Wood," said the captain.

From the battlements, the soldiers called down greetings, and the hunter waved to them.

"Back to it," called Curaswani. The men above turned around to face again the wilderness, while those on the ground continued on their errands.

The captain led Cley into the larger of the structures, a two-story building without windows. They entered a wide room lined with sleeping cots under which were stored the soldiers' individual trunks. Hanging on one wall were a rack of rifles and a rack of pistols. In the back corner there was a small kitchen and a long table for meals.

Passing through the barracks area, they entered a hall with a stairway off to the left. They ascended the steps and entered another dim hallway lined with rooms. The captain opened the first door on his left.

"Here you go," he said. "It's not exactly comfortable, but when the wind really starts to bite, I think you'll find it better than that cave."

Cley thanked the captain as he put his bow, the quiver of

arrows, and the empty book cover on the bed and sat down. "I haven't slept on a mattress in over a year," he said.

"Come down in a little while. They will be serving dinner. You'll smell it cooking. Let's hope the aroma cannot be mistaken for anything else. I will issue you a coat and a weapon. You can stand guard tonight," said Curaswani.

"Yes," said Cley.

"Can you shoot a rifle?" asked the captain.

"I can drill a swooping demon at a hundred yards," said the hunter.

"The demons are, luckily, in hibernation now," said the captain. "Can you drill a ghost at a hundred yards? That seems to be the question."

"I'll do my best," said Cley.

"Very good. Since you are an experienced hunter, I'm going to need you to lead a party out into the wilderness for game from time to time."

"As you wish," said Cley.

The captain bent over and patted Wood on the head. "If we make it until the spring, it will be something of a miracle. But you, Cley, strike me as one who has witnessed miracles."

"Indeed, I have," said the hunter.

■ Dinner was a venison stew, biscuits, and beer. The soldiers sitting around Cley at the table struck him as being no more than boys. He doubted that some of them had begun shaving yet. Still, the lot of them seemed energetic, strong, and good-natured. They had many questions for the hunter about his experiences in the wilderness, about his strange tattoo. He could sense that he was quite an enigma to them—someone who had thrived in a place that, from their limited vantage point, seemed impossible to survive in for any length of time.

They were also taken with Wood, calling to him, petting him, and slipping him chunks of meat under the table.

When asked about his earlier life, Cley told them that he had been a midwife in his village before entering the Beyond, and they all laughed good-naturedly at the idea of it. "From one harrowing occupation, staring into the wilderness, to another," he said.

They asked a hundred questions about the demons they had heard existed to the south, the strange flora and fauna, natural wonders he might have witnessed.

"It seems like a place from a fantastic storybook," said one fellow, whose name was Weems. He was a tall blond youth with wide shoulders and biceps that stretched the sleeves of his undershirt.

Perhaps from having lived so long away from people, Cley was reluctant to tell too much about himself. He was sly in his method of turning the questions back upon the soldiers and finding out about their lives.

"We heard that the Well-Built City had been destroyed in the east," said another young man.

"Yes," said Cley. "It succumbed to its own gravity."

The soldiers weren't sure what he was talking about, but in order to be polite, they nodded as if it were a foregone conclusion.

"How did your ship get to the inland ocean? We were unaware of its very existence back in the eastern Realm," said the hunter.

"There are channels through deep gorges, very dangerous to navigate, that lead from the oceans of our world to this one," said the soldier to Cley's left. Although he was not yet a man, he bore a wicked scar across his left cheek and an eye patch on the left side. The others called him Dat.

"How long is the voyage?" asked Cley.

"Four months," said Dat. "The inland ocean is enormous,

with many strange beasts, leviathans, and krakens and more. I was pleased to set foot on solid ground."

"But the strangest, Cley, was the ghost ship we found floating low in the water and wrecked as if it had met its fate in a typhoon. Some of the sailors boarded it and said they saw in the hold a block of ice with a naked woman trapped inside," said Weems.

"They said she was beautiful," said the largest of all the young men, a fellow named Knuckle. "I could see from their expressions when they returned to our ship just how beautiful she must have been. From that moment, they seemed to be lost in a daydream for the rest of the trip."

"And do you have wives and girlfriends back home?" asked Cley to change the subject.

Many nodded quietly and appeared to be daydreaming, themselves, in response to his question.

"And what of the Wraiths?" asked the hunter.

"We don't talk about them if we don't have to, Mr. Cley," said Weems. "Better not to dwell on them, says the captain. He says he doesn't want us going mad."

There was a moment of silence.

"After you see what they can do, you'll be as scared as we are," said Knuckle.

■ It was midnight, and Cley stood on the narrow catwalk of the northern wall of the fort, staring out across the moonlit field of new snow at the dark tree line of the forest two hundred yards away. It was cold, and he huddled inside the large yellow army coat they had given him. The rifle he carried was of inferior quality to those manufactured in the Well-Built City. It was a single-shot weapon with a double barrel, so that it held only two shells at a time. They had, though, given him a pocketful of shells. The western Realm had never been known for its technology.

The hunter still basked in the afterglow of the pleasant time spent conversing at the dinner table. His humanity had been revived somewhat from its desolation through the months wandering in the Beyond. He was very pleased with his new home and his status among the soldiers. It was a certainty that the captain could use his skills as a hunter. With a place to rest and a job to do, he looked forward, without dread, to the winter months.

He turned and peered back down inside the fort to see that all was well. Wood sat on the ground beneath the catwalk, watching Cley's every move. On each of the other three walls there was a soldier at sentry duty. In the yard within the compound there were another four men making their rounds. The hunter tried to picture the slaughter the recruits must have faced when first they arrived at Vordor. A brief scene of butchered corpses flashed through his mind. He remembered one of the young men telling him that they had spent the first week at the fort digging graves out in the earth fifty yards off the western wall.

He looked back over the field and spotted a deer moving. Although he soon became weary, he occupied his mind with thoughts of Anotine sailing haplessly from ocean to ocean, forever frozen in Time. He wondered now if she was the sign that Vasthasha had told him Pa-ni-ta had predicted he would find. "Could there be such a coincidence? The world is too large to grant such a meeting," he thought to himself. "But then, as the foliate had assured me, it is also too complex not to."

■ Wood quietly growled and Cley woke to the darkness of his new room. It seemed to him that he had only minutes ago come in from his watch. He heard the door opening slowly, and with that sound reached for his knife, which was hidden beneath the pillow. "Wraiths," he thought, but then a familiar voice sounded. It was that of Captain Curaswani.

"Cley," he said, and the door opened all the way. The hunter saw the light from a candle that the captain was holding. "Get dressed. I need your expertise."

The hunter was fully dressed, still not having had the time to shed his habits from a life in the wilderness. He slipped into his boots and was on his feet in a moment.

"What is it?" he asked, rubbing the sleep from his eyes.

"An emergency," said Curaswani.

"A Wraith?" asked Cley.

"Even that might be preferable at this juncture," said the captain.

He led Cley and Wood down the hallway, speaking over his shoulder in whispers.

"There are only three of the settlers left living in the fort," he said. "Two of them are women, and one, now a widow since her husband was separated from his head by a Wraith, a Mrs. Olsen, is inconveniently with child. Private Dat has informed me that you had been a midwife or something close to it in your previous life. I'm ordering you to deliver the child in question, if you don't mind."

The captain stopped in front of a door at the end of the hallway. From behind it, Cley could hear sounds of heavy breathing and muffled cries of pain as if someone was screaming into a pillow. Curaswani turned and patted Cley on the shoulder.

"Pull this off, and I'll see to it that you are awarded an honorary medal of honor in the armed forces of the western Realm." He saluted the hunter, then retreated back down the hall as fast as he could manage on his bad leg.

■ The room was cramped and very warm. The flames of the two candles sitting on the night table next to the bed guttered with the heavy breathing of the expectant mother. Shadows danced, a rocker creaked behind the hunter, and he turned quickly to see an old woman sitting with a bottle of spirits in her hand.

"Who the hell are you?" she asked in a cracked voice.

"Cley. I know something about delivering babies," he told her.

"Good, because as much as I know about it, you could fit in a flea's ass," she said, and took a pull at the bottle.

"What is the mother's name?" he asked.

"Willa Olsen," said the old woman, whose hair was done up in a silver pile atop her head. She was wearing a high-necked, green-velvet dress. Although the wrinkles at the corners of her mouth and eyes testified to her age, in the shifting shadows of the candlelight she appeared to him alternately beautiful and haggard.

"And what is your name?" asked the hunter.

"Morgana," she said.

"Will you help me?" he asked.

The old woman rocked the chair forward, and in one fluid motion, stood and rested the bottle on the table.

"I may need something to sew with, a needle and strong thread, and they must be boiled so they are sterile," he said.

"Where are you from?" she asked.

"The wilderness," he said. "Now hurry. I don't think we have much time."

"I'm already gone," she said, and passed through the open doorway.

Cley watched her leave, and saw her sidle nervously past Wood out in the hallway. Then he turned back and lifted one of the candleholders off the nightstand. He brought it up close to the face of the woman in the bed. His patient was sweating and breathing heavily in between quiet moans. At times her mouth opened wide, and he was reminded of the captain's pipe bowl. Her body was pitching back and forth. The face he saw gave him some trepidation about the delivery. Willa Olsen was not in the prime of youth—only a few years younger than Cley, himself. Advanced age was one of the factors, he remembered, that often gave rise to odd birth positions, anomalies, stillbirths.

"Willa," he called loudly to her. "My name is Cley. I have delivered a score of children, and I am going to deliver yours. You can help me by not moving so much. Regulate your breathing; you are wasting too much energy. It will make the pain worse. Above all, don't push until I tell you to. Do you understand all of this?" he asked.

For the first time, the woman in the bed opened her eyes and looked at him. Her breathing grew more regular, and she nodded.

"I am going to have to uncover you, touch you. It is the only way I can help your baby. Do you understand?" he said.

"Yes," she said through clenched teeth.

Cley reached down and lifted the covers off the woman. Amazingly enough, she was fully clothed. He slipped the stone knife out of his boot, and with a smooth maneuver that harkened back to his scalpel work as Physiognomist, he slit through three layers of fabric, baring her body. Besides her swollen stomach, she was somewhat plump, with wide hips, and Cley took this to be a good sign.

When the hunter put his hands on her stomach, she cried out and twisted in the bed.

"I am just feeling to see if the child is in the proper position," he said. "And it is. You have never given birth before, I suppose?"

She shook her head.

He breathed deeply and began to pry apart her knees.

■ In all, the delivery had been routine. The old woman, Morgana, was snoring in the rocker, the empty bottle lying in her lap. The mother was resting peacefully, with the child asleep between her breasts. It was a boy. Cley tried to remember now if he was ahead on boys or girls, and decided the score was perfectly even.

He sat for a moment on the edge of the bed, studying the features of the sleeping Willa Olsen. "This hour," he thought, "might be the last free of strife that she will have for some time. Her husband dead, on her own with a new baby in the wilderness in a fort that is under deadly attack . . ."

For a brief moment, he gave himself over to a casual Physiognomy, trying to predict from her sleeping visage if she had what it would take to survive. Her face was round and neither homely nor pretty, but plain in a way that could not be described. Her straight brown hair was chopped short, obviously in haste, as if it had been gathered into a tail and hacked with a knife blade. He tried to find some distinguishing feature, perhaps the nose or chin, that would give him a clue, but he ended by shaking his head.

The hunter put the knife back in his boot and blew out the one candle that had burned nearly to its base. He knew his work was done, and what would happen now was up to the new mother and the will of the Beyond. He closed the door gently as he left. Then, stepping carefully so that his boots did not tap the floor, he headed back for his room, with Wood following close behind.

■ Cley grew accustomed to life at Fort Vordor in the days that followed. Although the captain did not require him to perform any functions other than guard duty and hunting for game, he readily volunteered to help in all chores from keeping the weapons cleaned and oiled to peeling potatoes for dinner. There was a welcome monotony to the routine, and the work was by no means demanding. There was plenty of time to get to know the soldiers. The hunter had great respect for Curaswani, who knew how to balance authority and humanity, tempering both with a dry sense of humor. In the late afternoons, before dinner, he usually met the captain in his quarters for a drink of whiskey and a half hour of conversation. The old man lent him one of his pipes, and they would toke up a minor squall in the small office.

Beneath this idyllic life, there ran, constantly, an undercurrent of fear. The Wraiths had not struck for a full month and everyone knew they were due. In the course of building a cradle for the new baby one morning, the hunter realized that he could be the next victim. "I must not lose sight of the fact that this is only a short stop in my journey," he told himself.

He took some time out of each day to leave the compound and search the nearby forest for game. Unlike the demon forest, this stand of woods seemed to retain its deer population through the winter. They were not the white variety, but tawny brown and larger than their cousins to the south. Dat, the one-eyed, scarred soldier, usually accompanied him and Wood on these hunting forays. For having one eye, Dat proved himself an excellent shot. Occasionally, on their way back to the fort, if they had been lucky and were returning early, they engaged in a marksmen's competition, aiming at some twig or rock in the distance. The young man always won, and Cley laughed with the pleasure of his loss.

The hunter inquired as to the health of the new child as often as he could. He worried that the mother might be too inexperienced, too distraught with recent events to help the baby thrive. Willa Olsen had not shown herself in the compound since the delivery, so Cley questioned Morgana. The old woman reported that the nursing was going well and that the mother was keeping her sanity and health together. Her only concern was that Willa had not named her son yet. Through her cursing, drinking bravado, he caught glimpses of the duenna's concern for the mother and child and soldiers. She made the rounds daily, joking with the men. At night, from his guard post, Cley saw her stroll nonchalantly, with head down, across the compound to slip inside the captain's quarters. She told the hunter that someday she would read his fortune.

■ From the captain's window, Cley could see the snow driving down. Curaswani threw another log into the fireplace behind his chair and returned to his seat.

The hunter puffed at his pipe, and said, "I remember you telling me that there were five citizens left alive when you arrived, and that two have been killed since. Now I have met Morgana and Willa, but who is the third?"

"You don't miss a trick, Cley," said the captain. He took a drink of his whiskey and began to relight his pipe. "A fellow named Brisden."

Cley sat forward. "Brisden is here?" he asked.

"Oh, yes," said Curaswani. "He is in a jail cell in the cellar of the barracks across the way. A comfy little place for him next to the furnace. Do you know him?"

"I've heard of him," said the hunter.

"Then you know he is a monumental pain in the ass. It seems that he is one of the main reasons that the Beshanti attacked our people. He was famous for roaming through the wilderness, getting to know the different tribes. Well, he incited them to overthrow their oppressors, namely the citizens of the western Realm. The laggard lives to talk. Talk is his reality. At first, I thought of having him shot for sedition, but believe it or not, I didn't want it on my conscience, though heaven knows

I'd have been doing the entire world a favor. He is fed and kept, and that is the best I can do for him. We will return him to the Realm in the spring, and he can stand trial."

"Do you know where he hails from?" asked Cley.

"Well I prefer not to be indelicate, but he is not what I would call your best ambassador from the eastern Realm. He wandered west years ago and ended in the capital city of Belius. I believe he was at one time a compatriot of Drachton Below, the Master of the Well-Built City."

"In a very roundabout, convoluted way, he saved my life once," said Cley.

"Well, that's all the better, but as for me, I'd just as soon put a bullet in his head. He spins a dark reality with that tongue of his. His conversation is chaos and somehow those words of his insinuate themselves into the actuality of life and shatter lives. I predicted he would cause mayhem here in the Beyond when he first shipped out with the settlers. Truth is, the Realm was happy to be rid of him."

"May I see him?" asked Cley.

"No one sees him unless I accompany them. He is too wily. I'll take you down there someday," said Curaswani, and finished the rest of his drink.

"The Wraiths have been quiet," said the hunter, and made sure to rap on the wood of the tabletop.

The captain knocked on the wood also. "They don't come when it snows," he said. "By the way, the Olsen woman has named her child. She has named it Wraith." The captain raised his eyebrows.

"Odd," said the hunter.

"Not so very," said Curaswani. "She is a little touched from her travails. Perhaps she believes that if she names it after the thing she fears, it will not harm the poor little fellow."

Cley nodded. "What about my medal of honor?" he asked.

"Honorary," said the captain. "Get ready, here it comes," he said, and lifted the bottle to top off the hunter's drink.

■ Two nights later, Cley woke in his room to the sound of Wood growling, and a moment later, he heard a terrible scream from out in the compound.

By the time he got his boots on and was out in the dark, frigid cold, he found Weems kneeling next to a body lying on the ground. In the lamplight, he saw the red stain blossoming in the hard-packed snow. Another soldier stood over the scene, shivering, but obviously not from the cold. The captain stood a few feet off dressed in long johns and boots, brandishing his sword and pistol, his head bowed. Steam issued from each of the soldiers' mouths and literally poured out of the corpse, which, from its huge size, the hunter only then could tell was Knuckle.

■ Cley knocked on the door down the hall from his room. Under his arm, he carried the cradle he had crudely constructed from the planks of a crate that had once held canisters of cooking oil. It was a baby-sized box with hand-carved rockers attached to the bottom.

The door opened, and there was Willa Olsen, holding the squirming Wraith. "Yes?" she whispered, appearing both nervous and shy.

"I've made something for the child," said Cley, and held up the cradle for her to see.

"A coffin?" she asked.

"A cradle," he said, undeterred, "so that you can rock him to sleep at night."

She did not smile, but she nodded and opened the door for him to enter. Stepping back, almost against the wall, she motioned with her free hand for Cley to set the thing down on the floor next to the bed. He did, then rose to face her. She was wearing a kerchief around her head and a dark blue dress.

He put his arms out, and asked, "May I hold him?"

She hesitated, visibly shaken by his presence.

"I do charge for my services," he said. "I require one chance to hold the child." He tried to make his most sympathetic face but feared it was not going to convince.

Reluctantly, she took a step forward and handed him the baby. Cley took the bundled infant in his arms and looked into the small face. He was a handsome imp, with dark eyes and a shock of black hair. A waving hand came up and got tangled for a moment in the hunter's beard. Cley thought of Knuckle being lowered into the earth two days earlier and hugged the child to his chest. The mother reached out and took Wraith away from him.

"Thank you," said Cley, and turned to leave.

"Wait, Mr. Cley," she said. "I want to buy your dog."

"Wood?" he asked, surprised that she had spoken.

"Yes, I have money," she said.

"I can not sell him, madam," he told her. "But why?"

"Because he will smell the ghosts coming for my boy," she said.

Cley had a memory flash of Wood growling just before the death cry of Knuckle. Without speaking, he left the room and ran down the hallway to the stairs.

■ From sundown until the break of dawn, Cley and Wood patrolled the compound, waiting for the next invisible assassin to scale the wall. Instead of the rifle, the hunter carried two loaded pistols. Mrs. Olsen's theory that the dog might be able to sense the Wraiths even though they were camouflaged had caused the captain to order a second plate of food at mealtimes for him. Wood had become the hope of the fort, and had a disposition that was well suited for it. He gladly accepted all of the attention and extra tidbits of food, but never felt the stress of the others' expectations.

On this night, Cley crouched in the darkness, Wood beside him, staring out across the compound. He was thinking of Morgana at dinnertime, telling the men's fortunes with the use of a deck of playing cards. Her facade of intense seriousness had all of the youths convinced of the prophecies she made. Each of the young soldiers had wonderful adventures and lives of passionate love predicted for them. When they had insisted that Cley have his fortune read, he reluctantly agreed so as not to break the spell the old woman had woven. Morgana dealt the cards, and upon seeing them, had quickly whisked them off the table, claiming she had grown too tired to retain her concentration on the future.

Cley laughed to himself quietly at the absurdity of the show the old woman had put on.

"What was it she saw for us?" he asked Wood, and looked down to see that the dog was gone.

He immediately looked up and, in that second, heard barking. Drawing the two pistols from his belt, he moved cautiously out of the shadows and spotted Wood across the way, near the outhouse in the southeastern corner. He began to run.

"Weems, light," he yelled, and the young man lifted the lantern he held and dashed away from his post outside the captain's quarters.

Wood was lunging and barking at nothing, growling as if fighting a demon. Weems got to the dog before Cley, holding the lantern high as he went for his gun. The light spread across the front of the outhouse and, like some illusion in a magic show, Cley saw a knife blade suspended in midair.

"Down," said Cley to both the dog and the soldier. Wood backed off, Weems crouched, and, on a dead run, the hunter fired both pistols at once. One bullet chipped the outhouse door and one exploded into a spurt of blood. The very air appeared to be bleeding and the wound moved along the wall dripping red in its wake. Cley dropped the guns and reached for his knife, but as his own blade flashed in the light, Weems fired his pistol and there was a ghostly cry. Something weighty fell and made an impression in the crusted snow. The bleeding wound blossomed in the frozen white, spreading out from one static point.

In minutes, the compound was full of soldiers. The captain burst from his quarters in his usual nightly attire followed by Morgana, who was wearing only Curaswani's field coat.

"One Wraith less," said Weems, wiping his brow with his coat sleeve.

"The dog?" asked Curaswani.

Cley nodded.

The captain got down on his knees and put his arms around Wood. A shout went up from the men. Morgana had gone to the kitchen and returned with two handfuls of flour. She sifted the fine powder over the growing bloodstain and slowly, beneath this handmade snowfall, the shape of a body began to materialize.

■ In the next week, two more Wraiths were sniffed out by the dog and disposed of—one by Cley's pistols and another by a remarkable rifle shot from Dat, across the entire compound, from his perch on the eastern catwalk. All men on guard duty were now issued a pocketful of flour for each night's watch.

■ "In light of recent events, I was hard put to ignore your request," said the captain, as he led Cley down the stairs to the cellar beneath the barracks.

Underground, the ceiling was low and the expanse, stone walls and floor of packed dirt, ran the exact length and breadth of the structure above. Short torches burned in holders on each of the walls, and the area at the bottom of the steps was crowded with barrels of supplies. The dark, earthy smell reminded Cley of his cave in the demon forest. Curaswani led him through a winding path that ran amidst the supply crates and barrels to a far corner, in which sat a furnace. Crackling sounds of burning wood issued from behind its metal doors. Through the grate on the door to the contraption the hunter saw the red-hot sections of log that heated the barracks above.

"This furnace is a wonder," said the captain. "I stoke it myself once a morning, and through its special design it need not be filled until the next morning. An example of the technology of the western Realm."

Cley remembered having one like it in his childhood home. He did not tell Curaswani that his wonder was a primitive heat waster compared to the spire furnaces of the Well-Built City.

"And here," said the captain, turning to the left and sweeping out his arm to reveal a jail cell previously blocked from sight by his girth, "is the supreme hemorrhoid, the taskmaster of language, itself, the insipid Mr. Brisden."

The shadows were thick inside the cage, which had three sides made of bars and one the stone of the foundation. Cley could see someone sitting there, like a massive lump of laundry in a plain, high-backed chair. A sound emanated from inside the cell, a steady mumbling, like a child saying prayers quickly in order to be done with them. The captain reached back behind himself and pulled one of the torches out of its holder on the wall.

"Here you go, Cley. You've got to get the full show," he said, and held the light up to the bars.

Now Brisden became clear. The hunter could tell it was the same man he had encountered in Drachton Below's memory. He was not so heavy as he was before, and there was a stubbled growth on his chin and cheeks, but the small, deep-set eyes and the voice, the ceaseless voice, were remarkably the same. His thinning hair was wild and the once white suit he wore, ripped and torn at the elbows, the knees, the collar, looked like it had not been washed in years.

Cley listened as a steady stream of words poured forth, some obtuse invective concerning time and consciousness, fact and fable. It was a mighty cyclone of inexplicable terminology celebrating language as reality.

"He's leaking words like a stuck dictionary," said the captain.

The hunter nodded, struck speechless at the sight of this second memory come to life. "First Anotine, now Brisden," he thought. "I am haunted."

Just as Cley was pondering the living Brisden, the heavy speaker looked up suddenly, his jowls bouncing, and stared directly at the hunter. His voice rose a decibel, and he said, at a speed that sounded like a drawl in comparison to the normal rapid flow of his monologue, "Cley, did you really think you had escaped the evil?"

The hunter stepped back as if pushed. While Brisden again achieved his old speed and incomprehensibility, Cley looked to the captain, and said, "He knows me."

"He doesn't know the difference between his ass and his mouth," said Curaswani.

"But he knew my name," said Cley.

"I spoke your name first," said the captain. "He's playing with you."

The hunter shook his head and turned away from the cell. "I cannot contemplate what his statement suggested," he said in a whisper. Without turning back to look again, he told the captain he had seen enough.

"That certainly makes two of us," said Curaswani, replacing the torch in its holder. "Let's get out of here. The smell of his breath is all over the place. Good-bye, Brisden."

"You'll be seeing me soon," said the voice from the shadows.

Once out of the cellar, Cley asked Curaswani for a glass of whiskey. No demon or Wraith had ever upset him the way the sight of Brisden had.

■ During a very cold night watch, Cley and Dat crouched in the shadows beneath the southern catwalk, with Wood sitting between them. The stars and moon were brilliant, and there was a fierce wind whipping down from the north. The young man broke the silence and confessed to Cley that even though he had told all of the other soldiers that he had lost his eye in a knife fight over a girl, it had really been a beating from his drunken father that had blinded him.

The hunter's first thought was to ask why the youth was telling him this, but instead he held his tongue. When the wind finally died down for a short spell, he said, "I've heard you tell that story about the girl, and you tell it well."

Dat nodded.

"I'd stick with it," said Cley.

■ Willa Olsen walked through the compound now on those afternoons when it didn't snow. She carried Wraith bundled in three blankets. The soldiers nodded to her and smiled, but she said nothing in response. Like a sleepwalker, she trod the perimeter of the wall once, and then returned to her room.

■ Cley and Dat took a large buck in the marsh to the north of the fort one day. When the hunter cut into it, he found it had no heart.

■ At the same moment that Wood lunged across the compound, barking and growling after an invisible enemy near the eastern wall, a knife blade suddenly appeared out of nothing and, in one fluid movement, sliced the throat of Private Soames where he stood on the southern catwalk. Weems and Cley, through their practiced routine of lantern and pistol shots, dispatched the Wraith on the ground as the body of Soames fell from on high into the snow of the compound.

In the bright moonlight, Dat, on the northern catwalk, spotted the floating knife blade that had killed Soames. Praying for a right-handed Wraith, he quickly calculated the distance from the hand to the heart of a normal-sized man and shot. There was a scream and a dark spot of blood in the air, but he did not wait to see what would happen. In seconds, he loaded the rifle again, brought it to his shoulder, and without bothering to use the sight, fired. Only when the bleeding wounds appeared to fall upon Soames's body did he leap off his perch and run to join Cley and Weems.

"There may be more," said Weems, pointing to the still-barking dog. As he spoke, the door of the captain's quarters opened with a creak, as if of its own volition.

Before any of them could run to Curaswani's rescue, a pistol shot sounded from inside the low structure, followed by a scream from Morgana.

Cley, Weems, Dat, and the other men on sentry duty made for the open doorway, with Wood in the lead. As the hunter entered the one large room, he reloaded his pistol. There, in the far corner, next to the fireplace, the captain and Morgana were lying together on the large cot where Curaswani slept. The captain was in an indelicate position atop the old woman, whose legs encircled the military man. In her hand, she held a smoking pistol.

Cley looked down at the floor and saw, next to the table at which he and the captain took their afternoon whiskey, a fist-sized wound, leaking onto the planks.

Morgana was smiling broadly. "I saw it moving through the lingering pipe smoke," she said.

"That scream, though," said Cley. "I thought you were done for."

"That was her victory cry, so to speak," said the captain.

"I grabbed the pistol right out of his belt and just pulled the trigger," said the old woman.

"Nice shot, madam," said Cley, who tried to block the doorway so that the soldiers behind him could not see in.

"Cley," said Curaswani.

"Yes?" asked the hunter.

"Close the door."

Cley did as he was requested and a few minutes later the captain appeared, fully clothed in the compound. The other men were standing around the body of Soames, and Weems was telling the others how the dead private had left behind, in the Realm, a wife and two children.

Obviously wanting not to give grief a chance to set in,

Curaswani ordered the men to materialize the bodies of the dead Wraiths and burn them outside the fort. He told Weems to put together a detail to hack a hole in the earth off the western wall for Soames's burial. "Quickly," he said.

The soldiers moved slowly, and one young man was overcome with tears. The captain put his hand on the private's shoulder. "We've got to move, Private Hast," he said, "or we'll all wind up like Soames. Stay with me, boy. I need everyone." Hast nodded, and he and the others moved off.

"This is unusual, Cley," said Curaswani. "More than one Wraith at a time. They must be upset that we are getting the better of them."

"Is that good or bad?" asked the hunter.

"Everything here, at Fort Vordor, is bad," said the captain, rubbing tears from his own eyes.

"The spring is only about a month and a half away," said Cley.

Curaswani nodded and was about to speak, when he was interrupted by another voice. He and the hunter turned to find Willa Olsen standing behind them, staring as if in a trance.

"A ghost has taken my son," she said.

"What do they want with the child?" asked Cley.

"Perhaps they want Brisden," said the captain. "He had become very influential with the head man of the Beshanti."

"Get him for me," said the hunter. Then he turned to Willa, and said, "I'll go for the child."

She did not change her expression, but opened her mouth and released a sound like the howling of a wounded animal.

■ Cley and Dat, armed with rifles, moved through the woods as another frozen dawn broke over the wilderness. Tied to a tether with a noosed loop around his neck was Brisden. The young soldier occasionally gave the disheveled talker a vicious kick in the rear end whenever he slowed down. The words were spewing out like the blood from Soames's slit throat, and although they had threatened to shoot him as many times as yards they had traveled, it seemed impossible to shut him up. The hunter had reluctantly left Wood behind, the dog being too valuable to the protection of the others to risk bringing. They had picked up the trail of the fleeing Wraith, the only set of fresh tracks moving away from the fort. What Cley meant to do when he finally met the Beshanti, he had no idea.

■ After an hour of walking through the peaceful forest, the sun now fully risen, Cley noticed that the footprints of the kidnapper had disappeared. He stopped in a small clearing surrounded by white birches and got down on his hands and knees.

"What is it?" asked Dat.

"See here," said the hunter, and pointed to the ground. "They've tried to cover the tracks." He indicated a place in the snow that appeared unusually smooth in relation to the rest of the area.

Dat pulled Brisden along with him and bent over to look. "What does it mean?" he asked.

"They know we have come after the child," said Cley.

"So the village is nearby?" asked Dat.

"I doubt it," said the hunter. "I don't think they will let us get anywhere near the village. Their village is probably off in the opposite direction somewhere."

"What do we do?" asked the young man, now standing straight and looking around nervously.

"I don't know," said Cley, "my specialty is delivering babies. I believe, before too long, they will find us."

"If this bag of wind doesn't shut up soon, I'm going to have to kill him," said the soldier. With this, he took the butt of his rifle and slapped Brisden lightly in the back of the head with it. "Close that bunghole of yours," he yelled.

The lumpen prisoner winced with the blow, but continued to jabber.

"Easy, boy," said Cley. "He is our commerce. We are trafficking in Brisden today, as sorry a pile of goods as he is."

Cley remained on his haunches for a moment, thinking about how to proceed. As he was about to stand, he heard a sharp whistling noise that seemed to pass just overhead. The constant babble abruptly stopped, and the sudden silence was deafening. The hunter looked up and saw an arrow sticking out of Brisden's throat. Blood dripped from his mouth. There was a look of utter surprise on his face as if he had just discovered the end of language. Two more arrows flew through the air, one piercing his chest and the other lodging itself in his shoulder. He fell, in his dirty white suit, like a sack of molded flour.

Cley turned and began crawling back toward the tree line. At the same moment, Dat opened fire.

The hunter got to his feet, and yelled, "Run!" He heard the screams of the warriors behind him. Dat caught up to him and they had almost made it back among the trees, when the soldier fell forward with a low grunt. Cley turned to help him up, and discovered a stone hatchet wedged in the back of the young man's head. Blood and brain matter, slivers of bone were strewn in the snow.

The hunter wheeled around and brought his rifle up just in time to fire at a rushing warrior. The double-barrel shot ripped half the charging attacker's face off as if it were no more than a leather mask. As he fell dead, another charged behind him. Cley had no time to get up. He reached for his knife and secured it in time to stop, with his free hand, the new enemy's arm from bringing down a hatchet onto his own head. The weight of the body fell upon him, and the two began wrestling. Cley's hat flew off, and the younger warrior's grip, like the jaws of a ferocious animal, squeezed the strength out of the hunter's fingers. The stone knife dropped uselessly into the snow. The warrior raised his hatchet to finish Cley, and just as the weapon was beginning to descend, the Beshanti stopped. He leaped up off the hunter and backed away.

Cley did not understand what had happened, but he seized the opportunity to retrieve his knife and get to his feet. When he stood, he saw that he was surrounded by a contingent of twenty or so strong-looking men wearing deer-hide tunics and leggings fashioned from beaver pelt. Their hair was long and dark and worn in braids that reached to the middle of the back. In the midst of his dilemma, Cley noticed that even in the snow, they wore nothing on their feet.

The hunter turned cautiously, holding the knife thrust outward in as threatening a manner as he could muster. He thought to himself how pitiful he must look, and wondered which of them would finish him. A warrior stepped forward, a large man dressed in a derby hat and a maroon dinner jacket that one might wear to a party in the Realm. The sight was unnerving, and Cley could not help but blink his eyes.

The man walked slowly up to Cley, opened his hands to show he had no weapons, and then reached out and touched the hunter on the forehead between the eyes.

"The Word," he said, and Cley was amazed to hear the language of the Realm coming from the Beshanti.

The hunter remained silent.

"Yes, I know your tongue," said the man.

"Brisden?" said Cley.

The Beshanti nodded. "I am Misnotishul. In your language this means 'Rain.' "

"Why did you kill Brisden?" asked Cley.

"We called him the pale toad. I learned from his croaking, but now he is useless to us," said Misnotishul.

"And me?" asked Cley.

"You have been marked by the Word. If we had killed you, we would not have lived long," said the Beshanti.

"I've come for the child," said the hunter.

"I told the Shensel, the spirits, to bring me the baby so he would not be killed when we attack. Is the child yours?" asked the warrior.

"Yes, he is my son," said Cley, looking down so the man could not see his eyes. "He is to be marked by the Word this spring."

Misnotishul motioned with his left hand and pronounced a string of words in Beshanti. A man stepped out from a stand of birch trees, carrying the child still wrapped in his blankets. The bearer of the child handed him over to Cley.

"Tomorrow, we are going to vanish those of the western Realm from our land," said Misnotishul. "No one in the fort will be left alive. You may go your way with your son and your wife, but the others, I promise you, will die."

"Why must they?" asked Cley.

"They are an illness in the land. We tried to let them grow here, but they are like poisonous weeds. I am sorry, but I want the Realm, the home of Brisden and yourself, to know that no more should come. Once the last of them is dead, I must undergo a ritual to forget your tongue. I wanted the power that the Word have to know all language, but the pale toad has given me a destructive knowledge."

"But . . ." said Cley, and the Beshanti waved his hand in front of him as if erasing the hunter's voice. Misnotishul turned and motioned for his men to follow him.

The hunter stood in the clearing in the birches, holding the sleeping child. He looked down at Dat and shook his head, thinking of the times they had gone hunting, the young man's confession to him about his father, his amazing one-eyed aim.

Cley was confused, weighed down by grief and unable to move. Then the baby woke and started to cry. The hunter picked up his hat and put it on. With his free hand, he slipped the knife back into his boot. He took a slow, weighted step, and then another, and another, until Fort Vordor came into view.

■ Curaswani drew on his pipe, lifted his drink, and finished it all in one draught. "Then you will go," he said to Cley.

"The others, though," said the hunter.

"We will hold the fort," said the captain. "Three saved is better than none. It will be our victory."

Cley shook his head.

"An order," said the captain, as he poured them each another glass.

■ That night there was a party in the barracks. Captain Curaswani ordered whiskey be served and relieved all men from guard duty. Private Dean played his harmonica, and Morgana danced with each of the soldiers. Some of the men sang old songs from the western Realm while others sat about telling jokes and tall tales, smoking pipes and cigarettes. The captain was the barkeep, and he kept all drinks filled to spilling. There was venison cooking on the stove, and Morgana had, through kitchen alchemy, created a cake with icing made from melted sugar cubes and lard.

Willa Olsen had also come downstairs, carrying the baby.

She stood off to the side most of the time, staring blankly at the goings-on. She approached Cley, who was sitting on one of the soldier's cots, smoking a cigarette he had begged from Weems. The hunter looked up from his thoughts and took a sip of his drink.

"Thank you," she said in a voice that was nearly smothered by the noise of the party.

Now it was Cley who could think of nothing to say. He reached up and touched the baby's blanket. She began to turn away, and he called her back.

"Get some sleep," he said. "Early tomorrow, you and I and Wraith are leaving Fort Vordor. Say nothing to the others tonight about it. Pack whatever you can possibly carry along with the child."

She nodded quickly and walked away. He was uncertain as to whether she really understood what he had said.

■ The captain's voice was like thunder as he called the men to attention just before sunrise. They lifted themselves, groggy and disoriented, from the places where they had fallen but a few hours earlier. There was a lingering fog of tobacco smoke in the barracks, mixed with the smell of venison that had been left to char on the stove.

Cley had not slept, but was fully dressed, wearing his black hat and the yellow coat. His bow and quiver were slung over opposite shoulders. In his left hand he carried a rifle, and there was a pistol in his belt. The new pack that Curaswani had given him was filled with some food, the book cover, his fire stones, and as much ammunition as he could carry. He stood in the darkness of the compound, with Wood at his side.

As the soldiers came from the door of the barracks, limping into boots and buttoning their uniforms, Curaswani, dressed in full uniform and bearing all of his medals on his chest, issued them rifles and pistols he had gathered on the ground in a heap. He directed them to where he wanted each to take up a position on the catwalks.

Cley saw in the young men's faces that they knew something portentous was about to happen. One or two had tears in their eyes, and nearly all of them were trembling. No one questioned the captain, but all moved quickly to their assigned posts. On his way to the great door of the fort, Weems passed the hunter and slipped a pack of cigarettes into his hand.

"For luck," said the young man, and was gone.

From the barracks came Willa, carrying Wraith in her arms and a pack on her back. Morgana walked with them, her arm wrapped around the new mother's shoulders. They moved next to Cley in the middle of the compound.

Once his men were in place, the captain approached the hunter and women.

"Cley," he said, "if I were you, I'd head east to where the settlers had their homes. I believe a few of those structures are still standing. Finish the winter out in one of them and then move on if you must in the spring. It seems you are immune from the Beshanti ire thanks to your marking. Perhaps they will not change their minds and will leave you alone until the weather gets better. If I can, I will send some men in the spring to check up on you and fetch Mrs. Olsen back."

The hunter nodded. He was about to speak, when one of the men up on the Eastern catwalk shouted, "Beshanti at the tree line."

"How many?" asked Curaswani.

"I can't count them, sir," came the reply.

Then, from each of the walls came the same news, "Beshanti at the tree line."

The captain handed Morgana a pistol, and yelled, "Open the door."

Weems pulled the timbers back, unlocking the oak barrier.

The captain reached down and petted Wood on the head as Morgana leaned over and kissed the baby.

"Good-bye, Cley," said Curaswani.

"I'll see you in the spring," said the hunter.

"To be sure," said the captain.

The sun had begun to rise as Cley and Willa walked through the entrance of Fort Vordor. Wood took up the lead. They moved quickly, saying nothing, across the field toward the eastern tree line. Ahead of them, at two hundred yards, there was gathered a veritable sea of Beshanti warriors. Cley leveled the rifle in front of him in case he needed to fire it. When they reached the middle of the field he put his free arm around Willa as a sign to the natives that she was part of him.

As they approached the vast war party, Wood ran forward and the warriors fled from him with shouts of fear as if he was some kind of evil spirit. This created an opening in their ranks. Cley whispered to Willa, "Don't look at them. Just keep walking."

The hunter was overwhelmed by the great number of men he continued to pass, even though they had made the tree line and were now moving into the forest. Finally, after another fifty yards, they were alone among the birches.

Minutes later, there suddenly arose from behind them a deafening shout, like the very shout of the earth. Wraith woke and screamed at the noise. Soon after, there was the sound of gunfire in the distance. Cley made for a hill he had often seen from the eastern catwalk of the fort, peering over the tops of the forest trees. He and Willa and the dog climbed the gentle slope. When they reached its peak, they turned and look back.

The fort was under attack. There was the distant report of rifle fire, and the hunter saw puffs of smoke appearing everywhere along the battlements. Dozens of bodies lay strewn on the field between the tree line and the walls of Vordor. Some of the Beshanti were scaling the walls with long ladders made of tree branches. He looked for Curaswani and found him on the catwalk, his sword blade catching the sunlight, his white hair and beard making him look at that great distance like the image of Father Time.

"Enough," said Willa. She took Cley by the hand and pulled him toward the other side of the hill. As he descended back into the Beyond, he felt himself leaving behind a great sorrow. He remembered how much he truly was a man of the wilderness. As the sounds of the battle faded, a new emotion grew inside of him. It was neither joy nor grief. He could not describe it, and he was content that he had no word for it.

the knife

Tomorrow I return to Wenau under dubious circumstances, and because I have been too busy in recent weeks to revisit my vision of the Beyond, I feel I had better take this time tonight to recount another chapter in Cley's journey. The future, it seems, a phenomenon which had for so long been a certainty of dusty books and quiet, solitary contemplation, has become an empty page, itself waiting to be marked by those events that have yet to transpire. Its perfect blankness fills me with trepidation and at the same time pleases me with its enigmatic possibilities. I go to town as a sign of good faith in my humanity and hope to find, in return, a similar sign from the citizens there. As the beauty slowly percolates my mind toward transcendence, I will explain.

After my initial visit to the schoolhouse, word had apparently gotten around that I was not such an angry monster as had been advertised for so long. Those who had been present that night, Feskin and his friends, had obviously convinced more of their neighbors that I was to be trusted. Because of this, as soon as two days following, I began to receive guests at the ruins. On the first day, there were only a few, but I was pleased to find that these folks were not among those I had met at the schoolhouse. Yes, they also brought *their weapons in order to ameliorate their fears, but they came in good humor and were inquisitive and friendly. I led them around the ruins and entertained them with snatches of historical, architectural, and technological information.*

Every day following, more and more visitors came, on foot, on horseback, in wagons. As the days progressed, they did not bother with the weapons. They conversed with me openly without fear and told jokes, and I came to see that it was a mark of status for those who could engage me in conversation or make me laugh out loud. That part of me that loves myself grew beyond all measure with this realization, causing me to act more flamboyantly the role of scholar and raconteur. It also dawned on both myself and the visitors that the ruins were a large part of their lives too—the shattered remains of the eggshell that had given birth to their present culture and community. The distance of time now allowed them to look upon the Well-Built City with more curiosity than dread.

Each day, I improved the tour I would give and honed my store of anecdotes. Instead of writing at night, I spent my time wandering the ruins in search of more and more interesting locations to which I might guide my visitors. Early on, I added a trip through the underground, which culminated at the site of the wrecked dome of the false Paradise. I also no longer hesitated to show them the corpse of Greta Sykes, Below's original werewolf. Having dispatched her with my bare hands years ago when ridding the ruins of those onerous creatures, I had had the wherewithal to preserve her carcass in a glass vat of formaldehyde in a laboratory on the remaining second-floor structure of the Ministry of Science.

Since many of those who came for the tour were interested in Cley and his role in the downfall of the City, I took pains to include a visit to his office. Although the building that housed his living quarters was now in too dangerous a state of disrepair, the front having been torn completely away and the staircase leading up to his rooms having been obliterated, I would offer to fly anyone who wanted to see it up to the height of the rooms and let them gaze in upon where their hero had spent his domestic hours.

One evening, I gathered all of the remaining intact blue spire statues, which had once been living miners in Anamasobia and were brought to the city by Below together in one room in the remaining quadrant of the Ministry of Education. They made a powerful display, at the site of which I had an opportunity to wax philosophical on the dehumanizing tendency of a state-run economy. I fatuously enjoyed my own speech, but I believe the tourists preferred the spectacle of intricate beard stubble turned to stone. I could hardly blame them.

Every tour ended at my own Museum of the Ruins. This had become the highlight of the visit, and many would ask me anxiously at the beginning if they would get a chance to see it. How could I refuse to show them? They walked among the shelves and gaped in awe, for through that collection one could really get a sense of both the social complexity and technological prowess of the once mighty metropolis.

The only time that the hordes of visitors diminished instead of grew was last Thursday when it rained hard. On that day, I had only a small party show up. In fact, it was but two people; an old woman and her son, a large hulking fellow with dim affect. They had made the trip from Wenau in a wagon. When I greeted them at the walls of the ruins, the woman nodded curtly but did not offer her hand in greeting. The young man never changed his expression throughout the entire visit, but presented the same bland, bowl-of-cremat face, no matter what wonder I revealed to him and his mother. The woman, on the other hand, made many different faces, all seemingly disapproving. I did my best to be gregarious at every turn, but her nose remained constantly wrinkled back as if she were smelling something noxious. As I remember, she did a good deal of head shaking, as if saying a silent "No" to everything I told her. Dressed completely in black and wearing a black hat and gloves, she had become, for me, by the end of the tour, like a sick shadow of guilt I could not escape.

I did not bother taking her into the underground, and since she seemed repulsed by the remains of the monkey who had written, "I am not a monkey," five hundred times, I also passed on a viewing of the wolf girl's corpse. Finally, we arrived at the Museum of the Ruins, and I gladly left her and her dullard son to look around on their own while I went off to make myself a cup of shudder.

I did not stay away long, and when I returned to escort them back to the wall, I found that they were gone. The rain had increased, but I took the initiative to fly over the ruins. I spotted them in their wagon, moving as if fleeing across the fields of Harakun. "Strange," I thought, and then, "Good riddance." She was one neighbor I felt I could certainly live without.

It was not until that afternoon, when I returned to the room housing my museum, that I smelled the absence of an object from one of the displays. The woman had taken something, I was sure of it, but although I made a cursory inspection of the shelves, I could not ascertain what it was. Thievery was an aspect of the human condition I had never pondered too deeply. Its implications gave me much food for thought. I, myself, had stolen cigarettes from the villages, and that fact prevented me from becoming too self-righteous over the incident.

The following day, the sun was once more bright, the sky blue, and the number of visitors was again what it had been. Then, as the days that led into this week passed, the numbers of people began to diminish, and then trickled down to nothing. I wondered if I had done something offensive, searching my memory for a situation that could have been construed as lacking in taste. I decided that it must have been Greta Sykes' remains that put the tourists off. "Maybe I recounted the tale of dispatching her with too much relish," I said to myself. "Perhaps, in my eyes, as I spoke about her, they could somehow see that I had once made love to her."

Two days passed without even a visit from Emilia, who had come twice in as many weeks. I was a wreck, admonishing myself for my crudeness. I then wondered if the fly to my pants had been

unbuttoned at one of the tours, and I kept walking around in soli-
tude, checking the buttons every minute or so. Putting my hand to
my mouth, I tried to smell my own breath. I stared into the mirror
for hours on end, searching for the clue to my undoing in my own
physiognomy.

Luckily, Feskin showed up on the third day and ended my miserable self-torture. He roused me from a nap on that makeshift coral
chair at the pinnacle of a pile of rubble. I woke to the sound of his
voice calling me and flew down to greet him.

"Misrix," he said, and put out his hand in as friendly a manner
as ever.

I was happy to have him there and told him so. "I was beginning
to think that I had offended your people in some way to make them
stop coming to see me."

"There is a problem," he said, pushing his spectacles up his
nose. I unthinkingly did the same.

"No," I said.

"Yes, but I think we can use it to our advantage," he told me.

"Was it Greta Sykes?" I asked. "The fly of my trousers?"

He laughed. "Not exactly."

"What then? I must know," I said.

"Well, do you remember a woman coming to visit you a few
days back? I believe it was on the day that it rained," he said.

"Less than pleasant," I said, and shook my head as she had done.

"You don't have to convince me," he said. "She is Semla Hood.
It was to her that Cley left his second manuscript about your adventures in Below's mind. She knew Cley well, and her husband
Roan was a close friend of his in Wenau. Her husband was one of
the casualties of the beauty. He had been cured of the sleeping disease with it, and then when the supplies of it ran out, his addiction
had caused him to take his life because he could not conceive of an
existence without it."

"But I did nothing to her," I told him.

"That doesn't matter," said Feskin. "She does not trust any-

thing that has any relationship at all to the ruins or Below. And I'm afraid she automatically puts you in that category. Anyway, when she came to visit here, it was not with the best of intentions. She wanted to find some piece of evidence to in some way damn you. I think she was hoping you might eat her son or maybe bite her on the forehead."

"My appetite does not run to dust or mold," I said.

Feskin laughed. "What she brought back from the ruins, an item she had taken from your museum, was a bone knife that she claims was Cley's. She said that it was given to him by Ea, the traveler, and that Cley would not part with it unless he was dead. With this flimsy circumstantial evidence, she believes that you, yourself, have murdered Cley."

I was not, at first, able to grasp the enormity of what the school-teacher was telling me. Then, as it slowly dawned on me, I shouted, "Absurd. Cley and I were the best of friends."

"Listen, I know this is true. I read his account of how you saved him from the sheer beauty, but this is what she is saying, planting new seeds of doubt in everyone's mind. She has taken the knife to the constable and said she wants a full investigation. Do you remember the circumstances in which you found the artifact or what its history is?" asked Feskin.

"I don't even remember its being in the museum. I must have picked it up somewhere among the ruins and tossed it mindlessly onto one of the shelves," I said.

"She said she knows it was Cley's because it had on the handle an insignia of a coiled snake," he said.

"Now I will lose the trust of all of the new friends I have made," I said, and could feel tears welling in my eyes.

"I don't think so," said Feskin. "The constable is not about to launch an investigation based on one piece of evidence, but I do think you should come to Wenau and answer the charges of your de-tractors. I truly believe that if you were to do this, of your own vo-lition, it would be proof of your honesty. I will represent you in your

meeting with the constable. He is not an unreasonable fellow. You will be cleared, and it might be just the trick to convince the rest of the community who have not met you that you have a good heart and the best of intentions."

I did not think twice about his plan, knowing that if I did not take some action, I would soon return to my lonely life haunting the ruins. I could not let this hag take away my bid for humanity. "Yes," I said. "I will come to Wenau."

"Excellent," he said. "I will make arrangements for a place for you to stay. I will expect you at the schoolhouse two days from now in the evening, at the same time you last arrived."

I chatted then with Feskin for a while about how we might present my side of the story. He told me to try to remember where the knife had come from. Then I walked with him to the edge of the ruins, but hung back when he left so as not to disturb his horse.

Since then I have been searching my memory for a clue as to the origin of the primitive blade. I think I found it one day in the wreckage of the Ministry of the Territory. Yes, I believe I might remember vividly the morning I came upon it, sticking out of the coral wall as if someone had been using it to hang his coat on.

In my thoughts, I now pull that knife from the wall, pink granules of coral drifting to the floor like flakes of the snow flurry falling outside the window of warped glass. A baby is crying in a back room, a woman is singing softly, a fire is crackling in the fireplace, a black dog is curled up on the rug, and a man is sitting in a chair with a loaded pistol in his lap, waiting for the first sign of spring.

a ghost story

A month had passed since the fall of Fort Vordor, which marked the end of the incursion of the western Realm into the Beyond. Although there had been light snow twice in this time, there had been much more rain. The hard-packed shell of white that had covered the landscape was now slowly vanishing. It was obvious that the weather was getting warmer and that spring was very close.

Cley and Willa and Wraith and the black dog had taken refuge in what had once been the Olsens' log house. It sat fifteen miles east of the fort in a stand of birches at the edge of a lake. The dwelling was small but had two rooms, a fireplace, and the glass of both of its windows was still intact. The very existence of the place was, to the hunter, a miracle since on their journey to it they had passed at least three other similar structures that had been burned to the ground by the Beshanti.

Life at the edge of the lake was like a ghost story without a ghost—the rain-sodden hours, the lingering grief of the death of Curaswani and the others, the unnerving silence of Willa Olsen, and the sudden, piercing cries of the baby. Cley spent his days in the birch forest, hunting and reflecting on the tumult of events that had brought him to this place. Wood, although content to be out on the hunt when he must, had become Wraith's second guardian and spent all of his time while indoors standing sentry at the entrance to that second room, where the child slept.

■ It was evening, and Cley cooked some fresh-killed deer meat on the flames of the fireplace. As the house had been untouched, so were the barrels of supplies, and in them the hunter had discovered dry rice, flour, and a few potatoes with which he augmented the venison, partridge, wild goose, or rabbit he felled each day. Willa accepted her meal from him with a quiet, "Thank you," in return. They sat in silence at the small table in the corner and ate together. When the hunter inquired as to the child's health, the mother simply nodded. For the most part, she did not look up. This gave Cley ample opportunity to study her. He noticed that there was always a slight trembling in her hands. She had been greatly abused by life, but still she showed signs of a certain strength in her determination to care for Wraith. If not for the child, Cley believed she would open the door and walk straight into the lake.

As soon as dinner was finished, and Cley and she had cleaned off the table and put things where they belonged, she returned to the other room. The hunter stoked the fire and sat in the chair that had once belonged to her husband. He smoked a cigarette from the pack that had been given to him by Weems and stared at the flames, watching for scenes and faces and portents of the future in their frantic dance. Then, he heard from the back room, the mother talking in a high, sweet voice that drew murmurs of delight from the infant.

The demon killer, the tattooed slayer of invisible Wraiths, smiled at the sound and blew smoke rings at the ceiling. Wood lay curled up at the entrance to the other room and lifted his head from dreams every time the baby cooed. It was only in this brief hour before sleep that ghosts were banished and the future and past were forgotten. When the cigarette had been smoked into oblivion, Cley lifted himself out of the chair and lay down on the floor.

■ The sun had barely begun to cast its reflection on the waters of the lake. Cley stood in the quiet house at the window, staring out along the tree line, watching two Beshanti warriors surreptitiously moving through the shadows from tree to tree. He had a mind to send Wood out to chase them away as he had done on numerous occasions.

■ One night, after he had sat in the chair, staring into the fireplace longer than usual, Cley was lying on the floor, trying to decide whether he should return to the fort and see if anyone had been spared.

Just as he decided that he could not bear to discover Curaswani slaughtered, the door to the other room opened on creaking hinges. He looked up and saw, in the light of the dying embers, Willa Olsen moving around the central room. Her eyes were closed, and she trod softly and slowly in her thin cotton nightgown. She whispered in her sleep, the name *Christof*. Finally, she leaned down over the back of the chair the hunter had recently vacated and planted a kiss in midair. Then she returned to the bedroom, and he heard no more from her till the morning when the baby woke, crying.

■ Cley smelled the scent of the ocean on the breeze one bright afternoon while hunting a mile north of the house. He thought to himself how much easier his life would be if he were to just keep heading in that direction, making progress toward Arla Beaton and the true Wenau. Willa and the child were to him like Vasthasha's taproots, holding him firmly in one place. He daydreamed of the freedom he had once known and cursed in his loneliness. In his mind, he saw the green veil soaring above the Beyond.

■ The hunter discovered a fishing rod and tackle in a corner of the main room of the house. On a clear afternoon, he and Wood went down to the lake to try their luck. Chunks of venison were used as bait. In the first hour, Cley managed to hook himself once in the pants and once on his thumb. The line tangled and snarled every few minutes, and it took at least as long to unravel the maze of knots.

Finally, with great patience, he was able to cast and keep things in order. The wooden bobber, carved into the form of a small boat with a tiny fisherman in it, floated on the surface. Below, in the clear water, Cley could see large dark forms moving close to the bottom.

Hours passed, and there was not so much as a nibble. The day was peaceful, and the lake was so still its reflection was a perfect opposite of the world above. Cley was roused from his torpor by the sight and sound of a large fish leaping into the air out past where his line descended. Scales caught the sunlight in a ripple of iridescence before it splashed back beneath the surface.

"Over here," Cley yelled.

Wood was bored beyond reckoning and headed back to the house.

"Deserter," the hunter called after him.

More time passed, then, suddenly, Cley felt a tug at the line. He reeled in, but the reel was old and rotted and the handle broke off. Filled with excitement, though, he took the line in his hands and began pulling his catch ashore. From the monumental struggle, he knew that whatever was on the hook must be very large. The line ran back through his grasp, and cut his calluses until his palms began to bleed.

Cursing and struggling, he started to make headway. His nemesis, it seemed, had given in. With each tug a huge, black creature emerged more clearly from below. Dragged onto the shore, its slick skin glistened in the sun. The hunter approached and was met with an horrific sight. It was a blob of a fish, with large, unlidded human eyes, antennae that reached three feet from its head, and a big-lipped mouth so wide it could swallow a whole crow at once.

"Harrow's hindquarters," said Cley, staring down on the monstrosity.

The creature opened its mouth, spit out the hook, and made a loud noise like an old man in respiratory distress, its gasping interspersed with explosive farting sounds.

"All this work for this flatulent pig of hell," thought Cley, as he stepped forward and kicked the thing back into the lake. Then he looked down and saw the condition of his hands and the bloodstains on his yellow coat. He pitched the fishing pole out into the water and stormed away toward the house.

"Where's my gun," he said as he came through the door. But he was brought up short by the sight of Willa, naked to the waist, sitting in his chair by the fire, nursing Wraith. She gazed calmly at him. He looked from her breasts up into her face.

"How was the fishing, Mr. Cley?" she asked in a quiet voice.

A moment of silence passed, then he said, "Excuse me,

madam. Oh, yes, the fishing . . . It was something less than a triumph." He turned quickly away and found his gun. When he looked back to call for Wood to follow, he saw what he believed to be a subtle smile on Willa Olsen's lips.

■ He knew the Beshanti were stalking him as he stalked a deer through thick underbrush on the opposite side of the lake. Wood looked over to see if Cley wanted him to charge back into the birches and chase them away. Instead, the hunter ran as fast as he could, weaving in and out of the straight thin trunks of the trees. The black dog stayed even with him, as if knowing which way his companion would turn before he actually did.

Three Beshanti found Cley's hat lying on the ground. The leader of the party was a large muscular man with a painted face—two streaks of white cutting diagonals across either cheek. He wore the delicate skeleton of a hummingbird on a lanyard around his neck, and a black, sleeveless blouse decorated with red-dyed circles. His two partners were dressed in green tunics and wore their hair in triple braids as was the custom. The trio bent over Cley's hat as if it was an animal that might spring to life at any moment.

Wood suddenly appeared from behind the tree in front of them. Startled, they rose and turned to run. Facing them now, with his rifle aimed at the largest, was Cley.

"What do you want?" asked the hunter.

The leader of the Beshanti spoke in his native language, making signs that seemed to be imploring Cley not to shoot.

The hunter smiled broadly but did not relinquish his aim. He was about to speak again when an invisible force violently pulled the weapon clear of his hands. He stared in amazement as it floated in midair a few feet in front of him. Wood growled at the presence of a Wraith but remained standing behind the warriors.

Now it was the Beshanti's turn to smile. The large man spoke quickly in his own tongue. Cley shook his head, showing he did not understand. It was obvious that he was being lectured to. Then the leader took a knife from his belt and passed it in a cutting motion an inch from his own throat. When he was finished speaking, he motioned with his left hand to where the invisible Wraith stood, holding the hunter's rifle. From that empty patch of air, a white scrap materialized and unfolded into a sheet of paper. It floated slowly toward Cley, and when it was within his reach, the hunter took it.

As he turned it over and noticed the handwriting on one side, his rifle fell to the ground and the three Beshanti brushed past him and began to walk away. Intent on what he was reading, he did not watch them leave. The script was beautifully rendered and at the bottom of the page he saw the name *Misnotishul*. When he was finished with it, he tore it into small pieces and threw them to the muddy ground. Wood walked over and sniffed at the fragments.

■ It was morning. Cley had eaten and was preparing to go out into the forest to hunt. He called softly to Wood so as not to wake the mother and child in the other room. When he was putting on his hat, Willa appeared at the doorway.

"Good morning, Mrs. Olsen," he said, and opened the door to the outside.

"Mr. Cley," she said, and he was surprised that she had spoken.

He turned back. "Yes?"

"I need you to watch Wraith for me while I go out to get some fresh air," she said.

The hunter was silent, at first stunned by the request and then working mightily to come up with an excuse why this might be impossible. "I have to go hunting," he said.

"We've got enough salted venison here to last two months," she said. "I need to get outside in order to keep my health up. I've been in this house for weeks. I won't be gone long. Wraith is asleep. I doubt he will awaken for some time. All you have to do is listen for him."

"Very well," said the hunter. "But do not go far, the Be-shanti are about. And take my pistol with you."

Willa walked over to the windowsill where the gun rested and lifted it.

"I can send Wood with you," he said.

"No, I'd feel better with him here, with the baby," she said.

The door opened and closed, and she was gone.

Five minutes passed and Cley was still standing in the same spot, wondering about the change in Willa Olsen. Not only had she spoken to him, but it was more than a single sentence. She could almost have been said to be animated. A moment later, Wraith began screaming.

Although the hunter was a successful midwife, he had never been a baby-sitter. Delivering children was one thing; having to amuse them was something else entirely. He tried at first to ignore the cries coming from the back room, hoping the child would fall asleep again. The noise did not stop, though, and gave no indication of diminishing.

"Demons in their death throes send up a less obnoxious caterwauling than this baby," he said.

Wood ran into the other room and then back out to stare at Cley. The hunter stood his ground. The dog barked at him.

"May I first just say, shit," said Cley. Then he walked in and gathered up the squirming child.

■ Willa came through the door to find Cley sitting in the chair before the fireplace, the baby wrapped in blankets on his lap. Wood lay on the floor, watching the child grab at the hunter's beard. In his free hand, Cley held open the empty book cover. The house was quiet but for the low murmuring that was a story about a man fishing for the answer to a great problem through a hole in a frozen lake.

■ Cley and Wood were returning from the south. The day was waning as a beautiful golden light drenched the birches. They had taken a large rabbit and a partridge. The hunter thought about Vasthasha and where he would find him once the weather grew warmer. He wanted desperately to leave the woman and child behind, but now, after reading Misnotishul's letter of warning, he knew the Beshanti would not let Willa live.

Before the log house or lake came into view, he smelled a peculiar scent on the air. He feared it was the smoke of a fire, and the first thing he could imagine was that the Beshanti had torched the house with the woman and child in it. Whistling to the dog, who was lagging behind, he ran frantically toward the lake. As he neared the house, he stopped in his tracks, realizing it was not the aroma of a fire, but rather the smell of wild onions and venison cooking.

"She's making a home," Cley whispered to Wood with a look of great sorrow.

■ The meal was tragic in its excellence. Willa watched Cley carefully as he took each forkful. This night, it was the hunter who did not look up from his plate. He noticed out of the corner of his eye the small purple blossom floating in a bowl of water to his right. The venison had been cooked all day in some kind of rich gravy, but he could not enjoy it, for simmering in the back of his own mind was the fact that Willa and Wraith must again be displaced. His thoughts were ablaze with scenarios of how he would break the news.

"Did you ever wonder why the Beshanti did not destroy this house, Mr. Cley?" she asked.

He nodded.

"I'll show you after we finish eating," she said.

His curiosity getting the better of him, he looked up and saw her face illuminated by the candlelight. Her features were plain and honest and appealed to him more than ever before. He wanted to look away again, but knew he couldn't without seeming rude.

"The food is very good," he said.

"You have cooked so many meals since we have arrived that I thought it was only fair," said Willa.

"The house looks different too," said Cley, "less cluttered and jumbled."

"I had a chance today to clean. Wraith slept quite a stretch this afternoon," she said, and pushed the bowl of potatoes toward him. As he took one more, she said, "Please, Mr. Cley, will you try to knock the mud off your boots before entering from now on?"

Cley could not help but smile. "Granted," he said.

There was a long silence, and then at the same moment, they both said, "It was a beautiful day."

When Cley had finished his second helping, they cleared the table together. Willa then told the hunter, "Stay there, I'll be right back."

She moved off toward the other room, stepping over Wraith, who lay on a blanket on the floor next to Wood. A few minutes later, she returned carrying a three-foot-wide wooden platform with six-inch sides. It was open at the top, and there was something growing from within. As she set it down on the table, Cley looked inside and what he saw astonished him.

There was a miniature landscape, a slight grassy rise with two perfectly real diminutive pine trees growing at either end. At the top of the small hill, there sat a house carved from dark wood. It was incredible in its detail.

"The windows of the house are made from slivers of quartz," she said. "If you take the candle and look inside, you can see the people who live there."

Cley did as she suggested and leaned over with the candle close to his face. There, in the flickering light, he could easily make out a man and a woman and two girls sitting at a table. He blinked and saw that the woman had a miniscule pipe to her lips and, even more fantastic, there was a trail of smoke coming from it. The man was at work on a box, very similar to the one the house sat in, with a birch tree the width of a fly wing growing from it. One girl had long blond hair and the other had brown.

The hunter shook his head, and reached out to touch the delicate pine needles of one of the trees. Quickly, he pulled back his finger. "They are real," he said.

"Yes," said Willa. "Notice the lower branch of the one on the right."

Cley looked and, for the first time, noticed a boy, scrupulous of detail, swinging from the branch by one arm.

"The carving is miraculous," said the hunter, "but the trees, the trees . . ."

"My husband, Christof, grew them from the seeds of real trees, and then through some process I do not understand, that has to do with the twisting and pruning of their roots, stunted their growth. He was a master carver and created the house and the people. I remember him working always with two jewelers' loupes, one in each eye," she said. The excite-ment in telling about the small wonder was evident in her voice.

"He must have been an incredible artist," said Cley, now truly absorbed in the tableau.

"He was an unusual man," said Willa. "He was quite naive and open and somewhat strange. He would always tell me stories about the people who lived in the house. The Car-rols, he called them. Long, involved stories with happy end-ings about their everyday lives. There was a point where I believed they were real."

"Did the Beshanti know of this?" asked Cley.

"Yes, some of them would come with that one who knew the language of the Realm, and Christof would tell them about the lives of the Carrols. Their leader would in-terpret for them. They were mightily intrigued, to say the least, and somewhat leery of the little world. His stories were as detailed as his carving, and through them, the Be-shanti were convinced that this was a kind of magic they should not disrespect. This is why, though they killed my husband, they left the house, because they knew the minia-ture was here." She looked over at Cley when she finished speaking, and he could see that there were tears in her eyes, and she was smiling.

"Listen, Willa," said Cley. "We can't stay here."

"We can," she said. "Things are working out perfectly."

"No," said Cley. "We must leave in a few days. The other day in the forest I got a letter from the Beshanti, Misnotishul, in which he warned me that there is great agreement among his people that you should be disposed of."

Willa brought her hands to her face and turned away.

"Listen to me," said Cley, raising his voice. "They won't kill me, and they won't harm Wraith, but they know I was lying when I said you were my wife."

"You what?" she said, and looked at him as if he had betrayed her.

"I told them that the day I went with Dat to get Wraith from them. I did it to save you and the child."

"I can't go away from here," she said.

"Misnotishul, the Beshanti who knows the language of the Realm, has been protecting you. In the next few days, he will undergo a ritual to cleanse him of our language. He told me in his letter that while the words of the Realm still live in him, he has sympathy for us and because of this has made an attempt to warn me. Once this ritual has been performed, there is nothing that can save you. They will come for you," said the hunter.

"I don't care anymore," she said.

"Think of this, though," said Cley, pointing to the baby on the floor. "If you die, the child dies. There is no way for me to feed and care for him."

She walked over and picked the baby up. Cley heard her begin to cry as she moved into the other room.

That night, the hunter smoked all but one of the rest of the pack of cigarettes he had been rationing over their time by the lake. There was no pleasant murmuring from the back room. In the fire, he saw only nightmarish images. These and the sounds of the mother's distress followed him into sleep.

■ Two days later, Wood and Cley found the bloody, naked corpse of Misnotishul tied to a tree. His tongue, eyes, fingers, and nose were strung in a necklace that hung across his chest. Lying beneath him on the ground was a large slaughtered pig, wearing the maroon jacket. The derby hat was affixed to the animal's head with a knife.

■ It was a warm, moonless night, and they moved quietly through the dark. Cley now feared the Wraiths more than anything else and was counting on Wood to be vigilant. He knew they had to cover a great distance by morning, which at the rate they were walking, weighed down with supplies and weapons and the child, he knew was impossible. Misnotishul had told him in the letter that if they were able to cross a certain stream many miles east of the house, they would be free of the Beshanti territory, and the warriors would not follow them beyond that point.

Before they had left the house, as he was closing the door behind them, Cley remembered the sight of the Beshanti leader tied to the tree. This filled him with dread but also gave him an idea. He went inside and found the platform holding the miniature world. Without hesitation, he ripped off the roof of the little house and lifted the figures out carefully. Next, he found a needle and thread in one of Willa's boxes and made, from the diminutive family, a necklace of the mother, father, and boy for her to wear. With this charm around her neck, they set forth.

Willa had, somewhere in between his revealing to her the nature of their situation and the moment they had to leave, come to terms with the fact that she must endure more hardship. She traveled without complaint, carrying the child in one arm and a loaded pistol in the opposite hand. When Cley whispered to her, she whispered back, and he was at least pleased with the fact that she had again found the will to survive.

■ The cracking of twigs, the sound of footfalls—something was moving in the deep shadows to her right. Willa Olsen cocked the hammer of the heavy pistol, reached out toward the noise, and pulled the trigger. There was a blinding flash of fire and smoke, a deafening report from the weapon followed quickly by a high pitched squeal. Wraith woke and began crying.

"Cley," she called out just above a whisper. "Cley."

The hunter answered a moment later, but not from her left where he had been walking all night. His voice now came from the very spot at which she had fired. "Nice shooting, Mrs. Olsen," he said.

"Beshanti?" she asked, rocking the baby so as to quiet him.

"Deer," said Cley. "You drilled it right between the eyes."

"I'm sorry," she said. "I thought . . ."

"No need to apologize," said the hunter. "I appreciate your vigilance."

"Yes, but won't it draw them to us?" she asked.

"Perhaps," said Cley, "but I'm surprised we have gotten as far as we have. It will be morning soon. They may be waiting for us at the stream. Or they may not know we have left yet."

■ They traveled faster than Cley had suspected they might, but all of their efforts in this direction were circumvented when Willa had to stop to feed and change the baby. Wraith's cries of discomfort at being hungry and wet were like a siren moving through the forest, letting the Beshanti know of their position at every step. Once the child was again asleep, they continued as rapidly as before.

"Move as quickly as you can, Willa," he told her, "and when we cross that stream, you can rest all day if you like."

"You, the same," she said in response, and this drew a smile from the hunter.

■ The sun had risen within the hour, and when Cley turned and looked behind him, he saw a thick column of smoke emanating from the forest to the west, reaching high into the sky. He knew that the house by the lake was in flames.

"They are coming," he said to Willa, who had stopped alongside him.

"How much farther?" she asked.

"A mile maybe, a mile and a half," he said.

Wood barked at them to move, and they began to walk again, weighed down by the fatigue of the long night.

■ An hour passed and the stream came into view at the edge of the wide meadow they were traversing. Cley was exuberant that they had made it without incident. Wood bounded ahead and leaped over the narrow watercourse that was the gateway to their freedom.

The hunter turned and brought his rifle up. "You cross first, Willa, and I will watch our backs," he said. When there was no answer from her, he looked and saw the baby, wrapped in its blankets, lying on the ground next to the pistol. Willa Olsen was gliding backward, her feet off the ground as if caught up in a powerful current of air. She struggled and screamed.

Wood dashed back toward Willa, but Cley told him to stay where he was. The dog reluctantly stopped and began to growl as he took up a position next to the child.

Cley surmised there were at least two Wraiths carrying her and wondered how many more were in the vicinity. He knew his chances of saving her were slim, and that if he failed, she would meet the same fate as Misnotishul or perhaps worse. He remembered a distant time when his friend Calloo had put a bullet into Mayor Bataldo in order to save him the experience of being rent apart by demons. These thoughts passed through the hunter's mind in the instant that he took aim for her heart.

"Forgive me," he whispered, and as he was about to pull the trigger, a large bird swooped across his field of vision. Momentarily startled, he fired, and that element of surprise marred the shot.

A spout of red appeared to the left of Willa, and drenched her dress on that side. She moved her arm freely now and balling her hand into a fist, lashed out at the seemingly empty air to her right. Cley could not believe it, but she was free and running back toward him. Wood barked wildly, awaiting the order to attack. Cley saw a knife appear in the air three feet behind her as she closed the distance between them. Cley dropped the rifle and lifted the pistol from where it lay on the ground beside the baby.

Standing straight, he called to her, "Fall down." She did, and he aimed the gun and shot. A wound appeared in the air at the height of where a man's stomach might be. He had obviously hit his target, but the slug had not killed the warrior, and the knife kept slowly advancing toward the fallen woman.

"Now," said Cley, and Wood was off like an arrow. The dog covered the distance in seconds. He hit the ground just in front of Willa's head and sprang upward over her. The floating knife fell to the ground, and the dog wrestled with the unseen warrior. Where Wood's teeth closed, blood trickled out of thin air. Cley was by then beside the dog. He called him off and with his own blade in hand, went to his knees and viciously stabbed at the invisible body.

■ The cold water of the stream that seeped into their shoes and around their feet was refreshing after their long march.

Cley held back his hand and helped Willa and Wraith up onto the opposite bank.

"Nice shooting, Mr. Cley," she said, and gave him a curious glance.

"Indeed," said the hunter. When he looked back across the stream, he saw a large party of Beshanti, standing over the bloody patches of ground that were their brethren. Cley pushed Willa Olsen ahead of him and walked behind her in case one of the warriors had a mind to send an arrow over the boundary.

As they moved in among the trees and out of view of their pursuers, Cley took a moment to reflect on what had transpired. He realized that the large red bird that had thrown off his shot and resulted in the salvation of Willa was of the same variety that he had eaten on the boulder island in the flood.

He laughed wildly at this fact. The sound of his voice echoing among the trees woke the baby, who began to cry.

"Shhh," said Willa, admonishing the hunter.

Wraith fell back to sleep, and they moved on in silence.

■ At night, they had taken to sleeping together as an antidote to the cold. Beneath the two blankets they carried, Wraith rested between Willa and Cley. Wood curled up at their feet and added his own warmth. The hunter again made use of the flint stones for lighting fires and resurrected the practice of heating rocks in the flames, which he then buried beneath the ground to offer heat from below.

He slept poorly, always afraid that he would roll over on the child and smother it. Willa did not have this problem. The long days' walks exhausted her so that after dinner, she dropped to the ground and was immediately asleep. Wraith somehow knew the severity of the situation and usually did not stir before sunrise. The hunter was uncertain how long they could continue to press onward, and searched every day, to no avail, for the temporary shelter of a cave.

■ They crossed a plain, three miles wide, that was dotted with small pools of bubbling water. Great plumes of steam rose up and filled the air with the scent of sulphur. Cley was reminded of his labors in the mine of Doralice, and he warned Willa to keep the baby's face covered as much as possible. They saw, through the ambient mist, a herd of large shaggy beasts with humped backs and curved horns protruding from their mouths, lurking on the southern edge of this boiling land. The hunter had never before encountered this creature. From the size of it and the thundering roar of its voice, he had no desire to inspect it more closely. Wood, on the other hand, kept running off in the direction of the herd, and Cley had to call him back repeatedly.

■ In a forest of pines, Willa rested against a fallen tree, holding Wraith to her breast. Wood lay at her feet. The warm sunlight found its way through the breeze-shifted branches above and fell like rain on the carpet of dry, brown needles. Cley stood in front of her, his gaze directed anywhere but at Willa, and smoked the very last of the cigarettes. He was worried about the possibility of encountering demons, about being lost in the heart of the Beyond with a woman and child, about finding a permanent shelter for them, about the senseless nature of his journey.

"Where are we going, Cley?" she asked.

The hunter thought for a moment, took a long drag, and

said in a cloud of smoke, "Toward the future, where I have an appointment to keep."

"Shouldn't we be heading back to the ocean, so that we can meet the ship coming from the Realm? Spring is here, and soon they will arrive," she said quietly.

"Perhaps we should," he said, "but I can't. There is something I need to do."

"What of Wraith and me?" she asked.

He had no answer for her.

"Well?" she said.

"You had better stay with me, at least for a while longer," he said.

"Who is this person you are meeting?" she asked.

Cley gave a distant smile. "You'll know him when you see him," he said.

"So we are to follow you across the Beyond on your errand?"

"I'm sorry," he said. He turned and looked directly at her. "I'm very sorry." His face was haggard with weariness, and he shook his head as if in confusion.

"You are exhausted, come and sit down," she said, and touched the ground beside her with her free hand.

Cley dropped the burning cigarette and stepped on it. He moved slowly toward her. "Yes," he said, "I will." He leaned over, and then sat with his back against the fallen tree. Willa reached over and removed his hat. Closing his eyes, he said, "I promise, I will find a way to get you home. I . . ."

"All is well," she whispered, and put her arm around his shoulders. In minutes, he was asleep.

■ The hunter again took to using the bow so that he might conserve the ammunition he had taken from Fort Vordor. It had been some time since he had nocked an arrow into place and practiced his shot, so a rabbit and two deer were spared this day that in the previous year would have been dead.

Willa asked that he teach her how to use the weapon, and they spent a morning at target shooting. Wraith lay on the ground with Wood at a safe distance behind them next to the packs and supplies. Cley used his knife to chip off the bark of a pine trunk, and this mark served as a bull's-eye. He was impressed with Willa's strength, for she had no trouble pulling the bowstring back far enough to get the maximum tension. On her first attempt, she hit the tree only inches from the mark.

"Not bad," said Cley, and he stepped up behind her and put his hands on her shoulders. Gently, he pulled her back straight. "Watch with both eyes," he said. "I know there are those who might squint, but I keep both eyes open."

She let the string go, and the arrow flew wildly off course, striking the base of a tree ten yards beyond the target.

"So much for my instruction," he said.

"I blinked," she told him.

"No blinking," he said.

"I blinked because you touched me," she said.

"My apologies," he said.

"I didn't mind it at all," said Willa.

Cley looked at her, and she at him. She lowered the bow and he took a step closer to her. He was about to lift his hand to touch her again, but from the corner of his eye, he saw something move. He turned quickly to find Vasthasha standing next to them, holding the baby. When Willa screamed, he knew she had also seen the foliate.

■ The night sky was strewn with stars, and the travelers sat next to a fire in a clearing in the pines. Cley had convinced

Willa to take one of the foliate's leaves and place it under her tongue as he had done. She rocked the sleeping baby in her lap, and Wood lay next to Vasthasha, being stroked across the back of the neck by a leafy hand.

"I went to the fort to find you," said the foliate.

Willa looked around to see where the strange voice was coming from. She stared at the curious twin fires burning in the green man's hollow eye sockets.

"What did you find there?" asked Cley.

"Carnage," said Vasthasha, "and this." He straightened out his leg and, reaching down, drew something long and slim from within the thatch that was his thigh. He held it up. "I brought it as a gift for you."

Cley peered through the dim glow of the fire and saw Curaswani's pipe with the bowl that was the woman's head. The hunter reached out tentatively and took it. He remembered the white-haired man, and a wave of sorrow passed over him.

"Humans live a hard brief life," said Vasthasha.

"I have no tobacco," said Cley.

"Try this," said the foliate, and handed him a small ball of dried yellow leaves.

The hunter stoked the pipe and sparked it with a stick he lit in the fire. A cream-colored smoke gathered around the company as Cley exhaled. He passed the pipe to Willa, who took it and placed it to her lips. She coughed hard and passed it on to the foliate. After Vasthasha inhaled, he did not exhale. The smoke simply drifted out of the tangled foliage from his chest to the top of his head.

"We must start tomorrow in a new direction," he told them. "I know of a trail through the Beyond that will take us a hundred miles in a mile."

"What?" said Willa.

"A shortcut?" asked Cley.

"The wilderness is veined with passages that defy time

and distance. One simply has to know where they are. At the other end, I know of a place that the woman and child can stay," said the foliate.

"Ea, from the true Wenau, mentioned them to me," said Cley. "I could never really believe in their existence."

"The Beyond exists on many planes and in many times," said Vasthasha.

"I hope we are not going to another fort," said Willa.

"A house. It lies in a meadow of beautiful flowers near the edge of a forest, and there is a lake no more than a hundred yards from it. Many, many years ago, it was built by one of the party of men with the lighted hats. His name was Pierce, I believe, and he was lost on his journey to Paradise and lived for a long time in the wilderness by himself," said the foliate, and again accepted the pipe from Willa.

"One of the expedition from Anamasobia," said Cley. "The last companion of Beaton. He was a young man. I thought he had perished on an ice floe."

"Figuratively," said Vasthasha.

"Wraith and I are to be left alone?" asked Willa.

"For only a short time, while Cley serves Pa-ni-ta," said the foliate.

"Pa-ni-ta?" asked Willa, and looked at the hunter.

"Please," he said, "I cannot even begin to explain."

Later, when the mother and child were sleeping beneath the blankets, and the fire was dying, Cley and the foliate sat in silence. A warm breeze blew through the clearing. The hunter noticed something gently floating on the wind. It fluttered and twisted and came to rest on the grass a few feet away. He slowly got up, stretched, and went to inspect it. As he approached, he saw the veil, folded in half, one corner slightly flapping. When he leaned over to touch it, it changed before his eyes into a large leaf.

"Get some rest, Cley," whispered the foliate.

Vasthasha led the way to the head of a well-worn path through the forest. From where Cley stood, peering over the foliate's shoulder, he could see that it traveled straight like a road of the Realm for a quarter of a mile and then made a sudden turn to the left, out of sight.

"I have to warn you," said the green man, "once we are on this trail, no matter what you see, you must not make a sound. Entities human, animal, and vegetable, who have traveled here, who are, somewhere in Time, always traveling here, will pass you. To touch them, to speak with them, will cause you to shatter like the ice of a winter lake struck by a falling star."

Cley and Willa nodded, and then the hunter said, "But Wraith, how will we keep him from crying, from uttering a sound?"

"You must let me carry the child," said Vasthasha.

The hunter looked at Willa, who was shaking her head.

"Trust him," said Cley.

Vasthasha smiled as Willa reluctantly handed over her son to the foliate. He pulled Wraith up close to his chest, and the baby's eyes closed immediately in sleep.

"Wait, what about Wood?" asked Willa.

"The dog knows," said the foliate.

In the first few minutes they traveled the trail, a distinct humming sound, which rose and fell, could be heard coming from everywhere, as if the air itself was trying to recall a song. The atmosphere grew heavy and soft, and Cley felt like he was more floating than walking. There came a strong breeze from up ahead that lifted the bottom of Willa's skirt and held it, not rippling but like a painting of a dress in the wind.

When they made the first wide turn, they saw the entities Vasthasha had spoken of. Deer and fox and rabbits and birds, using the trail to travel to another day, another year, someplace a hundred miles away in the Beyond. These creatures glowed, encapsulated in a faint, silver aura. It was clear to Cley that his party most likely appeared the same to them.

They took another turn in the trail, and the hunter looked up to see a tall human figure approaching. It was Ea. The traveler from the true Wenau turned and smiled as he passed by. The hunter wanted desperately to speak, but he remembered Vasthasha's warning. "He is going to Anamasobia long ago to begin the story that has brought me here," Cley thought to himself.

Ea was only the first. As they continued on the path, they passed dozens of others, moving in either direction. At one point, Cley believed he saw the old body scribe of the Silent Ones, the Word, hobbling around a bend. He wanted to catch up to see if it was really he, but there Vasthasha moved to the side of the trail and signaled to the others to follow him.

A moment later, they were back in the woods, walking with the work of gravity. Vasthasha stepped up to Willa and handed Wraith to her. As she took her child, she leaned over and kissed the foliate on the slick green leaves of his forehead.

■ Pierce, minus his flesh, still stood dressed in tatters in the flowering meadow, resting on the handle of his pickax. One of the points at the head of the tool was dug into the ground. Around him there was the faint outline of a rectangle, indicating that he must at one time have kept a garden in that spot. His skull nodded in the direction of the house, a large, two-room log construction with a porch and a fireplace, much like the Olsens' home. All that was missing were the windows.

The owner had obviously been very handy, because the furniture, although fashioned from branches and trees and tied with animal gut, was sturdy, even stylish in its design.

On the large bed there was a mattress made from hide stuffed with soft fur. The pillows had been made in the same manner. As at the house back in Beshanti territory, there was also a high-backed chair, like a throne, that sat before the fireplace.

Candles made from animal fat stood in wooden holders on the table in the corner of the main room. The planking of the floor had obviously been swept clean the morning of Pierce's demise by the handmade broom that still rested against the side of the table as if the owner of the house had meant to put it away later. Luckily, Pierce had been a tall man and built the entire place to accommodate his size. He had been poor in companionship but rich in Time, and the patient nature of his work was consistently evident.

■ In the days that followed, Cley and Wood hunted in the forest in order to put up enough game for Willa to survive in their absence. Vasthasha accompanied them and gathered wild fruits, plants, and roots that both could be eaten and had medicinal value.

Willa worked on Pierce's house, cleaning it and discovering old supplies left by the dead explorer. She patched holes against the night wind in the mud-and-dried-grass layers that sealed the spaces between the logs. One of her most useful discoveries was a stone ax, which she used to chop large branches to be burned in the fireplace. On the northern side of the house, about fifty yards away, she found the remains of the scaffolding Pierce had constructed to build his chimney. The wood was old and rotted, but the sections were large and still dry enough to be burned for heat.

There was no use for it, but she also found a locket on a fine, golden chain beneath one of the pillows of the bed. The metal heart opened on tiny rusted hinges to reveal the yellowed portrait of a pretty young woman, no more than a girl. She put this around her neck along with the necklace of the Carrols Cley had made for her, and it became Wraith's favorite toy.

At night, after they ate and the baby was asleep, Willa and Cley and the foliate sat near the fireplace and discussed their plans for the future. The hunter smoked his pipe, passing it around to the assembled company, and Wood moved close at times, in order to imbibe their exhalations.

They decided that Cley and Vasthasha should begin on their journey at once, so that they might be able to return before the cold autumn weather set in. The days now were warm and beautiful, and even the rain, when it came, was gentle. The hunter decided to leave Wood behind to be what help he could—to offer some companionship to Willa and to guard the baby.

When the evening grew late and the fire subsided, Vasthasha left the house to sleep in the forest. Then Willa and Cley, who had not changed their routine from the cold nights in the wilderness, moved into the other room and got into the large bed on either side of Wraith. Once Cley started to snore, Wood, moving as cautiously as a cat, lifted himself onto the mattress and curled up at their feet.

■ "I am going now," said Cley, wearing his pack and holding the rifle in one hand.

Through the open doorway, Vasthasha could be seen standing on the porch in the bright morning sunlight.

Willa sat in the chair by the fire, holding the baby, and staring at the blackened logs. "Good luck," she said, but did not turn her face to him.

The hunter left the house, and he and the foliate headed

out toward the northern side of the lake. Wood followed, barking. Cley stopped and pointed back at the house, indicating for the dog to return. "Stay," he said. Wood sat and stared at him.

"Does he understand?" Cley asked of Vasthasha.

"No," said the foliate.

"Go," said Cley, and Wood turned and walked away with his head lowered.

"Come, we must hurry," said the foliate.

They walked a few more yards, and then the hunter said, "Wait for me." He put down his pack and gun and ran back toward the house, passing the dog on the way.

As he approached the structure, the door opened, and Willa stepped quickly across the porch. When Cley saw her, he stopped running and walked slowly up to her. He put his arms around her. They stood together, in silence, for a long time. When their embrace ended, and they each turned away, neither uttered a word.

▦ Like diminutive carved figures traversing a huge miniature in a box crafted by Christof Olsen, where the trees are dwarfed with tortured roots and the streams are real water that miraculously flows, Vasthasha and Cley journeyed through forests of oak, of pine, of shemel, of demons, across marshes and wastelands and meadows, down into valleys of flesh-eating plants, through ruins of lost cities, up steep hills and the sides of cliffs.

▦ It was the very apex of summer, when the days were longest and the nights offered a cool respite from the blazing sun. The two wayfarers sat by a fire beneath the stars and smoked the pipe. Vasthasha was in full flower, and there was a large, black, shiny fruit growing from a stem at the nape of his neck. Cley no longer needed the leaf beneath his tongue to understand the foliate, and he asked his companion the purpose of the dark plum.

"Tomorrow, we will arrive at our destination," said the foliate, "and then I will reveal everything to you."

"Very well," said Cley.

"You have brought the crystal given to you by the old man of the Word as I have instructed?" asked Vasthasha.

"It is in my pocket, here," said Cley.

"We will need that," said the foliate.

"And when I am finished with this task, I am guaranteed passage to Wenau?" asked the hunter.

The foliate said nothing, but looked overhead at the moon.

"Yes?" asked Cley.

"You will finally find Paradise," said Vasthasha.

The foliate closed his eyes, folded his arms in, his head down, changing his posture from green man to shrub, and slept. Cley tried to think about what he would say to Arla Beaton when he finally was reunited with her, but his thoughts always drifted back to Pierce's house by the lake. He missed Wood, and although the foliate was good company, a fine friend, the hunter felt as if he had left a piece of himself back by the lake in the meadow.

He put his hand in his pocket to check that the crystal was there. His fingers touched its hard smoothness, but he noticed there were other things in this pocket that he did not remember putting there—three very small objects along with the stone. He gathered them up in his hand and pulled them out. The Carrols, not all of them, just the woman and the little boy, rested in his open palm.

"Willa," said Cley, knowing this had been her work. He smiled and closed his fingers around the miniatures.

In the afternoon, they came to the foot of a mountain that had loomed on the horizon, appearing to grow bigger each day for the past week of their journey. Vasthasha led Cley through the trees that surrounded the base of the stone giant to the head of an old trail that angled upward along the southern face. The hunter marveled at the work it must have taken to carve the path into solid rock.

"Who was responsible for this?" he asked the foliate when stopping to catch his breath.

"Those from the inland sea. They created it in a single day. The inside of the mountain is hollow, and the peak that we cannot see has been removed so that the sun may shine down inside on the world they have made there. Their machines made light work of the impossible on more than one occasion," said Vasthasha.

"What were these machines?" asked Cley.

"Not the simple gear work of men," said the foliate. "The Water People have an organic technology that can manipulate the very particles that constitute reality."

"I'm lost," said Cley.

"Actually," said Vasthasha, "in being here, you are found."

"What is it, a hiding place for them?" asked the hunter.

"Not for them," said the foliate.

Before Cley could question the green man further, Vasthasha moved on ahead, continuing along the steep trail. The hunter shook his head and thought, "He's starting to sound like Brisden." As he hoisted his pack, he looked back over his shoulder and saw how far they had already climbed.

Spread out below him, to the south, was the wide plain they had crossed in the last three days. He took a few deep breaths and followed his guide.

A half hour later, and a few hundred feet farther up, they came upon what appeared to be the entrance to a cave. On closer inspection, though, Cley could see that the opening in the rock was too uniform along its edges, too perfectly engineered an archway to have been made naturally. Vasthasha stopped outside the gaping hole.

"We have arrived," he said. "You may rest, and I will now tell you everything."

Cley took off his pack and sat down. The foliate sat across from him, and they passed the waterskin, each drinking great draughts.

"This is the entrance to the garden inside the mountain. As I said, it was created by those from the inland ocean . . ."

"Do they have a name?" asked Cley.

"They do, but it is so long and complicated I could never remember it," says Vasthasha. "We will call them the O or Water People or those from the inland ocean."

"Agreed," he said, smiling.

"Inside the mountain there is a lush landscape that was created to hold the last remaining great serpent of the wilderness. Once these creatures roamed the entirety of the vast width and breadth of the Beyond. You could not travel a mile without encountering one. They were fearsome creatures, pink-scaled, with horns, and they slithered like snakes along the ground . . ."

"I have seen their remains," said Cley. "I call them Sirimon after the star constellation."

"Very good," said Vasthasha, annoyed at the interruption. "Now, these Sirimon, as you call them, were more than just death dealers, more than just the greatest fear of the peoples of the wilderness. They embodied the ability to transfer, to

project the very mind of the Beyond, itself. The distance between the points that were the Sirimon collectively created a
web or a net through which the consciousness of the Beyond
flowed. It was through them that the wilderness could be
aware of its own awareness."

"The wilderness thinks?" asked Cley.

"It did. It directed the course of its own existence. It had a
will, and it was good," said Vasthasha. "It was the war between Pa-ni-ta and the Water People that destroyed the Sirimon and depleted the will of the Beyond, so that now it is
contained in only the one creature that has been kept alive inside the mountain. The wilderness is dying."

"How did the war destroy the species?" asked the hunter.

"Pa-ni-ta circumvented the will of the Beyond and sent
the Sirimon against those from the inland ocean. In defense,
the Water People destroyed them with a disease in the same
way they killed off my brethren. When we were defeated, and
Pa-ni-ta was killed in her physical body, the Water People understood too late what they had done. They could smell the
wilderness dying. They saved the life of the last Sirimon and
trapped it here, in the mountain, for a time when they could
decide how to regenerate the species. When they decided to
expand their civilization to the land, they had never wanted
to inhabit a dying world."

"But the wilderness seems very alive to me," said Cley.

"To you, because you are not from it," said Vasthasha.
"You cannot notice all of the small complex ways in which
it is perishing just as you will not notice when it is
revived."

"I understand what you are saying, although it sounds
like a fairy tale, but what is my part in this?" asked the hunter.

"Pa-ni-ta has sent us to revive the serpent, to impregnate
it," said the foliate.

Cley laughed. "It's been a long time since I have made

love, but, still, I don't think I can generate the passion to join with a dragon."

Vasthasha turned his back to Cley. "Pick the fruit that grows at my back. Take it in your hands and do not let it go. This contains the seed that will cause the serpent eventually to spawn offspring."

The hunter reached out and grasped the dark fruit. When he pulled it away from the foliate there was a distinct snapping noise followed hard by a deafening scream that echoed across the mountainside. The cry was so unexpected, he almost dropped the large plum. When Vasthasha turned back to face him, Cley could see the green man sobbing.

"This is madness," said the hunter. "I'm sorry."

"Now," said Vasthasha, heaving, "you must tempt the serpent."

■ Inside the cave, there was a pool, and it reminded Cley of the water that was in the cave where he had discovered Pa-ni-ta's physical remains. A few yards beyond it there was another opening, covered by a very thin, blue membrane. Through this rippling blue window, he saw a beautiful landscape of trees and flowers and ferns. It was how he had pictured Paradise since the idea first presented itself to him years ago in Anamasobia.

His clothes lay in a pile on the floor, the black hat resting atop them. Cley was completely naked, holding the fruit in one hand and the crystal given to him by the body scribe in the other.

"Explain to me one more time why this is necessary," said Cley.

"The serpent distrusts anything from the Beyond, because the wilderness has become infected against it. That is why it is sealed in this garden chamber. The fruit has been in your hand long enough now to have taken on your scent. Also, that which has brought you so far, the desire that burns in you to rectify a great wrong, to achieve an equilibrium of peace with your conscience, recommends you for this task. The wilderness must reacquire that same balance. You will find the sleeping Sirimon and tempt it to open its mouth. Then, throw the fruit into its maw," said Vasthasha.

"What if I miss?" asked Cley.

The foliate did not answer.

"It might kill me, though," said the hunter.

Again, there was no comment.

"I see," said Cley.

"The crystal will give you passage through the blue entrance. Don't lose it, or you will never get out. Once you have delivered the seed, run as fast as you can. Do not look back. I will be waiting for you," said Vasthasha.

Cley stepped up to the blue membrane. It was like a window made of water. He passed one hand through it, then brought it back.

"This is the only way that you can complete your own journey," said the foliate.

The hunter held his breath as if he were about to dive into a wave, and stepped forward through the portal. He felt an intense cold and lost consciousness for a split second. Then he heard birds singing, felt the warmth of the sun and opened his eyes, knowing he had been born into Paradise.

■ Vasthasha stood in the cave, watching through the membrane as Cley walked off through the trees. Behind the foliate, from within the pool, two webbed hands appeared at its edge. A red-scaled being with the bubble eyes of a fish and fanlike fins at the sides of its head pulled itself up onto the dry rock of the cave. Water dripped off it, and its rasping, gilled breaths echoed through the cave. Barnacles grew on its arms and stomach, and its wide mouth was rimmed at the top lip by two long feelers that formed a kind of mustache. Hair, like yards of seaweed, flowed down its spiked back and tail, undulating as if still below the surface of the pool.

The creature slithered up next to Vasthasha in time to see Cley disappear around a flowering hedge.

"How did you convince him to come?" asked Shkchl, the scaled being.

"I told him a story," said Vasthasha.

"You lied," said the other.

"As you wish," said the foliate.

"Does he know we are all now joining together to revive the Beyond?"

"I didn't bother. Things were complex enough. Besides, as I understand his species' concept of a story, there must be a villain," said Vasthasha.

Shkchl's rasping increased, and the foliate knew he was laughing.

"Does he understand the sacrifice he must make—the other ingredient besides the fruit?"

The foliate shook his head.

"What if he escapes before the serpent tastes his blood?"

"He won't," said Vasthasha.

"don't be afraid."

I am certain that the use of sheer beauty is illegal in the town of Wenau, but I hid two vials of it and a syringe in the fold where my right wing meets my back. The only other belongings I brought with me were my pen and ink and the manuscript of the hunter's journey. What choice did I have, seeing as where I had last left Cley, about to encounter the great serpent? I knew I would be staying here for a few days, and I could not, in that time, forestall the story, which is now, I feel, at the point of some apotheosis. The tale had left my mind in great turmoil, which was probably a blessing in that it distracted me somewhat from concerns at facing Semla Hood and my other detractors.

I sit now, in a second-floor apartment, overlooking the main street of the flourishing town. This place that Feskin has arranged for me is very fine, even though the furniture has not been adapted for my idiosyncratic physiognomy. Now that it is late, and Wenau is asleep, I have taken the beauty. I am impatiently waiting, as usual, for signs of the Beyond to slither through my mind. In the meantime, allow me to describe for you the events of my own encounter with a serpent perhaps as dangerous as Cley's, namely the prejudice and ingrained suspicion of humanity.

I arrived this morning, as had been arranged, dressed in my suit and hat, trembling with a very real fear of being rejected. Feskin said I looked fine, but I went to the mirror in the small bathroom at the back of the schoolhouse no fewer than three times to check my attire and to do some last-minute practice at smiling without showing my fangs. Once I had remembered the exact facial contortion that was necessary for a convincing closed-mouth grin, I told the teacher that I was ready.

We left the sanctuary of the school and started down the street. The day was clear and very mild. Citizens of the town were out and about, shopping in the stores and standing on the corners engaged in conversation. I tried to pay no attention to the stares I was receiving, nor to the voiced insults. Some people moved to the other side of the street when they saw us coming, and a very brave few called out wishes of good luck and waved, albeit from a distance.

"We are going before Constable Spencer," said Feskin. "He is the sole proprietor of law and order in this town. I have always known him to be a fair and honest man, not given to rampant emotion but always working from the empirical evidence of any given case."

"And what will happen when we arrive?" I asked.

"There will be quite a few people there I suspect," said the teacher. "Do not be alarmed by the armed guards. Spencer will make sure that the spectators remain silent. Your detractors will enter and make their case against you. You will then have a chance to answer their charges. The constable will render the final verdict. I have already spoken to him, and he is greatly impressed that you are coming to stand up for yourself."

We turned into a side street and arrived at a large building that houses the court, the jail, and Spencer's office. There was a mob of people outside, two of whom carried rifles. My heart began to pound. Then Emilia broke away from the crowd and came running up to greet me. She put her hand out and I took it in mine and held it for a moment.

"Don't be afraid, Misrix," she said.

Of all those present, the child was the only one who could understand what it might be like to be me.

As we approached the crowd, the two armed guards ordered everyone to step aside and make way for us to enter. In passing through their ranks, I was reminded of Cley passing through the Beshanti lines when he left Fort Vordor, and it struck me that there was nothing that could prevent a disgruntled citizen from pulling out a hidden weapon and putting a slug into my head. At the last moment, before we could pass through the entrance, one angry-looking large fellow moved into Feskin's way, and the thin, bespectacled schoolteacher reached out and nonchalantly shoved the man out of our path.

"Step aside," said Feskin, and I was mightily impressed with his courage. I had been so wrapped up in my own fear I had not considered the chance that my friend was also taking by being my representative.

I whispered a word of thanks to him as I followed, but I'm sure it was drowned out by the sounds of voices cheering me while many more yelled, "Death to the Demon!"

My mind was literally swirling like a whirlpool, and it was all I could do to stand straight and not walk like I was drunk. We moved inside and across a spacious room. To the right there were rows of seats that were already filled with townspeople, and to the left was a large desk at which sat a man dressed completely in black. I realized that this must be Constable Spencer. He was much shorter than I had imagined but powerful-looking with a wide chest and shoulders. His hair was thinning and gray, and he had a bushy mustache of the same color. His expression was the lack of an expression, his mouth a straight line across a large, red face.

Upon seeing us, Spencer stood and lifted his hand high to bring it down hard on the desk top. The sound made me jump, and at the same time quieted those gathered behind us.

"Silence," he said to all. "If anyone interferes with these proceedings, he or she can expect to spend some time in jail," he said.

Feskin walked forward and shook hands with the constable. "This," said the teacher, "is Misrix," and swept his arm back toward me.

"Step forward," said Spencer.

I did and as I approached him he put his hand out. I, in turn, offered mine. He grabbed it, not seeming to fear the claws, and pumped my arm up and down. "I know you did not have to come, and this will be considered when I decide the outcome," he said.

I nodded to him and stepped back.

"State your case," said the constable, as he sat once more.

"We have come before you today for two reasons," said Feskin. "One is so that my friend, Misrix, answer the charges leveled against him by Semla Hood and others, namely that his having in his possession a certain stone knife that she believes once belonged to Cley proves he has murdered our town's most illustrious founder. Second, and more important, we come to ask that Misrix be given a chance to prove his goodwill and be allowed an opportunity to become a citizen of Wenau and to live among us."

"Two very distinct issues," said Spencer. "We will not decide the latter today, but I must add that Mr. Misrix's presence here can only improve his prospects for citizenship later on. Now, as to the charges leveled . . ." The constable waved toward the audience. "Come forward Mrs. Hood," he said.

I turned around and saw approaching the old woman who had visited me at the ruins. Three other gentleman followed her. She carried in her hand the knife she had taken from my museum.

"I understand that you bring with you a piece of evidence," said Spencer.

The old woman stepped up to the desk and placed the knife before the constable. "This," she said, "is Cley's knife. I know it, these men know it, and I am sure this creature, whom we foolishly entertain as a human being, has killed my old friend."

"And what makes you believe this knife once belonged to Cley?" asked Spencer.

"Beside the fact that I had seen him use it on numerous occasions when he and my husband were close friends, it has a distinct design on the handle, the image of a coiled snake. In addition, the blade is made of stone, not metal. It was given to him by the Traveler, that native of the Beyond, Ea. You know your history, I should hope, Constable Spencer."

"Yes, madam," said Spencer, smiling. Then he turned to me, and asked, "Was this knife in your possession?"

"It was in a collection I kept; a museum I have been constructing from items I have found in the ruins of the Well-Built City," I said, and bowed inanely when I was finished.

"And where in the ruins did you find it?" he asked.

"My recollection is vague, but I believe it was stuck in a section of remaining wall," I said.

"And why would a knife be stuck in a wall?" he asked.

I felt I was losing ground in the investigation, and blurted out, "And why would anything be anywhere in that jumbled offspring of explosions? I once found a child's skeleton embedded in a column of coral."

One of the men with Semla Hood spoke up. "I too knew Cley, and that is his knife. There were no others like it in the Realm until the Traveler appeared. I also know that Cley would not be separated from it, since he used it for all purposes from fishing to hunting to delivering babies. He showed me once that it cuts like a scalpel."

The other two men behind the old woman nodded in agreement.

"I see . . ." said Spencer, but here, Feskin spoke up.

"If you will allow me," said the teacher, who did not wait for a nod of approval but continued speaking. "When the Traveler was captured by Below, would he not then have been carrying a knife? He obviously would not have been allowed to keep it in his captivity. Perhaps this is the object we have before us now. It could have been left in one of the offices of a ministry and then been embedded into a wall as a result of an explosion. Ea must have made Cley a knife when they both lived in close proximity in the early Wenau."

"Then where is Cley?" asked the old woman.

"I left him in the Beyond. I could not go on, but he felt he had to deliver the green veil to Arla Beaton," I said. "We were friends. We helped each other. It was I who saved him from his addiction to the drug, sheer beauty. I saved his life. Why would I take it?"

Spencer called for quiet. He picked up the knife, one finger on the handle, one at the sharp tip, and twirled it with his thumb. A second later, a trickle of blood ran down his hand. He dropped the weapon on the desk and looked up. Taking a handkerchief from his coat pocket, he wrapped it around the wounded finger.

"If Cley is dead, where is the body? Where are the witnesses to this murder?" asked the constable. "What is the motive? What I find here is that you, Mrs. Hood, absconded with a piece of property that was not yours. Seeing that you truly believed it was valuable evidence used in the commission of a crime, I will not charge you with theft. As far as Misrix is concerned, he is free to go. In addition," he said, raising his voice so that all in the room might hear him, "anyone caught harassing, threatening, or attacking this visitor to our town will suffer the severest penalties. I should hope, you, Mrs. Hood, remember your history. This town was built with the idea in mind that all those of goodwill, no matter their economic or social standing in the community, be allowed to live here safely. Should we forget the lesson that was taught to us by Cley—that looks can be deceiving? Remember that Misrix came today of his own will, had saved Emilia from drowning, and that many of you have been in his company and found him to be a decent fellow. That is all."

Need I tell you I was ecstatic? Feskin actually tried to hug me. I flapped my wings, and my tail did a dance on its own. The constable tried to hand the knife back to me, but I held up my own hands and shook my head. "For you," I said, and he nodded, accepting the gift with a smile.

Semla Hood stormed out of the building, followed by her contingent, and I stood in the middle of a crowd of well-wishers. Somehow they all knew I would be found innocent. It was a moment I will never forget. Emilia's mother allowed me to put her daughter on my shoulders, and we went out into the sunlight.

Later, at the inn, over drinks, Feskin told me that the constable's word is well respected and that it will be a mere matter of weeks before I can officially join the community of Wenau. The bill was torn up by the innkeeper. As the day progressed into evening, I walked the streets of town, chatting with one and all. There were those who still shunned me, but it was obvious they were now in the minority. For the third time in my life, I was born.

Thinking about these events of today still gives me a great sense of satisfaction, and it is difficult to concentrate on Cley's journey even though I am beginning to feel the beauty at work. Instead of showing me the Beyond, as it has, it is showing me my future—Perhaps a small cottage on the edge of town. No need to rub their noses in it; I will always be different. But then I see friendship and easy, useless conversation for years to come. I will be of great help in performing feats of strength, in defending the community, and I should not forget my intellect. Maybe, with all of my reading, I could do some teaching at the school. I love Emilia and the other children. Even better, I could bring all of the volumes from the ruins and create a quiet, contemplative place where others could come to read, talk about philosophy, and tell stories. Yes, that is a stroke of genius.

I wonder now, beyond where I should, if someday, perhaps a woman of the town might learn to like me enough to be my regular companion. Can I even think it, a wife? What would the child of a woman and a demon look like? As my mind works feverishly to encompass the notion, I notice that there are ferns growing from the floor, vines hanging from the ceiling, a tree in the corner where there had been a cabinet with a clock in it. Wenau is becoming my own Paradise. What is this? The child? Pink and smooth and wriggling . . . But wait, it has scales instead of flesh, and, no, a horned head and a mouth of needlelike teeth. It stretches toward me, armless, legless, a terrible monster. The serpent has entered my Paradise, and I am off . . .

green veil on the wind

The world inside the hollow mountain was bounded by the inner slopes of granite that reached up and up to the wide opening above where the blue sky was like a distant dream of ocean. The lush garden appeared to be a nearly perfect circle, and although the circumference was predominantly in shadow, the center was bright with sunlight.

Cley was stunned by the beauty that surrounded him— the green of the foliage and grass almost glowing, the abundance of birds and butterflies, the brilliance of the flowers. It reminded him of the oasis in which he first met Vasthasha, but that was like a yellowed photograph in comparison to this vibrant reality. He felt a subtle breeze from above ruffle his hair and caress his body. Aromas mingled to create a perfume of fruit and blossom and earth that he believed must be the scent of life itself.

As he walked toward the center of the garden, he left behind the generously spaced trees that grew more like an orchard than a forest and came to the edge of a thick, green lawn. At a distance he saw a body of water, and at the center of this lake, an island with a narrow land bridge stretching out to it. He somehow knew that this was where he would find the serpent.

The grass was like velvet against his bare feet, and now that he was in full sunlight he felt as if he could lie down and sleep forever. He yawned and when he exhaled the silver-backed leaves of the trees across the lake seemed to sway with his breath. His thoughts no longer dwelt on Wood or Wraith or Willa or either Wenau. The image of Arla Beaton dissolved as did all his memories and self-recriminations from the past. Now there was but one thought in his mind and that was to tempt the serpent. He heard a sound like music, very faint chimes and voices, and he could not tell if it was oozing out of the air or coming from within his own ears.

Cley proceeded across the land bridge, holding the dark fruit in one hand and the crystal in the other. The weight of these objects in his palms was all that prevented him from drifting off into flight or sleep. Sunlight glittered on the clear water—a million sparks forming and re-forming geometric patterns before his eyes. Beneath the surface there were fat, orange fish, kissing out bubbles that burst into the air like notes from a flute.

Through the trees on the small island, at the very axis of the garden, he came upon the enormous, sleeping form of Sirimon. It was four times the size of any of those skeletons he had discovered in the Beyond. This one was as long and wide as the smoke serpent created by the body scribe—large enough to encircle an entire village. Its scales were a resilient pink, as if made of metal, like armor. The body of the creature was as thick as Cley was tall and the head nearly as wide as the Olsens' house. The horns were sharpened-bone tree trunks, and the mouth could easily devour a horse in one pass.

There was no fear in the hunter. He stepped up to the side of the great serpent and rubbed his hand along the length of its body. Its breathing was measured and altogether relaxing. Cley walked to the head and held the fruit forward, close up to the flaring nostrils. He watched the lidless eyes for signs of cognizance, but they remained fixed, like prodigious concave windows with yellow curtains inside opened just barely in vertical slits.

As he stood, swaying before the incredible entity, the hunter saw in his mind's-eye flashes of scenes from the ancient war in the Beyond. Foliates and dwellers of the inland ocean clashed in combat. Great black mollusks without shells, organic machines draped with seaweed, moved through the forests devouring trees. Vines ensnared some of these juggernauts, and flocks of crows swept out of the sky to tear at their flesh. Fleets of swelled leviathan bladders blocked the sun, pouring liquid fire that melted meadows into dry waste. Pani-ta sent swirling clouds of poisonous insects into the Palashize, and the Water People countered with a dozen different plagues.

Cley saw the Sirimon dying in great numbers, saw the Beshanti suffering, the Word, speechless in the face of destruction, and then an extraordinary thought entered his mind. "If the wilderness had consciousness, a will, then why did it turn upon itself? The inland ocean was as much a part of the Beyond as were the forests and the meadows and marshes. It did all of this to itself and now needed to be rescued."

The hunter stood enwrapped in visions as the body of the Sirimon rippled almost imperceptibly, tremors running its length. The serpent's nostrils twitched, and its eyes began to vibrate. Cley became aware that the monster was waking from its nightmare of loneliness and that it hungered for the fruit.

Without warning, there was a tremendous blast of air that threw the hunter backward onto the ground. The Sirimon screamed, and this cry changed everything, like a light going out in a room without windows. Cley came to his senses. At the last second, he rolled to his right as the creature arched its back with lightning speed, curled its body over its head, and stabbed the earth with its needle tail precisely where he had just fallen.

The Sirimon coiled inward upon itself in order to strike with its fangs, but the hunter was already up and running through the trees. It released like a spring and hit the earth only inches from Cley's heels. He stumbled and rolled and then was up and running again. He could feel the breath of the serpent on his back, and its voice was deafening.

Across the land bridge he fled and now fear uncoiled in his chest, his heart beating wildly, his pulse pounding. When he reached the opposite side, he turned to look behind. This, he told himself, was his only chance to accomplish what he had come for. The serpent slithered across the land bridge, rippling at top speed, its mouth open wide. Cley cocked his arm back and waited until he could wait no more. Just as the pink scales touched the lawn, he hurled the fruit. His aim was terribly off. The strange plum hit the ground in front of Sirimon, but as luck would have it, bounced into the cavelike mouth.

Now the hunter was sprinting, and the garden's placid beauty mocked his terror. The exotic music was drowned out by the roar of the creature. The perfume disintegrated into the stinking breath of the serpent. Ferns and shrubs lashed at his shins and ankles as he ran. The sun moved past midday, and the shadows grew more quickly than the memories rushing back into Cley's mind.

Just as he caught a glimpse of the blue, wavering portal and the form of Vasthasha standing on the other side of the membrane, the serpent struck, uncoiling forward with a desperate lunge. It caught Cley in its maw across his chest. The hunter felt the needle teeth sink into his flesh and heard the cracking of his own ribs. He tried to scream but blood filled his mouth. The Sirimon reared its head upward, carrying Cley's weight into the air, and then shook him back and forth, burying its fangs deeper into his vital organs. When it was done, it flung his body onto the rocks only a few steps from the blue portal. The creature turned then, like a bullwhip rolling backward, and slithered calmly away toward the island.

The blood poured from Cley's chest, nose, mouth, ears. When he tried to move, he could hear his bones cracking like a bag of glass shards rolling on a wooden floor. He pulled himself along with one arm and one leg, covering the distance to the portal. There was a slight rise, and he had no strength to lift his body the rest of the way. With one last effort he lurched forward so that only his hand, still holding the crystal, passed through the boundary.

His eyes closed and in his mind he saw the green veil on the wind. It flapped once, snapped everything into darkness, and he died.

I have little doubt now that not only the Beyond, but the entire world has a mind, and disbelieve me at your own peril when I say a cynical one at that. It deals in irony with all the subtle grace and sharp wit of a master storyteller, and just when you think the hero will succeed, a love might be fulfilled, a promise kept, it will flip your life like an hourglass and send an avalanche of trouble trickling down upon you.

I sit now in a jail cell, like some hairy, scribbling Brisden, at the back of the very building where only yesterday I was applauded for my veracity and goodwill. This concrete container is barely large enough for me to spread my wings, and always, everywhere, there are the vertical shadows from the bars at the doorway and the one tall window that looks out upon the town. The breeze slips in unimpeded through that back opening, carrying with it the sounds of the town I had foolishly dreamt would be my home. Thank goodness for this desk and chair. The bed in the corner is useless to me, and I will have to sleep standing up, as there are no bars on the ceiling from which to hang. What does it matter? Believe the following if you can:

Last night I was in the room that Feskin had gotten me, leaning over my manuscript, my hands covering my face, weeping uncontrollably at the loss of Cley. The very words, as if they, themselves, were snapping monsters, horrified me as I was describing my friend's demise. For that whole tortuous journey I had traced to end like this broke my heart. I wished that I could somehow erase what the Beyond had dictated and have the hunter move on to the true Wenau, but that would have been as false as Cley thinking he could change Arla Beaton's soul by changing her physiognomy. The discovery of his death was too sudden a reversal from the day's celebration, and I was without my usual defense of skeptical fatalism to protect myself from the pain.

When I could weep no longer, and had finally resigned myself to the fact that I would have to go on alone without the nighttime visions of Cley and Wood, there came a knocking upon my door. The hour was very late, but I thought nothing of it since my mind was a tangled skein of confusion and sorrow.

"Just a moment," I called, and tried to compose myself. Wiping the last of the tears from my eyes, I opened the door and pulled it back. There stood Feskin, and behind him Constable Spencer, and behind him a half dozen men with rifles aimed around the heads of the two in front and directly at my heart.

"Glad you could stop by," I said, thinking nothing of the rifles, since whenever I was in the presence of a human, there were usually weapons in sight. I stepped back in order to let my friends enter.

"Bad news, Misrix," said Feskin, and he looked down at the floor, as if unable to go on.

"What?" I asked, as the men with the guns came in and surrounded me. I sensed that they were very nervous, and this was my first indication that something had gone terribly wrong.

Constable Spencer, no longer the affable purveyor of righteousness, stepped forward with a grim look on his face. "Tonight, at precisely eight-thirty, Horace Watt, and those remaining from his expedition to the Beyond, returned to Wenau. With them they brought a corpse and also convincing evidence that you, Misrix, did indeed murder Cley."

It took a moment for Spencer's words to register, and even when they did, I was struck dumb by their message. "Impossible," I finally whispered.

"That will be decided in the court," said Spencer. "For the time being, you will have to come with us."

"Where are we going?" I asked.

"Jail," said Feskin, still unable to make eye contact with me.

My wings lifted, my tail snapped the air threateningly, and the men cocked the hammers on their rifles.

"Wait!" said Feskin, holding up his hands. "He will come peaceably, I know it. Allow him a moment."

"Will you?" asked Spencer.

Such was my frustration that for a brief moment I had considered tearing off a few heads and slicing the constable down the middle. I knew and they knew they could not have pumped enough bullets into me before I had killed at least half of them. Then I caught myself from falling back into the abyss of my discarded animal nature.

"Yes," I said. "It is the civilized thing to do."

"I will help you," said Feskin.

I nodded to him, then made a move to fetch my papers and pen and ink. Luckily I had already returned the sheer beauty paraphernalia to its hiding place beneath my wing or I'm sure more charges would have been leveled on the spot.

The guards would not let me pass.

"I'm bringing my manuscript with me," I said.

"What is it worth to you to have him come without incident?" Feskin asked Spencer.

The constable nodded. "Let him gather his things," he told the guards.

And so, here I am, a prisoner, falsely accused of a crime I did not commit. Feskin accompanied me to the cell and told me he would *represent me against the charges. I thanked him but admitted that I had little hope of battling those prejudices that had, in hours, blazed up from a dying ember.*

"Conspiracy," I told him through the bars.

"Not exactly," he whispered, so that the armed man sitting on the stool down the hallway could not hear him. "Watt has real evidence that could convince a jury. Not only did they find Cley's remains only two days into the Beyond, but they found a diary, kept in his handwriting, the last entry of which states that he is in mortal fear of you. He writes that you had already made one attempt on his life while he was sleeping, and he believes you will eventually kill him as he suspects you have already done to the missing dog."

"I don't recall Cley even keeping a diary," I said.

"Well, they all know he was a scribbler," said Feskin. "Think of the two manuscripts he left that recount his history. They have the artifact."

"A fake," I said.

"Perhaps something else, but I know Watt. He is not a dissembler. And besides, he just arrived this evening. He had no time to be inculcated into any plot. There are seven other men with him, who all attest to the discovery and its veracity," said the teacher.

"How could they find Cley in the Beyond?" I asked.

"They took bloodhounds and some of Cley's possessions from his house. The dogs followed the scent. Listen, Misrix, this looks bad. If I am going to help you, you must assure me that you had no part in Cley's death," said Feskin.

"I have proof that I did not kill him," I said.

"What?" he asked.

"My writings," I told him.

He shook his head. "I hope that you are right," he said.

"If I did not believe in my own innocence, then tell me why I am putting up with this charade. You know as well as I know as well as they know that I could bend these bars apart with my hands and fly *away from here. Not to mention the fact that I could slay quite a few in the process if I so desired."*

"Yes, I know," he said. "There is definitely goodness in you. I will do all I can to help."

Then he left, and I was alone with my torment. Last night lasted almost forever. The first thing I did was slough off the ridiculous clothes. They were uncomfortable to begin with and now they were torturing me with an extra confinement beyond the most obvious one. There were tears and cries of pain, I will admit. There is no anguish worse than being falsely accused and having the entire world believe you are guilty. I paced as well as I could around this mausoleum, banged on the concrete walls, and tested the metal of the bars.

Finally, near dawn, I fell into a fitful sleep in which I was visited by dreams of Cley and me in the Beyond. It was wonderful to be with him again, to speak of books and notions about life. He was recounting for me the story of when he and Calloo and Bataldo had first ventured into the wilderness. He spoke of his old friends with great passion as we sat next to a fire at night, listening with one ear for sounds of predators. Then I dreamt of Wood and how bravely he had fought against the other demons. I tell you it was as if I was there. In the midst of this recollection, though, came sudden bursts of a vision of Cley lying disemboweled beneath me. Three times this scene flashed and as quickly passed, and then I woke up, shivering.

It took me a few minutes to clear my head. At first, I was disoriented by finding myself in the cell when a moment before I had been in the limitless Beyond, but once I had my wits about me, I realized that the ugly, momentary nightmares were a result of unfounded guilt at the false accusations against me and the recent discovery in my writing that Cley had been savagely killed by the Sirimon. Still, the experience had been unnerving.

There was only one thing to do. I did my contortionist act, and retrieved from its hiding place the sheer beauty. It was a comfort to see that I had enough left for at least two more bolus doses. Care-

fully, I prepared the injection, and the intricacy of the work took my mind off my troubles for a few minutes. I needed fast relief, so I went for a spot under my tongue that I had seen Drachton Below access in times of great stress.

As my luck would have it the guard had just woken up and come down the hall to check on me. He saw what I was doing and his eyes went wide.

"You can't do that," he said.

I pulled the needle out and told him, with a partially numb tongue, "Stop me." I suppose I shouldn't have smiled in the way I did, as if daring him to take action.

He grew red in the face and went for his keys. I bobbed my tail toward the bars, flexed my arm muscles, and laughed my true laugh, showing every ripping fang in my mouth. As I knew he would, he thought better of it.

As he walked away, he said, "You'll soon be dead."

"Likewise," I told him, knowing he would not tell anyone about my having the drug. If he did, he would have to explain why he did not take it from me.

Some time passed before the beauty began to do its work, but slowly I felt its caress, easing the tension in my back muscles. I had taken quite a bit, and it brought with it colors and memories and far-flung philosophical notions that crowded the anger right out of me.

When I looked up once, I saw my father, Drachton Below, before me. He was inside the cell, sitting on the edge of the bed in the corner. There was a wry smile on his face, and he was shaking his head.

The sight of him brought tears to my eyes, and I feared his anger, as I had when newly born into consciousness.

"Misrix," he said. "What is this ridiculous turn of events? Haven't I taught you to comport yourself with more dignity than this?" He closed his eyes as if unable to face his disappointment.

"I'm sorry," I told him. "But I did nothing wrong."

"I know you are innocent," he said. "I know how it feels to be misunderstood. You are a good boy. No," he smiled, "you are a good man. Think of this—since you have been arrested, since you have been charged with a crime, since you have decided to argue your case, this is proof of your humanity. Do they arrest beasts? If a horse goes wild and tramples its master, do they bring it to court? These trying times, though regrettable, are conclusive proof of your humanity."

He stood up from the bed, and his image wavered slightly in the breeze from the window. When he was solidly before me again, I saw that he had opened his arms.

"Come closer, my son," he said.

I stepped up to him, and I could feel his arms close around me. I could smell the horseradish on his breath as I had when I was a child. He rested his head upon my chest.

"I love you," he said. "I am proud of you."

I closed my arms around him too late, for he had vanished at the sudden sound of some commotion in the hallway.

"You can't go down there," I heard the guard calling.

"Okay," said a child's voice.

I turned, with tears still in my eyes and the beauty coursing through me, to see Emilia standing outside my cell. She, I knew, was real, but the drug had affected my vision so that I saw a faint golden glow around her figure. She was smiling, and for her sake, I smiled back.

"Misrix," she said, "I know you could never have done what they say. I wanted to tell you."

The guard stepped up behind her. "Come miss, you cannot be here. It is against the law."

"Okay," she said again, but remained where she was. She lifted her arm and put her hand between the bars. In it, she held a stick of candy. The guard tried to pull her away.

"Touch her, and I will kill you," I shouted.

The man backed off.

"Try not to be afraid," said Emilia, as I looked at her offering. When I reached down to take the candy, something very peculiar happened. *Her hand appeared to be that of a man, and the candy transformed before my eyes into a clear stone, a crystal. My own hand was no longer hairy and clawed, but had somehow changed into a mitt of twisted root and foliage.*

As the guard ushered her out of the hallway, a series of events flashed before my eyes in rapid succession. All I could think was, "How will I remember all of this?" But I do. I remember it all. Considering its fantastic nature, I don't think I will ever forget.

The foliate stepped closer to the blue membrane and reached out his leafy hand as if to grab Cley by the wrist but, at the last second, he stopped and looked back at Shkchl, the dweller from the inland ocean. The red-scaled being twisted the very end of his antennae mustache with webbed fingers, stared for a lengthy spell through the portal at Cley's corpse, then nodded. With this sign, he moved next to Vasthasha and together they grabbed the arm of the dead hunter and pulled his bleeding, wrecked body into the cave.

Once Cley was inside, Vasthasha rolled him over so that his blank eyes stared at the rock ceiling. The foliate got down on his knees next to the body so that he was leaning over the mordant face and began to make quiet choking sounds. Shkchl shook his head.

A long, thin stick, twice thinner than the stem of a rose, was slowly growing straight out of Vasthasha's mouth. Its end was needle-sharp, and it did not stop until it was as long as a man's hand. The Water Being averted his gaze as the foliate thrust his head downward, the end of the probe piercing Cley's left eye to lodge in the brain. The process took less than a second, and then with a quick zip, like the sound of a fly buzzing past your ear, the stick retracted back into Vasthasha's mouth.

"Do you have it?" asked the Water Being.

The foliate nodded.

"Then go, quickly," said Shkchl.

But Vasthasha was already gone, out of the cave, running along the trail that wound down around the side of the mountain. Loose blossoms flew off him as he sprinted in the heat of late afternoon. He had to reach his destination before the cold winds of mid-autumn brought snow. His thatched legs were powered by the knowledge that if he stopped to slake his thirst for more than a heartbeat at a time, took the wrong path once, was forced to delay to battle some creature, or even gave himself over to memory too often, he would never arrive. What waited for him at the end of this impossible race, he knew full well, was Death.

■ Willa walked with Wraith in her arms along the southern side of the lake. Inside the cabin it was sweltering, and she had come to catch the breeze that usually began to blow out of the forest in the afternoon. Wood ran in front of her, blazing a path through the tall meadow grass and flowers, making sure there were no snakes.

She had been trying for the past weeks not to think of Cley, but had found the hunter was always on her mind. Life at Pierce's cabin was not the hardship she had at first feared it would be. There was plenty of food for their survival and then some, but the loneliness was always with her, an unfriendly spirit that made her talk to herself, stare for long sessions into the small cracked mirror in the bedroom of the cabin, cry at night instead of sleeping.

As she moved along the lakeside, she felt the wind begin

to stir. On this day it came not from the south but instead from the opposite direction. She watched the ripples on the water and the rhythmic swaying of yellow flowers that hung in the shapes of bells from a central green stalk. Soft white clouds sailed by in the deep blue above.

She finally called to Wood to return. There was a meal to prepare for herself and the dog, and before she could get to that she knew she must nurse Wraith, who was growing larger by the day. Expecting the dog to dash past her, she waited. A few minutes passed, and he still had not come. Just as she turned to call him again, she heard a haunting noise that momentarily stopped her heart.

Wood was standing by the edge of the lake, his head lowered, his hackles raised, tail straight. She watched as he lifted his head and again howled mournfully with a voice that chilled her. The baby woke and began to cry. Willa clutched the child to her and ran for the house. She did not notice the necklace holding the wooden figurine break, spilling the remaining wooden man onto the ground.

■ The body scribe, in the village of the Word, made the last precise jab with the bone needle, completing another blue image on the left buttock of the queen. The figure he had created by covering over the face of Brisden was that of a dog howling. With that final dot of color, the queen herself howled, and the old artisan knew it was time to begin his journey.

■ Shkchl took the corpse by the legs and pulled it toward the pool in the center of the cave. He slowly backed into the water with a hissing sigh. He had been too long out of his natural medium, and the feel of it upon his scaled flesh was soothing. Slowly, he submerged, and as he did, he dragged Cley's body beneath the surface with him.

■ Willa sat before the fireplace in the high-backed chair with Wraith on her lap and the loaded pistol in her left hand. Wood, who had only given up his lament with the fall of night, lay on the floor at her feet. She was singing softly to the baby while watching the flames ripple. Cley had told her once how, at times, he thought he could see things in the fire, and she now searched for signs of him in the orange blaze. Every now and then the dog whimpered and kicked a back leg as though running in his dreams. Suddenly a scorched log dropped, and there was a burst of fire that appeared to carry a portrait of the hunter. She leaned forward and said his name, but he was gone before she realized it.

■ The foliate dashed through a deep forest of gnarled trees that bore fruit like lanterns. The drooping branches held at their ends large, glowing globes that attracted swarms of insects. A fox darted across his path, and so as not to trip over it, he leaped, flipped in the air, and hit the ground running. Somewhere in the canopy above, the monkeys applauded his performance.

■ In the murky waters at the bottom of the pool, in a clearing surrounded by huge, black, tuberous flowers that grew on stalks anchored in the sandy bottom, Shkchl went to work on Cley's corpse. He had all of his instruments handy in valises that were giant oyster shells.

First, he secured the body so it did not float away on the strong current by tying it at the wrists and ankles to long tentacle vines that grew from the bases of the black flowers. Rummaging through his things, he found a hollowed-out fish, wide mouth open, that was used to store a thick, gooey substance that shimmered like quicksilver.

He grimaced as he dipped his webbed hand into the mouth and swiped up a big gob of the stuff. Holding his hand out to the side as if he was carrying excrement, he approached his patient. He covered every inch of Cley's form so as to prevent decomposition. When a thin film had been applied to the hunter, he took another gob from the fish and crammed half of it into Cley's open mouth. The other half, he used to plug the remaining apertures of the body.

Now came forth the swordfish saws, the fish-bone needles, and other tools that were living organisms: minute, all jaw and fangs, to be used as clamps. There was cutting and bone-breaking, and it was hard to see what was happening because blood spewed forth in billowing red clouds.

■ Cley was huddled inside a tiny bubble, his legs drawn up, his arms around his knees. There was no room for anything else, save the voice of Pa-ni-ta, which was telling him tales of the history of the wilderness. In his mind, he saw everything vividly, and the ancient sorceress spared no details. The flow of words was infinitely fascinating. It was the very air he was breathing. When she spoke of the will of the Beyond, he lost the story for a moment and remembered Pierce's cabin by the lake. Images of Willa and Wood and

Wraith appeared and disappeared only to reappear against the backdrop of the brutality and grace that was the evolution of the vast territory.

"Am I dead?" he shouted.

"You are waiting for spring," said the voice.

With this, he pictured Willa sitting in the chair before the fireplace, holding the baby. She was staring directly at him, and her look of sadness and confusion made him want to be with her. Desire became frustration, like an itch that could not be attended to.

"Sleep now," said Pa-ni-ta.

"Wait," Cley cried, but just then a fallen tree trunk appeared out of thin air directly in the path of the coursing foliate. Vasthasha tripped over it and fell, the thin stick at the bottom of his throat, at the end of which the bubble of Cley bobbed, hit against the hard vines of his inner vegetable skeleton. The hunter smashed against the boundary that was his prison and lost consciousness.

Vasthasha leaped to his feet and began running again. He cleared the edge of the forest and passed into the moonlight of a desert he would have to cross before the rising of the sun.

■ In the confines of the walls of Fort Vordor, a crow ripped the remaining flesh from Curaswani's neck. It had come every day of the summer to feast on the remains of the soldiers, not knowing that their dead meat harbored a parasite that had already, very slowly, begun to sap its life.

■ Willa chopped wood with the stone ax out behind the cabin. The day was overcast, and a misty drizzle fell. Wood and Wraith lay on a blanket behind her. The child rolled over and pulled himself along, sliding on his stomach. When he reached the edge of the blanket, Wood lifted him by the back of the overalls his mother had sewn for him and returned him gently to the center of the large blue rectangle.

■ Shkchl had been at his work for days, setting bones, cauterizing arteries with the charges of electric eels and everywhere probing the corpse with a three-pronged wand that he held with the ends of his antennae mustache. Wherever the triple points touched a sudden torrent of bubbles erupted.

He retrieved from his store of implements a small snail shell. With the sharp tips of his webbed fingers, he dug into the shell and pulled out a wriggling yellow creature, like an inchworm with delicate horns. Using his thumbnail, he made an incision across Cley's exposed heart and shoved the creature inside the muscle. That done, he replaced the plug of bone into the sternum and welded it with the triton. Next, he applied the living clamps to the flaps of chest flesh, sealing shut the thoracic cavity.

When Cley was again in one piece, Shkchl cut the vines that held the body in place. Lifting the hunter under the arms, he swam with him up above the tall tubelike flowers. He chose one that would accommodate the measurements of the corpse and shoved Cley down inside the dark blossom. Then he gathered the top and wrapped and tied it with a piece of vine.

The Water Beings' work was done, but before gathering his tools, he looked up at the flower that now was a shroud and mentally calculated the rate of disintegration for the vine, the goo that covered the body, and the snail whose life, when it ebbed, would give life to Cley.

Shkchl shrugged. "Close enough," he thought. As he collected his oyster-shell baggage, he wondered if the great serpent yet knew it was pregnant. He pictured the blue membrane that blocked entrance to the garden above, and with a directed thought turned it off. With this, he took to the underground waterways that led back to the inland ocean.

■ The old body scribe ambled through the oasis where Cley had first met Vasthasha. At the heart of the lush forest he found, in a clearing beneath a tree with wide leaves, the remains of a campfire. He knelt and brought his face within inches of the burned wood. In the charred pile, he smelled the word for Cley.

■ Bad dreams plagued the Beshanti. Misnotishul walked through the nightmares of too many warriors, spewing the poisonous drivel of Brisden. They decided to burn Fort Vordor and erase its existence from their memories.

■ On the other side of the desert, Vasthasha ran through the crumbling remains of an ancient city. The ruins of the buildings still gave evidence that they had been constructed in imitation of human heads—the mouths, the doorways; the eyes, the windows; the smoke tunnels, merely the tops of elaborate hats. When the wind blew, these rotting stone heads conversed in low murmurs, and the foliate believed they were discussing the fact that he would never make it to Paradise.

■ The fort burned, the crow flew north, Willa laughed out loud at Wraith's baby language, and the body scribe passed along the seashore, looking at the wreck of an old ship foundering in the surf off a distant sandbar.

■ Cley heard a story, in all the languages of the Word at once, about the creation of the world. It was like an impossibly complex joke, involving a bird, a fish, a tree, a snake, a man and woman, and the punch line, he knew, although it was still an eternity away, had to do with the hatching of an egg.

■ The summer dozed in its own heat, sleepwalking through blue days and cool nights. Its lethargy slowed Vasthasha in his race, and the foliate felt as if he were running across the bottom of the inland ocean. He stopped one afternoon, for only a moment, to drink from a green pool, next to which lay the carcass of a dead deer. As he lifted himself to continue, water dripping from the leaves of his face, he smelled it—the first hint of summer's demise.

Later that afternoon, he passed the mouth of a cave. If he had had the time to stop and explore, he would have found inside the remains of the adept, Scarfinati, who, in his self-imposed exile from humanity, had discovered the secret of immortality only to eventually choose suicide by cutting his throat with a razor.

■ Two turns of the vine that held the top of Cley's shroud disintegrated from the nibbling of one-celled organisms and the inherent catalytic processes of water.

■ Shkchl, on his long return to the inland ocean, was swimming through a swiftly moving underground channel when he decided to stop for a moment's rest. He wedged his webbed feet against an outcropping of rock and let the rush of water move around him. He had not been resting long when he was struck squarely in the back by a pointy piece of debris. Reaching out, he grabbed the projectile before it could be swept away.

"What is this?" he wondered as he studied it. He saw it was a man-made tool, strung with line, at the end of which was a dangerous hook. A round spool where the line was wound had rotted badly. "A pathetic human device," he said to himself. "Pollution of the worst sort." He let the fishing pole go on ahead of him in the flow. "May they all, every one of them, sit on one of these and spin," he said, and his words flew away in bubbles that would not find air against which to break for days.

■ One night when Wraith would not sleep, Willa wrapped him in blankets and took him out of the bed to go sit by the fire. She threw on a few more large branches she had cut that day and settled down in the high-backed chair. The child was wide-awake, but not crying, only gurgling in baby language.

At the sound of Wraith's voice, Wood woke up. He went into the other room and returned with the book cover.

Willa smiled upon seeing it, remembering the day at her old house when she had come in from a walk and found Cley reading to Wraith and the dog from the empty book. Wood set the leather cover in her lap and took his place at her feet, looking up. And so on this night, she began telling the story of her life: "I was born in the town of Belius in the western Realm . . ." Wraith went quiet, and the dog was asleep before she finished describing her parents, but she continued on and got as far as her first day of school.

■ Although the days were still warm, the nights grew cold, and the leaves started to change at their tips from green to red. The great serpent sensed the seasons shifting as the clutch of eggs grew inside of her. Twenty replicas in hard white cases, twenty transmitters that would leave the cave and spread out to form a web that would widen the consciousness of the Beyond and then multiply every spring to expand it further until it knew, again, every inch of itself. Each of the tiny Sirimon was curled in its bubble like Cley, listening to tales of the wilderness.

■ The body scribe found the remains of the Olsens' house. He stood amidst the ruins, the blackened wood reeking with the word that was Cley. Watching him from a distance were the Beshanti, who knew they dared not disturb him. Beneath the remains of a curious platform full of dirt still holding the brown-needled remains of two dwarfed trees, he found a pair of miniature wooden carvings in the shapes of young women. He took them in his hand and put them in a deerskin pouch he wore on a lanyard around his waist.

■ The leaves that were the foliate's arms and legs would soon begin to change color. All of his blossoms had drifted away in his wake, and now violet berries began to show where the flowers had been. At night, bats sought him with flawless sonic precision, swooping out of the dark to steal this sweet fruit. During the day it was the sparrows that swarmed down upon him in migrating flocks. He ran through both night and day, beset by pecking, grasping scavengers, and the pain of each theft was like the jab of a body scribe's bone needle, the stab of a fishing pole carried by a rushing current.

■ The crow, whose eyesight was failing, whose beak was softening, and whose feathers shed as a result of the parasitic disease he had contracted from feasting on the flesh of Curaswani and his men, turned in its flight one morning and followed a path through the Beyond that defied time and distance.

He sailed into the wind of passing years and miles, above the heads of the other glowing creatures that were on their way somewhere far from where they had begun. In its flight, a feather came loose and fell. It drifted down like a bright idea and struck, on the head, Scarfinati, who years earlier had passed this way on his pilgrimage to the cave farther into the heart of the wilderness. Instantly the shining form of the adept shattered like fine glass beneath the tap of a hammer at the same moment that, years in the future, he pulled the razor across his throat. In the intervening time, he no longer existed.

■ The meadow lost its flowers, and the grass had turned from green to the color of wheat. In the late afternoon, when the sunlight broke through openings in the mountainous clouds above, streaming down in distinct shafts, the field, all the way to the lake and beyond, appeared a rippling sea of gold. A herd of six-legged shaggy behemoths with oblong heads, wide nostrils, and blunt faces, ambled out of the forest to graze.

At first, Willa feared them for their size, but eventually it became evident that they were as afraid of her as she was of them. Wood took great pleasure in running among them and rounding them up into a tight group. The dog barked wildly, as if shouting orders to the lumbering creatures, and they responded with uncharacteristic speed to his commands.

The beasts lingered for a week, grouped together on the southern shore of the lake, and then one morning Willa woke to find them gone.

■ The underwater blossom that shrouded Cley's body began to change. The large, soft petals stiffened; the soft plant matter became hard and coarse. The stalk that held it upright bent a little more with each passing day.

■ Vasthasha was pursued by troubling thoughts through a forest of tall trees whose leaves fell around him in a yellow blizzard. He could feel his energy diminishing. Each step took a conscious effort, but whenever he slowed, he felt the notion of failure nipping at the backs of his legs, and this served to spur him on. His own leaves had gone red at the tips, and one or two were singed brown. The vines that had made up his hair had already died and turned to short stubble.

■ ". . . and we went hand in hand out behind the town hall, the sound of the violin following us in the dark. We hid beneath the weeping willow that stood next to the bronze statue of the great horned God, Belius, and there, Christof, your father, first kissed me," said Willa. She closed the empty book cover and sat, staring into the fire. The night was very cold, and she was feeling lonely. She thought about Cley, and decided that if he did not return, she would try to make it back to the seashore in the spring.

Before her emotions could get the better of her, she diverted her attention by making a mental list of all the chores that needed to be done the next day. Laundry, chopping wood, fetching water, sweeping the floor, preparing meals . . . She listened to the noise of the old crow that had taken lodging in a hole under the roof of the house. It wheezed when it breathed, and at night the sound was like a distant whistling. When she fell asleep, these respirations were transformed in her dreams into the music of a violin.

■   ■   ■

■ Cley, in his thoughts, walked with Arla Beaton along the night streets of Anamasobia. Bataldo waved hello from across the lane, and they passed the open doors of the tavern wherein Frod Geeble could be seen pouring drinks behind the bar.

"I heard that you were killed in the Beyond," she said to him.

"Mere rumor," said Cley, and when he looked at her she was now wearing the green veil.

"What exactly happened?" she asked.

"I was trapped in a block of unmelting ice at the bottom of a ship," he said. "No, wait, that wasn't me," he said. When he turned to her this time, she had become Anotine. "That was you," he said.

"No, Cley, it was me," said Willa Olsen, who took him by the arm and led him out of town, into a meadow where a log house sat by a lake.

■ Shkchl reached the inland ocean and was greeted by his fellow Water Beings.

"Is there hope?" asked their leader.

The weary traveler lifted his shoulders and momentarily looked up to where the waves rolled a half mile above. "Let's eat," he said.

■ And now the snow fell, a light flurry that powdered the meadow and left traces on the bare branches of the trees at the edge of the forest. The sight of it was beautiful, but it filled Willa with a paralyzing dread as if it was a sign that Death was on its way.

■ Vasthasha, brown-leafed and showing great patches of bare thatch, moved along bent at the waist, traversing a glacier, the last obstacle to his destination.

■ The Sirimon slithered through the opening where the blue membrane had always been and curled itself into a coil defined by the edge of the pool. Over the course of three days, it fell into a heavy sleep that would last until spring.

■ The crow gathered berries and insects enough to last for weeks and huddled inside the hole beneath the roof in a nest made of dead meadow grass. Its mind was addled with disease and it believed that the small wooden object (a miniature carved man) it had found in the field, was its young.

■ Vasthasha limped through the valley of Paradise at the heart of the Beyond. His right foot was missing; his left hand had cracked and fallen off. Both lay in a scatter of sticks out on the glacier that ringed the mythical place. Disembodied lights flew through the perfect trees. He wanted so desperately to lie down and sleep forever, but, after having traveled through the enchanted place all night, he saw with the first light of morning, the one true flower. Its blinding petals were spread outward in a vast radius from a center that was an eye of utter darkness. The stem that held the blossom was bent beneath its weight at a right angle to the ground. Its yawning middle appeared to the foliate to be a wide tunnel.

He gathered his strength, and even though he had only one foot, he attained the speed he had at the very beginning of his journey. As Vasthasha dashed toward the flower, dry and rotted branches flew from him. The flames in his eyes died out, and tiny streams of smoke whipped away from the empty eyeholes and trailed behind him. He leaped as his life left him, and while propelled through the air, he came apart in a rattling of dry vines and dead leaves. His head and neck flew forward into the open center of the blossom, and the tiny bubble of Cley descended into the womb of the plant.

■ There was a knocking at the door, and Willa screamed with the suddenness of it. She put the baby down and lifted the pistol, which she always kept loaded.

"Cley?" she called. "Cley?"

"A visitor," said a strange voice.

Wood left Wraith and went to the door. He wagged his tail and barked.

"Who are you?" she called, thinking of the snow.

"A friend," said the voice.

"Come in," she said and cocked the hammer.

The door opened, and the body scribe entered.

■ The wilderness slumbered inside its shell of snow and ice. Also asleep were the great serpent, the crow, the demons of the forest, and Cley. Even the Beshanti dreamt peacefully now. Misnotishul had made one last appearance during the mushroom ceremony in the last hours of autumn, and as his spirit hovered near the ceiling of the longhouse, he spoke only Beshanti. The tribe rejoiced that they had been able to save his soul.

■ From the moment she first saw the old man's face she knew there was nothing to fear. He was a great help with Wraith, and though bent and slow-moving, he could hunt and did not seem to mind the bitter winds and deep snow. She was amazed that he spoke to her in the language of the Realm. But what was more astonishing was that he also seemed capable of communicating with the baby in a babbling tongue and with the dog in a pattern of high-pitched whines. Sometimes, when she saw him standing outside in the swirling powder, she believed he was talking to the very earth itself.

Each night after dinner he asked her to please read more of her life story from the empty book. At times he would amuse them all by tossing small pinches of powder from a little pouch he carried into the fireplace. Then smoke images trailed out of the flames and came to life in the room. On one night he produced a pink cat that engaged Wood in a wrestling match before dissipating into thin air. He had drawn the first true laughter out of the child, and eased Willa's anxiety. She wanted to ask him about Cley, but she didn't, afraid of what he would tell her.

The body scribe convinced Willa that it would be in the child's best interest for him to tattoo Wraith's forehead. When she finally nodded, he took out his tools and set to work. Even though blood ran in rivulets across the baby's face, he smiled through the entire operation. When the work was done, there was a minute image of a crow in flight over the left eyebrow.

"Your boy will know the language of the birds," he said when he was finished.

■ Snow blew in great gusts across the meadow. It covered over the charred remains of Fort Vordor and blocked the cave entrance wherein lay the great serpent. A long stretch of boring white underscored by the distant howling of the wind only momentarily interrupted by a glimpse of the one true flower in the heart of the Beyond. *Then more white, on and on, until I almost lose the vision as the guard down the hall coughs and clears his throat. When I turn back, the snow has stopped, the wind now whispers, and there are patches of earth showing through the frozen crust. There, growing up through Curaswani's rib cage, is a blade of grass, and I know that, in an instant, spring has come.*

■ In the forests to the south, the demons flapped their wings and snapped their tails, driven from sleep by hunger.

■ The serpent laid her eggs, and eighteen survived the birth.

■ The crow under the roof, though insane, and having lost nearly all of its feathers, still lived, having forced itself not to die so that it might care for its weak, silent offspring.

■ Wraith said his first word, "Woo," meaning the dog.

■ The last of the vine holding closed the hardened dead flower encasing the hunter's body broke off and floated away. The petals sprang open and launched the silver-slicked corpse into the underground current.

■ In the Earthly Paradise, the one true flower spewed forth a cloud of pollen like a smoker coughing out a huge drag that tickled the throat. Amidst this sparkling gossamer flock of seed flew the morsel of Cley. Inside the boundary of his infinitesimal prison he was awakened by the voice of Pa-ni-ta. "The time is near," she told him, as he was lifted by the wind high up over the rim of the glacier and sent floating southward.

■ The snail in Cley's heart was almost completely dissolved, and the muscle twitched with its absorbed energy as his body was carried along in the swift flow.

■ "... And that," said Willa, "was how I came to the Beyond."

■ The rotted hull of the wrecked ship that had drifted upon the inland ocean for years finally split open, and a block of unmelting ice drifted down to the sandy bottom.

■ After a day in the forest, the body scribe returned with a handful of thin, twisted roots. Willa watched as he, methodically and meticulously, cut them into a fine powder with his stone knife.

■ The moving water had almost entirely washed away the silver goo from Cley's form. Only a very thin film remained, covering his nostrils, and a tenuous bubble guarded his open mouth. Slowly, the hunter rose toward the faint sunlight above.

■ The wind rushed from the north, carrying with it the particle of Cley. It met in its flight a piece of green fabric. The veil twisted, gathered into a ball, and then snapped outward like a whip. With its very tip it struck the seed, which lost its lift and plummeted toward the earth.

■ Moving the high-backed chair into the corner of the house, the old man climbed upon it. He lifted his pipe to his mouth, the bowl of which held the powdered root he had chopped the previous day.

"Now," he said to Willa, who walked forward with a short branch she had lit in the fire. She got up on her toes and dipped the flame into the bowl of the pipe. The body scribe toked at the mouthpiece, and a small cloud soon encircled his head. He drew in a huge lungful of it, and, aiming his lips at the small crack in the corner of the ceiling, he released the smoke in a thin stream.

■ The body breached the surface of the lake and drifted toward the bank.

■ Eighteen broken eggshells and as many slithery trails through the soft dirt snaked out of the cave and into the wilderness.

■ The crow feared the smoke. Gathering up its young in its mushy beak, it pushed through dried grass that had been its comfort all winter. It flew away weak unto death and circled erratically before it dropped its charge and spiraled into the lake.

■ The seed from the one true flower drifted slowly down and was passed in its descent by the falling wooden man. The miniature struck the blue tattoo of the coiled snake directly at the center of Cley's forehead. This collision vibrated outward through the body, settling the wildly pulsing heart into a steady rhythm. The chest heaved for air, bursting inward the remaining bubble of silver, and the seed was drawn down into the hunter's right nostril.

■ "Go to the door," said the old man, stepping down from the chair.

Willa walked across the room and did as she was told. She went out onto the porch. Across the meadow, the green grass was sprouting all around stubborn patches of old snow.

Down by the edge of the lake was Cley, standing naked, shivering with new life and the shock of being born.

"It's him," she cried, and ran to the bedroom to get a blanket. Wood darted out of the house. The old man lifted the child off his blanket on the floor and, smiling, headed toward the lake. Willa rushed past the body scribe and reached the hunter first.

"Where have you been?" she asked, throwing the warm cover over him and wrapping her arm around his shoulders to keep it in place. She suspected from the distant look in his eyes that he had been to Paradise.

He grunted but could not yet speak the word, *Dead*.

consumed by the wilderness

The last two days have been a whirlwind of activity, not all good, some actually dreadful, but to my delight, swirling around a central axis that is yours truly. Ladies and gentlemen of the jury, I have been to court, and seeing as how tomorrow they will pronounce my guilt or innocence as concerns the murder of Cley, I thought I had better get back to work and make one more trip to the Beyond. Feskin has told me he believes that the prosecution has built a good case, although much of their evidence is circumstantial. It is our hope that I will walk out of the courtroom tomorrow a free man.

The guard down the hallway is snoring like a warthog, and I have just administered my remaining dose of the beauty. What a respite it will be after such frantic goings-on. Before I leave myself behind here in my cell and go to find Cley in the wilderness, I will take a few minutes to record for you the events that have transpired in the court of Constable Spencer.

Feskin had assured them that I would not need to be handcuffed, and they accepted his promise. Still, they sent no fewer than ten men with rifles to chaperone me down the short hallway into the court. My usual lethargic guard came the morning following my pitiful first day of incarceration and turned his big key in the lock of my cell. *Stepping free of the confines of the barred cubicle reminded me of Cley being reborn into the wilderness. When I stretched my wings, all of the ten guns came up in alarm. Had they fired, I think they most likely would have shot each other.*

Feskin was to act as my attorney, and he had begged me to wear my outfit, so I did. I felt I was looking rather good as I strode down the aisle between the two rows of benches facing the constable. I wondered which of the people of the gallery I passed were among the crowd outside my window through the night, calling for my immediate execution. I turned and smiled to one and all. Emilia and her mother were seated in the back. The girl waved to me and I to her.

The prosecutor was a true believer, if you know what I mean—a rancorous rail of a fellow named Jasweth Frabone, a name I can't believe any mother would have given her son. He wore a brown suit that shimmered in its cheapness. His hair was failing mightily, though a few wispy strands were overtaxed in an attempt to suggest otherwise. It was obvious that he was too righteous even to eat. Yellow nails, yellow teeth, and skin the color of toadstools. When the constable called him forward to make some preliminary remarks, he bombastically lambasted me personally with religious quotation. I, in turn, corrected his botched recitation of a line from Saint Ilfus, and both Spencer and Feskin told me to keep quiet. So I did.

As was the law in the court at Wenau, the prosecution was given the first day in which to lay out its case, and on the following day the defense had the opportunity to rebut the charges. On the morning of the third day, a decision would be rendered by the constable. Frabone began by first introducing Semla Hood and again getting her story about the stone knife. The old woman had a self-satisfied smile on her face as she stood in front of the room, holding the weapon up for all to see. While she was speaking, Feskin leaned over to me and whispered that he planned to demand her arrest for theft. I had to laugh. Spencer admonished me with a glance, and I heard whispers roll through the sea of onlookers.

Semla Hood was followed by her compatriots, the three wise men, dullards all, who in turn gave their meandering testimonies. The court was in a doze by the time they were done. But when Frabone next brought forth the small red-covered book that was supposedly Cley's diary, I could feel the tension begin to build. He also produced a page from one of Cley's famous manuscripts and laid it beside the book on Spencer's desk.

"Notice," said the prosecutor, "the overall similarity of writing styles."

Spencer looked and looked and then nodded. "Can you be more specific?" he asked.

"Certainly," said Frabone, and launched into a painstaking comparison of i dots and the tails of y's. "The M in Misrix, most fittingly, Your Honor, has these points like the horns of a demon," he said and, as Spencer bent forward, the prosecutor glared back at me in a show of arrogance. In response to him, I lifted my tail and curled the end into a perfect likeness of a question mark. I heard laughter come from the gallery of citizens behind me.

"If you would, Constable, please read this passage, here," said the prosecutor, pointing to the open diary.

"As you wish," said Spencer. He cleared his throat and then proceeded to recite in his gruff voice: "The black dog has been missing now for two days, and I fear the demon has devoured him. I woke last night and found the creature standing over me with a ravenous look in his yellow eyes. Saliva dripped from his lips, and I am quite sure that if I had not come to in time and quickly pulled my knife, he would have dined on me also. As it is, I think it will be only a matter of days before he does me in. The Beyond has a powerful hold on him, and he has told me on more than one occasion that he longs to be one with it. I have suggested that we split up, but he assures me that I will come to no harm. Through the course of the days, though, I see him sizing me up the way I might the caribou steaks I have longed for since entering this damnable hell."

"Very good, Your Honor," said Frabone, when the constable paused. "And there are two more entries in which Cley's suspicions turn to certainties and he says his good-byes to the world . . . If I may, I will read the longer of the two." As the prosecutor took the diary from the desk, Spencer nodded. Frabone began reading and took a step toward me.

"I have been hiding from Misrix in this cave for the past week. Wood has never returned. I write only to relieve my anxiety. As I sit, knife in hand, always waiting for the sound of his hooves on the rocks outside, the sweep of his wings from above, I wonder if I ever really returned from Below's memory. Last night I dreamt of Anotine and Arla and another woman on the streets of Anamasobia. The past is flooding in, brimming with suggestion but utterly pointless. To be consumed by the wilderness, is that not what I wanted all along?"

The prosecutor snapped the diary shut in front of my face, then turned on his heels and walked back to Spencer. "Now that you have heard these, you must want to know the last," said Frabone.

"Well?" said the constable.

The prosecutor paged slowly through the book toward the end. When he arrived, he shook his head sadly. "Cley's last written words, his last communication to us was, 'I don't understand.' "

There was a moment of silence before Frabone said, "I don't understand. I don't understand why we are trying a creature. This is better settled out of doors, somewhere off in the woods outside the town. This is an insult to Justice itself."

"Conserve your energy, Jasweth," said Spencer, then called a recess for lunch.

I was taken back to my cell, and the guard asked me what I would have to eat. Eventually I ordered my usual meal of vegetables and fruit, but before I gave my real order, I said, "How about Frabone, with a baked apple in every orifice?" The ten gunmen laughed heartily.

It was only while sitting in my cell that the morning's performance by the prosecutor began to irritate me. All lies, as if he was talking about some other reality. I admonished myself by thinking, "You were there with Cley, you know what has happened to him. Don't let their trumpery confuse you."

Feskin came soon after to visit me in my cell. The gunmen had gone to lunch and only the heavy, tired guard remained down the hall. We whispered our communications in case he might be listening. The schoolteacher sat on the bed precisely where my vision of Below had.

"What have you got in that manuscript of yours that is going to offset Frabone's evidence?" he asked.

"Proof that Cley lived for many years after I left the Beyond, and might still be alive today," I told him.

"Is the writing not subjective?" asked Feskin.

I explained to him how I came upon Cley's story by sampling the elements of the wilderness. When I was done with a synopsis of the hunter's tribulations, Feskin's hands were shaking.

"You know," he said, "after lunch, Frabone is going to call Horace Watt to testify. He comes before them with a body. Is your story going to be that convincing?" he asked, getting to his feet.

"I will demonstrate my abilities to the court," I said.

"I half wish now that I had never told you to come to town," he said.

I walked up to him and put my hands lightly on his shoulders. "You are a good man," I said.

■ Horace Watt, looking every bit the fearless explorer his reputation suggested, stepped forward, towering over Frabone. He was a young man, perhaps not quite as old as Feskin, but wider in the shoulders than he by two. He had long blond hair that went untended in a wild, matted tangle. The wilderness was still in his eyes, and yet he was as calm as Frabone was annoying.

"We traveled to the Beyond," said Watt. "There were eleven of us when we crossed the boundary. We returned from the wilderness

with seven live men and one partial corpse. The demons, looking like
this one here," he said pointing at me, "devoured, like mindless
dogs, four of my friends. We shot and killed scores of them, but there
were always more, and they hunted relentlessly. With us we had two
bloodhounds, who in the first week of our stay led us to a cave where
we discovered what I believe to be Cley's remains. It took us two
weeks to fight our way back out. Once the Beyond has you, it does
not want you to leave."

"About the body," said Frabone. "What did you find?"

"It had been ravaged and partially eaten. Greatly decom-
posed, but the bite marks on the bones, the holes in the sternum
where it was gored by a pair of horns, were consistent with the
wounds my men suffered at the hands of the creatures. We also
found the diary, a pair of boots that have been identified as Cley's,
and a black, broad-brimmed hat with three wild-turkey feathers in
the band."

I could do no more than listen in silence to the entire tale. Although seemingly told true by the young Watt, it was to me as if he
was talking about someone else, some vicious criminal who also
piqued my own sense of terror. When he was through speaking, I
wept at the unjustly persuasive character of his testimony. If I was
ever going to forsake humanity and let loose the demon inside me, it
would have been precisely there. Instead, I breathed deeply, buried
my urge to strike back, and went quietly to my cell when the proceedings were over.

All that night, I could think of only one thing. Say, for argument's sake only, that I had done this thing to Cley. Would it not be
the ultimate irony that in losing myself so completely to the Beyond,
shedding so completely my human nature, that I committed an act
that would eventually, conclusively prove my humanity? As Below
had said, "Do they arrest beasts?" The trial, as ugly as the accusations are, is to be my salvation.

The day of my defense came after a sleepless night. Feskin arrived early, filling me in on his strategy.

"All of their evidence," he told me in my cell, "is real, but the logic that is applied is skewed. They cannot prove beyond a doubt that it was not some other demon who finished off Cley. Even if you were stalking him, another could have beaten you to the kill. The presence of the stone knife in your museum means little. An accusation based on the dubious memories of the elderly."

"The diary?" I asked.

"There is no place in it where he states that you killed him. How could there be?" he asked.

I had other questions, but before I could voice them the guard and the gunmen appeared outside my cell. We again made the short journey to the courtroom, but this time I was not so self-assured. I could feel my heart racing, and I did not look at the faces in the gallery of citizens.

Feskin did his utmost to sew a seed of doubt into Spencer's mind. He told the constable all of what he had told me, but in a much more elaborate and well-argued presentation. The only answer he got to all of his questions was that there was no definitive proof of my guilt. The sole setback occurred when he inquired of Watt about the bloodhounds. He wondered how these dogs could trace a trail after the passage of so many years. The explorer told him, matter-of-factly, that the dogs were raised from a line that had originated in the Well-Built City. "They can track a grain of pepper across a continent after twenty years," said Watt.

When Feskin tried to broach the subject of having Semla Hood arrested for theft, Spencer dismissed the idea by saying, "We have traveled that road, and I am not going down it again." This brought a squall of whispers from the crowd, but the constable squashed them by slamming his open hand upon the desk and calling for silence.

During lunch, I convinced Feskin to call me as a witness for myself. He told me it was dangerous but that he would honor my wish. When we returned to the court, I carried with me these pages and did not look at the floor. I went forth from my cell with my head held high and a great determination to reveal the truth as I believed it to be.

After the room had quieted down, I was called to come before the constable. Feskin simply said, "And now, Misrix, the accused, would like to address you all." After introducing me, I noticed that he returned to his seat in the front row and sat very still, with his eyes closed.

I wasted no time but launched directly into my explanation as to how I came by the knowledge that Cley lived long past my time in the Beyond. I detailed my trip to the wilderness and my gathering those things I would need to decipher the story. When I related the part about my sampling the elements and finding information concerning Cley's life in them, the gallery broke out in howls of laughter.

"But it's true," I said, my voice lost amid the storm of jeers.

Spencer quieted the room, then turned to me. "I also find this hard to believe," he said. "Is there any way that you can prove this special ability of yours?"

"I can enter your memory by simply placing my hand on your head," I told him. There came more tittering from the crowd.

"Prove it," he said.

His command made me lose my nerve. In my head were spinning all of the horrible masks of derision in the gallery.

"Tell me something about me only I could know," said Spencer.

As I stepped over to him and reached out my hand to cover his head, one of the gunmen stepped forward and raised his rifle to aim at my chest.

"It's all right," said the constable, and the man backed away.

There was sweat on my hand and my thoughts were unfocused. My nervousness was making it impossible for me to initiate what I have come to call "the dreaming wind." Instead, I was visited again by those flashes of a disemboweled Cley lying beneath me. I shook my head and tried to catch some minor stirring of the breeze that would carry my mind into Spencer's memory. Many moments passed. In my mind's eye, I saw Anotine in the block of ice, Wood howling by the lake, Misnotishul's tortured corpse.

"Well?" said Spencer, looking impatient to have my clawed hand off his head.

Just then I caught a spark of what I believed to be a fragment of his memory. I was certain I had something and stepped away from the constable. "Your wife," I said, turning toward the audience so as better to see their reaction to my revelation, "is a woman with dark hair and green eyes. Her name is Lilith Marnes."

There was total silence.

I began to smile, and then Spencer said, "I have never been married."

I spun around to face him, and a wave of shouts broke against my back. The constable slammed his hand repeatedly on the desk.

"Now," he said, not unfriendly, "what else have you for us?"

"These are the writings," I said wearily, "of my insights into the Beyond."

"Inadmissible," he said.

I was in shock. Feskin had to come and fetch me. As he ushered me back to my cell, he turned, and told Spencer, "We are finished for the day."

All was a blur to me as we passed through the throng of people crowding out of their seats. I felt I was drowning in a sea of voices, shouting, "Murderer," and far fewer proclaiming, "Free the demon." Somewhere in the crush of people, Emilia appeared. I leaned down to hear what she was saying, but I couldn't make out a word of it. She reached her hand up to mine and pressed a scrap of paper into it. I closed my fist around her message, and then she was whisked away in the swiftly moving human current.

Feskin did not accompany me inside the cell this time. "Don't worry, Misrix," he said. "Things may work out without your having to read your tale of Cley. We have to trust Spencer."

"I was ready to read," I said to him from what seemed a great distance.

"I know," he said. Then he shook his head and walked away down the hall.

It was only later tonight that I read Emilia's message. Written in her neat hand were the words: "There is something I know that might help you."

Now, through the filter of the drug, I see all of this clearly in perspective. I was truly a man earlier today, shaken by language and logic, and this pleases me. Tomorrow, should I be found guilty, even that will please me. There is no trail emanating from the corners of this cell that defies Time and Distance. I leave myself no alternative but to carry on with dignity.

square of paradise

Cley's hair and beard were streaked with gray and the look of determination with which he had begun his journey had softened considerably. He lifted himself from the high-backed chair before the fireplace and crossed the room for his hat and bow.

Leaving the house, he went down to the edge of the lake, where Willa was picking onion grass for salad. She watched him approach and straightened, brushing the back of her hand across her forehead.

Cley drew close and kissed her on the cheek. "I'm going hunting," he said.

"Get a rabbit if you can," she said.

He nodded.

"Do you need Wraith to go with you, today?" she asked.

"No, I'll go alone today," he said.

"He'll be disappointed," she said.

"I'll explain it to him," said Cley.

"Be back before sundown," she said, and bent over to pick some more of the bright green spirals.

The hunter passed the house. Fifty yards away, there was

a huge pen made of long thin tree trunks. Inside it moved eight "oxen," as Cley called the behemoths that came out of the forest every year at the end of autumn to eat the golden grass of the meadow. The cows gave milk and the meat of one was worth ten hunting trips.

As he neared the pen, he saw Wraith wielding a pitchfork fashioned from branches. The boy dug into the pile of meadow grass and shoveled the load over the side of the pen where four of the oxen had gathered to eat.

Wraith, for all of the troubles of his early years, had grown up tall for his age and was very thin, with blond hair. "Only six more years and he'll be a man," thought Cley, and shook his head.

The hunter watched as the boy lifted another pile of hay over the side of the pen. There was a slight rippling of muscle down the slender left arm and a distant look in the eyes. For some reason, this one glance at the boy filled Cley with great satisfaction.

"I'm going hunting," he said.

"I'll go," said Wraith, dropping the rake.

"Not today," said Cley.

"Why not?" asked the boy.

"I'm going far, and you have too much to do."

"All right," said Wraith. He walked over and hugged Cley. The hunter wrapped his arm tightly around the boy.

"Tomorrow," said Wraith, taking a step back.

"Tomorrow," said Cley, as he turned and headed for the tree line.

It was late spring, and the day was mild. The forest was brimming with life. Birds and squirrels moved through the new foliage, and the scent of deer was everywhere.

On his way into the heart of the forest Cley stopped at a small clearing circled by shemel trees. A tall pile of brown stones sat in the middle of it. The hunter approached the marker and stood quietly. He thought about the black dog, remembering its brutal death in the jaws of the Sirimon.

They had taken Wraith along and gone out hunting in the forest. It was early autumn in the sixth year of their stay at Pierce's cabin. Cley was preoccupied, aiming at a deer off in the distance, when the pink column of monster rose up from behind some bracken. If Wood had not leaped, the Sirimon would have taken Wraith. By the time the hunter felled the great serpent, with one perfect shot (the last of the rifle bullets) to the head, Wood was lifeless. It had been the boy's idea to bury him with the cover of the empty book.

For years after the tragedy, Cley had wondered if this had been his repayment for saving the Beyond. The body scribe, who came back to visit from time to time, had suggested one summer night that perhaps something else would have happened if the dog had not been killed by the serpent.

"Like what?" asked Cley.

"The boy," whispered the old artisan.

Now the anger was behind him, and he was left with only a longing to see his hunting companion again. Sometimes, when he was deep in the forest, he heard a very distant sound like barking. The first time he heard it, he tracked it for five miles before he realized that it never grew any closer. On other occasions he might feel something brush lightly against his leg. When he was alone in some unknown tract of the wilderness, he still found himself whistling to call the dog to his side.

For the past few nights, he had been dreaming of hunting a strange creature through the forest. Wood was with him, and they traveled through an unfamiliar landscape, tracking the thing that always, at the last minute, eluded them. When the hunter woke, he tried to remember what the animal had been, but the image was jumbled in his mind, a winged whirl of feather, fur, beak, and claw in myriad colors. The sounds that came from it were sometimes high-pitched squeals, sometimes the huffing of a pig, and once it rumbled in a human bass voice from behind the undergrowth, "I don't understand."

The dreams were so vivid that Cley had come to believe that he would actually find this creature out in the real forest of his waking days. There was something portentous about it, and it was for this reason that he left Wraith safely behind. He had the sense that if he was able to succeed in felling the enigmatic prey, many things would become clear to him.

So the day passed as Cley hunted the dream creature, listening carefully for its cry and peering long and hard at any rustling of leaves. In the afternoon, he missed twice trying to get a rabbit for Willa. As he had told her from time to time, "My shot is not worth a word from Brisden anymore." He fetched the arrows and continued on his way.

As the sun descended, he realized he must turn back to the house. He now had two rabbits strung over his shoulder, so the day had not been a total loss. Traveling down the gently sloping side of a hill, between the trunks of birches, he noticed that at the bottom there was a tall bush whose branches were swaying. There was something within, behind the leaves.

Cley stood still, and at the same moment the bush stopped moving. The hunter raised his bow and placed an arrow. Cautiously, he advanced, waiting for the thing to dart out in either direction. When he was five paces away, he pulled the bowstring back, aiming for the spot where the commotion had been. An instant before he decided to release, something rushed from the back of the bush in a blur of color and disappeared behind trees a hundred yards away.

The hunter could not believe how fast the creature moved. He could have sworn it made a sound as it fled, a quiet screech that still echoed in his memory. Cley started after it, moving slowly toward the stand of trees. He tried to remember if he was really hunting the creature or dreaming he was hunting it. He had a vague sense that he had done this before, more than once.

All was silent within the trees. The creature had not moved. As he approached with great stealth, Cley expected the thing to either fly or run. Even after having seen it, he had no idea how it traveled. Now he wished he had the boy with him to help flush it out. He lost his concentration for a moment and pictured himself presenting the carcass of the exotic creature to Wraith.

"It takes many, many years of hunting to be able to fell a beast like this," he said in his daydream.

"Why?" asked the boy.

"You have to learn to understand the wilderness," he said.

He was pulled back into the here and now by a low croaking coming from the thicket. Cley focused again, and worrying that he might have been distracted too long, charged. As he plunged into the trees, something flew above him in the opposite direction.

Only a crow.

Cley felt as though he was sinking into his own chest, and then laughed.

Night was close by, the moon already shining. The hunter looked back over his shoulder at the thicket. He squinted and peered into where light failed and shadows brewed. For the first time in years, he felt lost.

On his way back to the house, with night a heartbeat away, Cley noticed a movement, like a wing flapping, off to his left. He raised the bow and quickly released. The arrow struck the side of a fallen tree. As he went to fetch it, he cursed. When he drew close, he saw the wing again slowly lifting. The sight of it surprised him and he reared back, afraid it was the dream creature poised to strike.

When the wing deflated, he saw it was not a wing at all.

He walked over to the fallen tree and lifted the green veil off the end of a broken branch. Muttering to himself, he stuffed the scrap of material into his pocket.

The hunter broke through the tree line at the edge of the forest and out into the meadow. The moon was shining full, directly over the house. Willa was calling to him from the porch, as she did when he was late. He ran slowly, short of breath, beneath the stars, while from behind him, deep in the forest, came the sound of a dog barking.

In the days that followed, Cley said nothing to Willa about finding the veil. She did not know of his earlier life, and he did not want that to change. He thought often of getting rid of the green scrap, perhaps burning it in the fireplace late at night when the others were asleep. When he was in the forest, alone, he took it from his pocket and studied it. The wind of the Beyond had worn the fabric so thin that no face could now hide behind it. It was badly torn, and the entire edge was frayed. Every time he gathered it up to shove in his pocket, he feared it would crumble like a dead leaf.

■ Cley, Willa, and Wraith were sitting on the porch, their legs hanging over the side. It was midday, and the view out past the lake was incredible. Flowers of every color filled the meadow, and the clouds moved in the still water. Cley was telling a story about me to the boy.

"That's right," said the hunter, "an island in the sky. It was all in Below's mind."

"And you flew in the demon's arms?" asked Wraith.

"Over the Beyond, to the Palashize, a vast spiral of hollowed-out mounds, where I met a ghost who told me about dancing with his ghostly wife by the seashore," said Cley, smiling.

"Were you afraid of the demon?" asked Wraith.

"Yes, but he saved my life more times than I can count," said Cley.

"Where do you get this fluff, Cley?" asked Willa, leaning forward.

The hunter laughed. "I make it up to amuse myself."

"None of it is true?" asked Wraith.

"It's all true," said Cley.

"I see a story coming right now," said Willa.

"No, I'm done for today," said Cley.

"I mean, out there," said Willa, as she pointed toward the meadow.

Coming along the northern shore of the lake was a figure that was too far off to see clearly.

"The body scribe?" asked Cley.

"Too tall," said the boy.

"Besides," said the hunter, "he has not come for years now. I'd better go and get the pistol."

"Get in the house, Wraith," said Willa.

The hunter started out toward the lake. The Traveler kept advancing with long strides. By the time Cley reached the shore, he knew that the visitor was Ea.

Cley stood still as his old friend closed. He lifted his arm and waved. Ea waved back, smiling.

"Have you found Paradise, here?" asked the Traveler.

"I've been to Paradise, and now I'm back," said Cley.

"I heard the wilderness thinking your adventure," said Ea.

"Arla?" asked the hunter. "What has become of Arla Beaton?"

"She is as she is," said the Traveler.

"Jarek, Cyn?" said Cley.

"They are very strong," said Ea.

Walking back to the house, Cley told the Traveler that he had seen Below again. Ea laughed and slapped himself in the side.

"One time, in my conjuring pool, I saw you having tea with a demon," he said.

"Conjuring pool," said Cley, and laughed. "You're full of tricks."

Creepers sang in the meadow, and a night bird called from out of the forest. Cley lit his pipe with leaves from Ea's pouch. The Traveler sat in the high-backed chair before the fireplace, and Willa and Cley were sitting on the floor with their backs to the flames. Curaswani's screaming woman spewed green smoke. They did not know that Wraith was still awake in his bed in the corner.

When the bowl was empty, Ea handed the pipe to Cley, and said "I came for a reason."

"I know," said Cley.

"Arla is not well. She will not live through the next winter," said the Traveler.

"Is this my chance to reach Wenau?" asked Cley.

"It would seem," said Ea. "We heard from an old man, a member of the Word, that you were here. The trip to Wenau will take you six months there and back. But I will guide you, and my son Jarek will return you."

"I found the veil the other day," said Cley.

"Good," said the Traveler.

"You aren't going away again, are you, Cley?" asked Willa.

"I may have to," he said.

"I wish you wouldn't," she said.

"This is important, though. It is the reason I came to the Beyond. I've got to finish it," he said.

"I don't understand," said Willa. She got up off the floor and left the room.

"There will not be another chance, Cley," said Ea.

"Dad?" said Wraith from the corner.

"Yes," said Cley.

"Don't go away."

"Go to sleep," said Cley.

The hunter then got to his feet and went into the bedroom. The weary Traveler smiled, searching the flames for the face of Arla Beaton. Wraith eyed the huge man in the chair through lowered lids.

"Please turn over and let me speak to you," said Cley, as he lay on the bed beside Willa.

He rested his hand lightly on her shoulder. She turned to face him.

"What is it you are going to find?" she asked, a hint of anger in her voice.

"It is a very old debt," said Cley. "I don't want to leave you two here, but this will be my last chance to set things right. I will find out who I am," he said.

"Where do you know this woman from?" asked Willa.

"The past," he said.

"Why do you need to see her?" she asked.

"Listen to me," said Cley. "Just listen, and I will tell you everything . . ."

The next morning at breakfast, Ea told Cley, "We must leave soon if we are going to make the mountain pass before it becomes choked with snow."

Cley looked over at Willa. "What do you say?" he asked, secretly hoping she would tell him not to go. Since telling her the entire saga of his life as the Physiognomist, he felt free of it.

Willa sat with tears in her eyes. She said, "You must go."

■ The day before they were to leave, Cley took Wraith hunting in the forest.

"I don't understand," said the boy.

"Don't worry, I'm coming back. I promise," he said. He had a brief memory flash of having told Anotine the same thing as she lay on the path next to Dr. Hellman.

"What if you don't?" said Wraith.

"There is no question that I will," said the hunter. "Let's find a deer, now."

They crouched together behind a blind of tall ferns, having tracked a large buck through the underbrush for two miles. Now that it was time to take a shot, Cley gave the bow to Wraith.

"Remember," whispered Cley. "You've got to watch with both eyes."

With the arrow in place, the boy slowly stood, and pulled back on the string. He held the shot for a moment, aiming, and his form looked perfect. Cley thought to himself, "He will be fine."

Wraith released, but the arrow sailed harmlessly over the buck's head and embedded itself in the trunk of a pine tree. With two bounding leaps, the animal was gone.

Neither of the hunters spoke for the rest of the afternoon. Only on their way back to the house through the gathering dusk did Wraith turn to Cley.

"By the time you return," said the boy, "I will be able to make that shot."

"I know you will," said the hunter, and put his hand on Wraith's head.

"If you don't return after the winter, I will come for you," said Wraith.

Cley could not speak. He moved on toward the edge of the forest. When they reached the meadow, the boy ran ahead to the house.

■ It was early morning, and Willa and Wraith were still asleep. The hunter wore his hat and held his bow and quiver. His pack was filled with food and the tools of survival. He looked around the room, at the fireplace, Pierce's old broom leaning against the table, Wraith sleeping in the corner.

"The time has come," said Ea.

Cley walked over and leaned down to kiss the boy. Willa appeared at the entrance to the other room. She was smiling.

"Please be careful," she said. She took Ea's hand in hers. Then she went to Cley and touched his shoulder.

"When you fire the pistol . . ." said Cley.

"No more about the pistol," said Willa. "I'm a better shot with it than you are." She laughed.

The hunter smiled. "Yes, I'm an old man," he said.

They embraced.

The door opened, and Willa watched Cley and Ea heading off toward the north.

■ Cley's years by the lake left him in poor shape for a journey. Ea, too, was now much older, and did not move with the same grace as in his youth. The companions made slow progress, taking much the same route that Vasthasha had on Cley's journey to save the Beyond. Two months passed them in the opposite direction before they came to the foot of the mountain range they must cross.

It took three arduous days to ascend to the head of the pass, which was the only route through the maze of towering stone giants. As the temperature began to plummet, they made camp one night at the mouth of the mountains' gullet. After they ate the wild goat Cley had killed that afternoon, they sat by the fire, talking aimlessly about the past.

When Cley brought out his pipe, Ea said, "Along the way today, I found some of these." He held out his hand and showed Cley six little brown pellets.

"Rabbit turds?" asked Cley, and smiled.

"Put them in the pipe," said Ea.

"I've smoked my fill of shit in this life," said Cley, waving a hand at Ea's offering.

"They are the seeds of a weed that grows only in these lonely mountains," said the Traveler.

"What will I see in the smoke?" asked Cley. "I'm tired of the consciousness of the wilderness."

"It does not tire of yours," said Ea.

The smoke of the seeds was bitter, but also very relaxing. Before Cley took his third toke, he was ready to bed down.

"Are you tired?" asked Ea.

"Exhausted," said Cley as he leaned back and pulled the blanket over himself.

The hunter's body lost all its tension. The muscles and joints that had ached for days now, miraculously, had no complaints. He felt warm and tired, on the verge of sleep. Before drifting off into a dream of arriving at the true Wenau, he had two very vivid thoughts. The first was brief. He was back at the house by the lake, in bed with Willa. She lay facing him, her breasts against his chest, her hand on his back, her quiet, steady breathing near his ear. He ran his open palm down the skin of her shoulder, her side, her hip.

The second thought, briefer still, was of Wraith, aiming the old bow. He released the arrow and it flew over the leaf-strewn ground, threading between two tree trunks, and struck the buck directly in its heart. The beast released its life in a torrent of steam, and, as it fell, Cley fell into Wenau and landed beside the reclining form of Arla Beaton.

The next morning the companions woke before sunrise.

As they prepared to leave Cley found, in his pack, the

green veil. He took it out and opened it, laying it flat upon his upturned palm.

"See, here," he said to Ea.

The Traveler smiled. "Your square of Paradise."

Cley lifted the veil in both hands and held it up to cover his face. Through it, he saw the wilderness clearly, save for a green tint that slightly changed the color of everything.

"Are you ready, Cley?" asked Ea.

"No," said the hunter. "I'm not going."

"We've come so far," said Ea.

"I'm sorry," said Cley. "It has been very fine to see you again. I wish I could see Arla before she dies, but I need to return. I'm needed more urgently elsewhere."

"There will be no other opportunities," said the Traveler.

"I know," said Cley. "I'm going home."

Ea stood in silence for a long time, watching the hunter lift his pack and sling it over his shoulder. Cley still held the veil in his hand. "It is your decision," said the Traveler.

Cley walked over to his friend from Wenau and shook his hand. "Thank you," he said.

"The wilderness loves you, Cley," said Ea.

"I couldn't tell," said the hunter, and they both laughed.

"I should make it back before the snow," said Cley.

"You will," said Ea.

The hunter turned and began to walk away.

"Cley," called Ea. "I have to give you a message from Arla."

Cley stopped but did not look back.

"She is dead," said Ea. "She died a few months before I came to see you. We knew you were living by the lake with the woman and the boy. The old tattoo master of the Word told us everything. In her last days, she made me promise to come to you and offer passage to Wenau. She told me, 'If he makes the long journey here, he should find my grave. Only if he turns back, and goes to the woman and the boy, are you to tell him that I forgive him for everything.' "

Cley began walking again. He knew it would be a long and difficult journey, and he did not need the extra weight. Holding the veil above his head, he opened his fingers, and the wilderness took it from him.

I tried to explain to them that it was folly to attempt to hang a man with the power of flight, but they continue building the gallows. If I look out the barred window at the back of the cell, I can see it under construction. Yes, I have been found guilty—sentenced to death. This is to be my last night.

I could bend the bars on that window like they were long blades of grass and take to the sky in less than a minute, but I won't. The instant I pass through the portal to freedom, I will again be a creature. It is all in the choosing.

Spencer had a choice to make, too, and he was about to pronounce his decision, when Frabone stood up and interrupted the proceedings. Everyone in the court turned and looked at the wretch.

The constable was clearly angry at his intrusion.

"Before you slam the desk, sir, I have one more piece of evidence to present," said the prosecutor. "It will give the truth."

"The truth," said Spencer and smiled. "I doubt it."

"In the name of Justice," said Frabone.

"No," said Feskin.

"He's had his day, Feskin, I agree, but I want to see this evidence for my own decision. Stay calm, I'm still at the tiller," said Spencer.

Feskin leaned over to me, and whispered, "This won't be good."

"What part has been?" I asked.

Frabone stepped to the side of the room so that both judge and citizens could see him at once. He wore a look of death with ambition as he held up his hand for everyone's attention.

"Yesterday afternoon," said the prosecutor, "in this court, as the defendant was being escorted to his cell, he was approached by a girl who slipped a note into his hand. My associates witnessed this and warned me of it. I instructed them to follow the little girl, keep her under surveillance until the trial was over.

"They followed her home and watched her house for an hour before they discovered she was gone. They gently persuaded her mother to reveal the daughter's destination. She finally told them that Emilia had taken a horse and gone to the ruins.

"My associates hired horses and rode through the forest, over the fields of Harakun to the Well-Built City. It was evening when they approached the remains of the old wall. A hundred feet off the ruins, they apprehended the girl. She was on her horse, and she carried something under her arm. My associates investigated this object and found it to be a box done up with fake jewels. It had sat on the demon's writing desk, back in the Well-Built City.

"When they opened the box, they found this inside," said Frabone. He reached into his pocket and pulled out the green veil. "Guilty," he said and stood there holding it in the air for all to see.

The doors opened then, and two of Frabone's associates escorted Emilia into the court. She was shown to a spot near the constable's desk, and she stood there, looking at the floor.

The prosecutor approached her, and said, "You were taking the veil in order to destroy evidence, weren't you?"

Emilia looked up. She stared at the back of the room. "I went to the ruins to get the box for Misrix. He told me that it was special to him. That is why I went."

"At least, if you are innocent, you found the evidence we needed when you took the box," said Frabone.

"The veil as I have told you over and again," said Emilia, "was not in the box." She glared at the prosecutor. "I told you, I was coming through the ruins, and I saw it floating downward through the air. It drifted almost to my hand but the wind tried to grab it away at the last second. I was too fast for it. I put the veil in the box before leaving through the wall."

"Emilia," said Frabone, coming close to her, and laying his hand on her shoulder, "we know that is a lie."

This was a defining moment for me. The urge to tear Frabone's head off was very great all throughout the trial, but when Emilia's composure crumbled and she began to cry, Feskin had to put his arm across my chest to hold me steady. They never got another word out of her. She cried for a half hour in front of the town of Wenau, and when she was finally ushered out of the building, she was still weeping uncontrollably.

The allegations, as I have told you, are not true. Frabone wants to convince you that I murdered Cley. I have shown you Cley. Does he not live? He is remembering me, right now, somewhere in the Beyond.

Before I sat down to record these final thoughts for you, I heard a voice outside the back window of my cell. I pulled myself up on the bars and looked down. Emilia was standing there, looking up at me.

"I wanted to help," she said.

"You did," I told her.

"Are we still friends?" I asked, as my grip slipped and I fell back to the floor. When I managed to pull myself up again, she was gone.

I have also seen the hangman from my window. He has been overseeing the building of the gallows. I swear to you, the man bears an uncanny resemblance to Brisden.

Tomorrow, I will understand.